The Rumor:
Did Sir Harry Valentine kill his fiancée?

The Secret:
Could Lady Olivia Bevelstoke
be spying for the Russians?

The Mystery:
Why is he tossing so many papers
into the fireplace?

The Gossip:
Is she going to marry a prince?

The Scandal:
None whatsoever.

Because What Happens in London . . .
STAYS IN LONDON

By Julia Quinn

JULIA QUINN

What Happens In London

AVON

An Imprint of HarperCollins*Publishers*

This is a work of fiction. Names, characters, places, and incidents are products of the author's imagination or are used fictitiously and are not to be construed as real. Any resemblance to actual events, locales, organizations, or persons, living or dead, is entirely coincidental.

AVON BOOKS
An Imprint of HarperCollins*Publishers*
10 East 53rd Street
New York, New York 10022-5299

First Avon Books paperback printing: July 2009

Avon Trademark Reg. U.S. Pat. Off. and in Other Countries, Marca Registrada, Hecho en U.S.A.
HarperCollins® is a registered trademark of HarperCollins Publishers.

Printed in the U.S.A.

10 9 8 7 6 5 4 3 2 1

For Gloria, Stan, Katie, Rafa, and Matt.
I don't have in-laws. I only have family.

And also for Paul,
even though he has all the dominant genes.

The author wishes to thank Mitch Mitchell, Boris Skyar, Molly Skyar, and Sarah Wigglesworth for their expertise in all things Russian.

Prologue

By the age of twelve, Harry Valentine possessed two bits of knowledge that made him rather unlike other boys of his class in England of the early nineteenth century.

The first was his complete and absolute fluency in the languages of Russian and French. There was little mystery surrounding this talent; his grandmother, the extremely aristocratic and opinionated Olga Petrova Obolenskiy Dell, had come to reside with the Valentine family four months after Harry's birth.

Olga loathed the English language. In her (frequently expressed) judgment, there was nothing in this world that needed to be said that could not be expressed in Russian or French.

As to why she had gone and married an Englishman, she never could quite explain.

"Probably because it needs explaining in *English*," Harry's sister Anne had muttered.

Harry just shrugged and smiled (as any proper brother would) when this got her ears boxed. Grandmère might disdain English, but she could understand it perfectly, and her ears were sharper than a hound's. Muttering anything—in any language—was a bad idea when she was in the schoolroom. Doing so in English was incredibly foolish. Doing so in English whilst suggesting that French or Russian was not adequate for the verbal task at hand . . .

In all honesty, Harry was surprised Anne hadn't been paddled.

But Anne loathed Russian with the same intensity Grandmère reserved for English. It was too much *work*, she complained, and French was almost as difficult. Anne had been five when Grandmère had arrived, and her English was far too entrenched for anything else to gain an equal footing.

Harry, on the other hand, was happy to speak in whichever language was spoken to him. English was for everyday, French was elegance, and Russian became the language of drama and excitement. Russia was big. It was cold. And above all, it was *great*.

Peter the Great, Catherine the Great—Harry had been weaned on their stories.

"Bah!" Olga had scoffed, more than once, when Harry's tutor had attempted to teach him English history. "Who is this Ethelred the Unready? The *Unready*? What kind of country allows their rulers to be unready?"

"Queen Elizabeth was great," Harry pointed out.

Olga was unimpressed. "Do they call her Elizabeth

the Great? Or the Great Queen? No, they do not. They call her the Virgin Queen, as if *that* is anything to be proud of."

It was at this point that the tutor's ears grew very red, which Harry found quite curious.

"She," Olga continued, with all possible ice, "was not a great queen. She didn't even give her country a proper heir to the throne."

"Most scholars of history agree that it was wise for the queen to avoid marriage," the tutor said. "She needed to give the appearance of being without influence, and . . ."

His voice trailed off. Harry was not surprised. Grandmère had turned to him with one of her razor-sharp, rather eaglish stares. Harry did not know anyone who could continue speaking through one of those.

"You are a stupid little man," she pronounced, then turned her back on him entirely. She fired him the next day, then taught Harry herself until they were able to find a new tutor.

It wasn't precisely Olga's place to hire and fire educators for the Valentine children, who by then numbered three. (Little Edward had been added to the nursery when Harry was seven.) But no one else was likely to involve themselves in the matter. Harry's mother, Katarina Dell Valentine, never argued with her mother, and as for his father . . . well . . .

That had rather a lot to do with the second bit of uncommon knowledge tumbling around Harry Valentine's twelve-year-old brain.

Harry's father, Sir Lionel Valentine, was a drunk.

This was not the uncommon knowledge. Everyone

knew that Sir Lionel drank more than he ought. There was no hiding it. Sir Lionel stumbled and tripped (on his words *and* his feet), he laughed when no one else did, and, unfortunately for the two housemaids (and the two carpets in Sir Lionel's study), there was a reason the alcohol had not caused his body to grow fat.

And so Harry became proficient in the task of cleaning up vomit.

It started when he was ten. He probably would have left the mess where it lay, except that he had been trying to ask his father for a bit of pocket money, and he'd made the mistake of doing so too late in the evening. Sir Lionel had already partaken of his afternoon brandy, his early-evening nip, his wine with supper, his port immediately following, and was now back to his favorite, the aforementioned brandy, smuggled in from France. Harry was quite certain that he had spoken in complete (English) sentences when he made his request for funds, but his father just stared at him, blinking several times as if he couldn't quite comprehend what his son was talking about, and then promptly threw up on Harry's shoes.

So Harry really couldn't avoid the mess.

After that there seemed to be no going back. It happened again a week later, although not directly on his feet, and then a month after that. By the time Harry was twelve, any other young child would have lost count of the number of times he'd cleaned up after his father, but he had always been a precise sort of boy, and once he'd begun his accounting, it was difficult to stop.

Most people would have probably lost count around

seven. This was, Harry knew from his extensive reading on logic and arithmetic, the largest number that most people could visually appreciate. Put seven dots on a page, and most people can take a quick glance and declare, "Seven." Switch to eight, and the majority of humanity was lost.

Harry could do up to twenty-one.

So it was no surprise, that after fifteen cleanings, Harry knew exactly how many times he'd found his father stumbling through the hall, or passed out on the floor, or aiming (badly) at a chamber pot. And then, once he'd reached twenty, the issue became somewhat academic, and he *had* to keep track.

It had to be academic. If it wasn't academic, then it would be something else, and he might find himself crying himself to sleep instead of merely staring at the ceiling as he said, "Forty-six, but with a radius quite a bit smaller than last Tuesday. Probably didn't have much for supper tonight."

Harry's mother had long since decided to ignore the situation entirely, and she could most often be found in her gardens, tending to the exotic rose varieties her mother had brought over from Russia so many years earlier. Anne had informed him that she planned to marry and "be gone from this hellhole" the moment she turned seventeen. Which, incidentally, she did, a testament to her determination, since neither of her parents had made any effort by that point to secure her a match. As for Edward, the youngest—he learned to adapt, as Harry had. Father was useless after four in the afternoon, even if he seemed lucid (which he generally did, up 'til suppertime, when the wheels came off entirely).

The servants all knew as well. Not that their numbers were legion; the Valentines did well enough with their tidy home in Sussex and hundred per year they continued to receive as a part of Katarina's dowry. But this did not translate to splendid wealth, and the Valentines' staff numbered but eight—butler, cook, housekeeper, stable boy, two footmen, maid, and scullery girl. Most chose to stay with the family despite the occasional unpleasant alcohol-related duties. Sir Lionel might be a drunk, but he was not a mean drunk. Nor was he stingy, and even the maids learned to deal with his messes if it meant an extra coin here and there when he remembered enough of his activities to be embarrassed by them.

So Harry wasn't really sure *why* he kept cleaning up after his father, since he certainly could have left it to someone else. Maybe he didn't want the servants to know how often it happened. Maybe he needed a visceral reminder of the perils of alcohol. He'd heard that his father's father had been the same way. Did such things run in families?

He did not want to find out.

And then, quite suddenly, Grandmère died. Nothing so peaceful as in her sleep—Olga Petrova Obolenskiy Dell would never depart this earth with so little drama. She was sitting at the dining-room table, about to dip her spoon into her soup, when she clutched her chest, made several gasping noises, and collapsed. It was later remarked that she must have had some level of consciousness before she hit the table, because her face missed the soup entirely, *and* she somehow managed to hit the spoon, sending a dollop of the scalding liquid flying through the air toward Sir Lionel, whose reflexes were far too dulled to duck.

Harry did not witness this firsthand; at twelve, he was not permitted to dine with the adults. But Anne saw the whole thing, and recounted it breathlessly to Harry.

"And then he ripped off his cravat!"

"At the table?"

"At the table! And you could see the burn!" Anne held up her hand, her thumb and forefinger pinching out a distance of about an inch. "This big!"

"And Grandmère?"

Anne sobered a bit. But only a bit. "I think she's dead."

Harry swallowed and nodded. "She was very old."

"At least ninety."

"I don't think she was ninety."

"She *looked* ninety," Anne muttered.

Harry said nothing. He wasn't sure what a ninety-year-old woman looked like, but Grandmère certainly had more wrinkles than anyone else of his acquaintance.

"But I'll tell you the strangest part," Anne said. She leaned forward. "*Mother.*"

Harry blinked. "What did she do?"

"Nothing. Not a thing."

"Was she seated near to Grandmère?"

"No, that's not what I mean. She was across and diagonal—too far away to be helpful."

"Then—"

"She just sat there," Anne cut in. "She did not move. Did not even start to rise."

Harry considered this. It was, sad to say, not surprising.

"Her face did not even move. She just sat there like *this*." Anne's face assumed a decidedly blank expression, and Harry had to admit, it was precisely like their mother.

"I shall tell you something," Anne said. "If she were to collapse in her soup in front of me, I would at the *very* least look surprised." She shook her head. "They are ridiculous, the both of them. Father does nothing but drink, and Mother does nothing at all. I tell you, I cannot wait until my birthday. I don't care if we're supposed to be in mourning. I'm marrying William Forbush, and there is nothing either one of them can do about it."

"I don't think you have to worry about that," Harry said. Mother would likely possess no opinion on the matter, and Father would be too drunk to notice.

"Hmmph. You're probably right." Anne's mouth pressed together into a rueful frown, and then, in an uncharacteristic show of sibling affection, she reached out and gave his shoulder a squeeze. "You'll be gone soon, too. Don't worry."

Harry nodded. He was due to leave for school in a few short weeks.

And while he felt a little guilty that he got to leave while Anne and Edward had to remain behind, this was more than drowned out by the overwhelming sense of relief that washed over him the first time he rode off to school.

It was *good* to be gone. With all due respect to Grandmère and her favorite monarchs, it might even have been great.

* * *

Harry's life as a student proved just as rewarding as he'd hoped. He attended Hesslewhite, a reasonably rigorous academy for boys whose families lacked the clout (or, in Harry's case, the interest) to send their sons to Eton or Harrow.

Harry loved school. *Loved* it. He loved his classes, he loved sport, and he loved that when he went to bed, he did not have to detour to every corner of the building, doing his late-evening check for his father, fingers crossed that he'd passed out before making a mess of himself. At school Harry took a straight journey from the common room to his dormitory, and he loved every uneventful step of the way.

But all good things must draw to a close, and at the age of nineteen, Harry was graduated with the rest of his class, including Sebastian Grey, his first cousin and closest friend. There was a ceremony, as most of the boys wished to celebrate the occasion, but Harry "forgot" to tell his family about it.

"Where is your mother?" his aunt Anna asked him. Like Harry's mother, her voice betrayed no trace of an accent, despite the fact Olga had insisted upon speaking to them only in Russian when they were small. Anna had married better than Katarina, having wed the second son of an earl. This had not caused a rift between the sisters; after all, Sir Lionel was a baronet, which meant that Katarina was the one called "her ladyship." But Anna had the connections and the money, and perhaps more important, she had—until his death two years prior—a husband who rarely indulged in more than one glass of wine at supper.

And so when Harry mumbled something about his mother being a bit overtired, Anna knew exactly what he meant—that if his mother came, his father would follow. And after Sir Lionel's spectacular display of stumbling grandiosity at Hesslewhite's convocation of 1807, Harry was loath to invite his father to another school function.

Sir Lionel tended to lose his *s*'s when he drank, and Harry was not certain he could survive another "Thplendid, thplendid thchool" speech, especially as it had been delivered whilst standing on a chair.

During a moment of silence.

Harry had tried to pull his father down, and he would have been successful had his mother, who was seated on Sir Lionel's other side, aided in the endeavor. She, however, was staring straight ahead, as she always did at such times, pretending she heard nothing. Which meant that Harry had to give his father a lopsided yank, setting him rather off balance. Sir Lionel came down with a whoop and a crash, striking his cheek on the back of the chair in front of Harry.

This might have set another man into a temper, but not Sir Lionel. He gave a stupid smile, called Harry a "thplendid thon," and then spit out a tooth.

Harry still had that tooth. And he never allowed his father to set foot on the school's campus again. Even if it meant he was the only boy without a parent in attendance at the graduation ceremony.

His aunt insisted upon seeing him home, for which Harry was grateful. He did not like having guests, but Aunt Anna and Sebastian already knew all there was to know about his father—well, most of it. Harry hadn't shared the bit about the 126 times he'd mopped up after him. Or the recent loss of Grandmère's prized samovar, whose enamel cracked right off its silver core when Sir Lionel had tripped over a chair, done a curiously graceful leap through the air (presumably to catch his balance), then landed on his belly atop the sideboard.

Three plates of eggs and a rasher of bacon had also been lost that morning.

On the bright side, the hounds had never been so well fed.

Hesslewhite had been chosen because of its proximity to the Valentine home, and so after only ninety minutes in the carriage, they turned onto the drive and began the last short stretch.

"The trees are certainly well leafed this year," Aunt Anna remarked. "Your mother's roses are doing well, I trust."

Harry nodded absently, trying to gauge the time. Was it still late afternoon, or had the day made its way into early evening? If it was the latter, he'd have to invite them in for supper. He'd have to invite them in in any case; Aunt Anna would want to say hello to her sister. But if it was late afternoon, they'd expect only tea, which would mean they could be in and out without a glimpse of his father.

Supper was a different story. Sir Lionel always insisted upon dressing for supper. It was, he liked to say, the mark of a gentleman. And no matter how small their dinner party (just Sir Lionel, Lady Valentine, and whichever of their children were in residence, 99 percent of the time), he liked to play the host. Which generally meant quite a lot of storytelling and *bon mots*, except that Sir Lionel tended to forget the middle bits of the stories, and his "mots" weren't terribly "bon."

Which in turn meant quite a lot of pained silence on the part of his family, who spent most of the supper pretending they didn't notice when the gravy boat was knocked over, or when Sir Lionel's wineglass was refilled.

Again.

And again.

And then, of course, again.

No one ever told him to stop. What was the point? Sir Lionel knew he drank too much. Harry *had* lost track of the number of times his father had turned to him and sobbed, "I'm thorry, I'm tho, tho thorry. Don't mean to be a trouble. You're a good boy, Harry."

But it never made a difference. Whatever it was that drove Sir Lionel to drink, it was far more powerful than any guilt or regret he might muster to stop it. Sir Lionel was not in denial about the extent of his affliction. He was, however, completely powerless to do anything about it.

As was Harry. Short of tying his father to his bed, which he was not prepared to do. So instead he never invited friends home, he avoided being in the house at suppertime, and, now that school was done, he counted the days until he could depart for university.

But first he had to make it through the summer. He hopped down from the carriage when they came to a stop in the front drive, then held up his hand to aid his aunt. Sebastian followed, and together the three of them made their way to the drawing room, where Katarina was pecking at her needlepoint.

"Anna!" she said, looking as if she might rise to her feet (but not quite doing so). "What a lovely surprise!"

Anna leaned down to embrace her, then took a seat opposite. "I thought I would give Harry a ride home from school."

"Oh, is the term finished, then?" Katarina murmured.

Harry gave a tight smile. He supposed he deserved the blame for her ignorance, as he had neglected to tell her that school was done, but really, shouldn't a mother keep up on such details?

"Sebastian," Katarina said, turning to her nephew. "You've grown."

"It happens," Sebastian quipped, flashing her his usual lopsided grin.

"Goodness," she said with smile, "you'll be a danger to the ladies soon."

Harry very nearly rolled his eyes. Sebastian had already made conquests of nearly all the girls in the village near Hesslewhite. He must give off some sort of scent, because the females positively fell at his feet.

It would have been appalling, except that the girls couldn't *all* dance with Sebastian. And Harry was more than happy to be the nearest man standing when the smoke cleared.

"There won't be time for that," Anna said briskly. "I have purchased a commission for him. He departs in a month."

"You shall be in the army?" Katarina said, turning to her nephew with surprise. "How grand."

Sebastian shrugged.

"Surely you knew, Mother," Harry said. Sebastian's future had been decided several months earlier. Aunt Anna had been fretting that he needed a male influence ever since his father had died. And since Sebastian wasn't likely to come into a title or a fortune, it was understood that he'd have to make his own way in the world.

No one, not even Sebastian's mother, who thought the sun rose and set on her boy, had even *suggested* he consider the clergy.

Sebastian wasn't overly excited about the prospect of spending the next decade or so fighting Napoleon, but as he'd said to Harry—what else could he do? His uncle, the Earl of Newbury, detested him and had made it clear that Sebastian could expect no perks, monetary or otherwise, from that connection.

"Maybe he'll die," Harry had suggested, with all the sensitivity and tact of a nineteen-year-old boy.

But then again, it was difficult to offend Sebastian, especially when it concerned his uncle. Or his uncle's only son, the heir to Newbury. "My cousin's even worse," Sebastian replied. "Tried to give me the cut direct in London."

Harry felt his brows rise with shock. It was one thing to abhor a family member; it was quite another to attempt public humiliation. "What did you do?"

Sebastian's lips curled into a slow smile. "Seduced the girl he wanted to marry."

Harry gave him a look that said he did not believe him for a second.

"Oh, very well," Sebastian relented, "but I did seduce the girl at the pub he had his eye on."

"And the girl he wants to marry?"

"Doesn't want to marry him any longer!" Sebastian chortled.

"Good Lord, Seb, what did you do?"

"Oh, nothing permanent. Even I'm not foolish enough to tamper with the daughter of an earl. I just . . . turned her head, that's all."

But as his mother had pointed out, Sebastian wouldn't have much opportunity for any sort of amorous efforts, not with a life in the army awaiting him. Harry had tried not to think about his departure; Seb was the only person in the world he trusted, completely and absolutely.

He was the only person who had never let Harry down.

It all made sense, really. Sebastian wasn't stupid—quite the opposite, actually—but he wasn't suited to academic life. The army was a much better choice for him. But still, as Harry sat there in the drawing room, uncomfortable in the too-small Egyptian chair, he couldn't help but feel a bit sorry for himself. And selfish. He'd rather Sebastian went to university with him, even if it wasn't the best thing for Sebastian.

"What color shall your uniform be?" Katarina asked.

"Dark blue, I should think," Sebastian answered politely.

"Oh, you shall look smashing in blue. Don't you think so, Anna?"

Anna nodded, and Katarina added, "As would you, Harry. Perhaps we should buy you a commission as well."

Harry blinked in surprise. The army had never been discussed as a part of his future. He was the eldest, due to inherit the house, the baronetcy, and whatever monies his father didn't drink before his death. He was not supposed to be put in harm's way.

And besides that, he was one of the few boys at Hesslewhite who actually *liked* studying. He'd been dubbed "the professor" and hadn't minded. What was his mother thinking? Did she even *know* him? Was she suggesting he join the army to improve his sense of *fashion*?

"Eh, Harry couldn't be a soldier," Sebastian said wickedly. "He can't hit a target at close range."

"That is *not* true," Harry shot back. "I'm not as good as *he*," he said with a jerk of his head toward Seb, "but I'm better than everyone else."

"Are you a good shot, then, Sebastian?" Katarina asked.

"The best."

"He's also exceptionally modest," Harry muttered. But it was true. Sebastian was a freakishly outstanding shot, and the army would be thrilled to have him, so long as they managed to keep him from seducing the whole of Portugal.

The half of Portugal, that was. The female half.

"Why *don't* you take a commission?" Katarina asked.

Harry turned to his mother, trying to read her face, trying to read *her*. She was always so maddeningly blank, as if the years had slowly washed away everything that had given her character, that had allowed her to *feel*. She had no opinions, his mother. She let life swirl around her, and she sat through it all, seemingly uninterested in any of it.

"I think you would like the army," she said quietly,

and he thought—*Had she ever made such a pronouncement?* Had she ever offered an opinion as to his future, his well-being?

Had she only been waiting for the right time?

She smiled the way she always did—with a tiny sigh, as if the effort was almost too much. "You would look splendid in blue." And then she turned back to Anna. "Don't you think?"

Harry opened his mouth, to say—well, to say something. As soon as he figured out what. He had not planned on the army. He was to go to university. He'd earned a spot at Pembroke College, in Oxford. He thought he might study Russian. He'd not used the language much since Grandmère had died. His mother spoke it, but they rarely had complete conversations in English, much less Russian.

Damn, but Harry missed his grandmother. She wasn't always right, and she wasn't even always nice, but she was entertaining. And she'd loved him.

What would she have wanted him to do? Harry wasn't sure. She would certainly have approved of Harry going to university if it meant that he would spend his days immersed in Russian literature. But she'd also held the military in extremely high regard and had openly mocked Harry's father for never serving his country.

Of course, she had openly mocked Harry's father for any number of things.

"You should consider it, Harry," Anna pronounced. "I am certain Sebastian would be grateful for your company."

Harry shot a desperate look at Sebastian. Surely he would understand Harry's distress. What were they thinking? That he might wish to make such a decision over *tea*? That he might bite into his biscuit, consider the matter for a brief moment and decide that yes, dark blue *was* a splendid color for a uniform.

But Sebastian just did that tiny one-shoulder shrug of his, the one that said: *What can I say? The world is a foolish place.*

Harry's mother lifted her teacup to her lips, but if she took a sip, it was undetectable by the tilt of the china. And then, as her cup descended toward its saucer, she closed her eyes.

It was just a blink, really, just a slightly longer than normal blink, but Harry knew what it meant. She heard footsteps. His father's footsteps. She always heard him before anyone else. Maybe it was the years of practice, of living in the same house, if not precisely in the same world. Her ability to pretend that her life was something other than it was had been developed right alongside her ability to anticipate her husband's whereabouts at all possible moments.

It was far easier to ignore what one did not actually see.

"Anna!" Sir Lionel exclaimed, appearing in, and then leaning against, the doorway. "And Sebastian. What a fine surprise. How're you doing, m'boy?"

"Very well, sir," Sebastian replied.

Harry watched his father enter the room. It was hard to tell yet just how far along he was. His gait was not unsteady, but there was a certain swing to his arms that Harry did not like.

"S'good to see you, Harry," Sir Lionel said, giving his son a brief tap on the arm before making his way to the credenza. "School's done, then?"

"Yes, sir," Harry said.

Sir Lionel splashed something into a glass—Harry was too far away to determine precisely what—then turned to Sebastian with a sloppy grin. "How old r'you, now, Sebastian?" he asked.

"Nineteen, sir."

The same as Harry. They were only a month apart. He was always the same as Harry.

"Are you serving him tea, Katy?" Sir Lionel said to his wife. "What are you thinking? He's a man now."

"The tea is quite adequate, Father," Harry said sharply.

Sir Lionel turned to him with a blink of surprise, almost as if he'd forgotten he was there. "Harry, m'boy. It's good to see you."

Harry's lips tightened, then pressed together. "It is good to see you, too, Father."

Sir Lionel took a hearty swallow of his drink. "Is the term finished, then?"

Harry gave a nod, along with his customary, "Yes, sir."

Sir Lionel frowned, then drank again. "You're done, though. Aren't you? I received a notice from Pembroke College about your matriculation." He frowned again, then blinked a few times, then shrugged. "Didn't realize you'd applied." And then, as an afterthought: "Well done."

"I'm not going."

The words emerged from Harry's mouth in a quick tumble of surprise. What was he saying? Of course he was going to Pembroke College. It was what he'd wanted. What he'd always wanted. He liked studying. He liked books. He liked numbers. He liked sitting in a library, even when the sun was shining and Sebastian was yanking him out for rugby. (Sebastian always won this battle; there was little-enough sun in the south of England, and one really did have to get out when one could. Not to mention that Sebastian was fiendishly persuasive, about all things.)

There could not be a boy in England better suited for life at university. And yet—

"I'm joining the army."

Again the words came forth, no conscious thought involved. Harry wondered what he was saying. He wondered *why* he was saying it.

"With Sebastian?" Aunt Anna asked.

Harry nodded. "Someone's got to make sure he doesn't get himself killed."

Sebastian gave him a dry look at the insult, but he was clearly too pleased by the turn of events to make a retort. He'd always been ambivalent about a future in the military; Harry knew that, for all his bravado, he'd be relieved to have his cousin along with him.

"You can't go to war," Sir Lionel said. "You are my heir."

Everyone in the room—all four of them his relations—turned to the baronet with varying degrees of surprise. It was, quite possibly, the only sensible thing he'd said in years.

"You have Edward," Harry said bluntly.

Sir Lionel drank, blinked, and shrugged. "Well, that's true."

It was more or less what Harry would have expected him to say, and yet deep in his belly he felt a nagging pit of disappointment. And resentment.

And hurt.

"A toast to Harry!" Sir Lionel said jovially, lifting his glass. He did not seem to notice that no one else was joining him. "Godspeed, m'son." He tipped back his glass, only then realizing that he had not recently refilled. "Well, damn it," he muttered. "That's awkward."

Harry felt himself slumping in his chair. And at the same time, his feet began to feel itchy, as if they were ready move forward. To run.

"When do you leave?" Sir Lionel asked, happily replenished.

Harry looked at Sebastian, who immediately spoke up. "I must report next week."

"Then it shall be the same for me," Harry said to his father. "I shall need the funds for the commission, of course."

"Of course," Sir Lionel said, responding instinctively to the tone of command in Harry's voice. "Well." He looked down at his feet, then over at his wife.

She was staring out the window.

"Jolly fine to see you all," Sir Lionel said. He plunked down his glass and ambled over to the door, losing his footing only once.

Harry watched him depart, feeling strangely detached from the scene. He'd imagined this before, of course. Not the going into the army, but the leaving. He'd always supposed that he'd head off to university in the usual fashion, packing his things into the family carriage and rolling away. But his imagination had indulged in all sorts of dramatic exits—everything from wild gesticulations to ice-cold stares. His favorites involved flinging bottles against the wall. The expensive ones. The ones smuggled in from France.

Would his father still support the Frogs with his illegal purchases, now that his son was facing them down on the battlefield?

Harry stared at the empty doorway. It didn't matter, did it? He was done here.

He was done. With this place, with this family, with all those nights steering his father into bed, placing him carefully on his side so that if he did vomit again, at least he wouldn't choke on it.

He was done.

Done.

But it felt so hollow, so quiet. His departure was marked by . . . nothing.

And it would take him years to realize that he'd been cheated.

Chapter One

They say he killed his first wife."

It was enough to make Lady Olivia Bevelstoke
cease stirring her tea. "Who?" she asked, since the
truth was, she hadn't been listening.

"Sir Harry Valentine. Your new neighbor."

Olivia took a hard look at Anne Buxton, and then
at Mary Cadogan, who was nodding her head in
agreement. "You must be joking," she said, although
she knew quite well that Anne would never joke
about something like that. Gossip was her life-
blood.

"No, he really is your new neighbor," put in Philomena Waincliff.

Olivia took a sip of her tea, mostly so that she would
have time to keep her face free of its desired expression, which was a cross between unabashed exaspera-
tion and disbelief. "I meant that she must be joking

that he killed someone," she said, with more patience than she was generally given credit for.

"Oh." Philomena picked up a biscuit. "Sorry."

"I *know* I heard that he killed his fiancée," Anne insisted.

"If he killed someone, he'd be in gaol," Olivia pointed out.

"Not if they couldn't prove it."

Olivia glanced slightly toward her left, where, through a thick stone wall, ten feet of fresh spring-time air, and another thick wall, this one of brick, Sir Harry Valentine's newly leased home sat directly to the south of hers.

The other three girls followed her direction, which made Olivia feel quite foolish, as now they were all staring at a perfectly blank spot on the drawing-room wall. "He didn't kill anyone," she said firmly.

"How do you know?" Anne responded.

Mary nodded.

"Because he didn't," Olivia said. "He wouldn't be living one house away from me in Mayfair if he'd killed someone."

"Not if they couldn't prove it," Anne said again.

Mary nodded.

Philomena ate another biscuit.

Olivia managed an ever-so-slight turn of her lips. Upward, she hoped. It wouldn't do to frown. It was four in the afternoon. The other girls had been visiting for an hour, chatting about this and that, gossiping (of course), and discussing their wardrobe selections for the next three social events. They met like this frequently, about once per week, and Olivia enjoyed their company, even if the conversation lacked the heft she enjoyed with her closest friend, Miranda née Cheever now Bevelstoke.

Yes, Miranda had gone and married Olivia's brother. Which was a good thing. A marvelous thing. They had been friends since birth, and now they would be sisters until death. But it also meant that Miranda was no longer an unmarried lady, required to do unmarried lady sorts of things.

Unmarried Lady Sorts of Things
By Lady Olivia Bevelstoke, Unmarried Lady

Wear pastel colors
(and be quite glad if you possess the correct
complexion for such hues).
Smile and keep your opinions to yourself
(with whatever success you are able).
Do what your parents tell you to do.
Accept the consequences when you don't.
Find a husband who won't bother to
tell you what to do.

It was not uncommon for Olivia to formulate such epigraphic oddities in her mind. Which might explain why she so frequently caught herself not listening when she ought.

And, perhaps, why she might have, once or twice, said things she really should have kept to herself. Although in all fairness, it had been two years since she'd called Sir Robert Kent an overgrown stoat, and frankly, that had been far more charitable than the other items on her mental accounting.

But digressions aside, Miranda now got to do married lady sorts of things, for which Olivia would like to have formed a list, except that no one (not even Miranda, and Olivia still had not forgiven her for this) would tell her what it was that married ladies did, aside from not having to wear pastel colors, not having to be accompanied by a chaperone at all times, and producing small infants at reasonable intervals.

Olivia was quite certain there was more to the last bit. That was the one that sent her mother fleeing from the room every time she asked.

But back to Miranda. She had produced a small infant—Olivia's darling niece Caroline, for whom she'd happily throw herself under hooves, equine or otherwise—and was now on her way to producing another, which meant that she was not available for regular afternoon chitchat. And as Olivia *liked* chitchat—*and* fashion *and* gossip—she found herself spending more and more time with Anne, Mary, and Philomena. And while they were often entertaining, and never malicious, they were, slightly more than occasionally, foolish.

Like right now.

"Who are *they*, anyway?" Olivia asked.

"They?" Anne echoed.

"They. The people who say my new neighbor killed his fiancée."

Anne paused. She looked at Mary. "Do you recall?"

Mary shook her head. "I don't, actually. Sarah Forsythe, perhaps?"

"No," Philomena put in, shaking her head with great certitude. "It wasn't Sarah. She only got back from Bath two days ago. Libby Lockwood?"

"Not Libby," Anne said. "I would have remembered if it were Libby."

"That's my point," Olivia interjected. "You don't know who said it. None of us does."

"Well, I didn't make it up," Anne said, a touch defensively.

"I didn't say you did. I would never think that of you." It was true. Anne repeated most anything uttered in her presence, but she never made things up. Olivia paused, collecting her thoughts. "Don't you think it's the sort of rumor one might want to verify?"

This was met with three blank stares.

Olivia tried a different tactic. "If only for your own personal safety. If such a thing were true—"

"Then you think it is?" Anne asked, in a rather pinning-you-down sort of voice.

"No." *Good heavens.* "I don't. But if it *were*, then surely he would not be someone with whom we would wish to associate."

This was met with a long beat of silence, finally broken by Philomena: "My mother has already told me to avoid him."

"Which is why," Olivia continued, feeling a bit as if she were slogging through mud, "we should ascertain its accuracy. Because if it's *not* true—"

"He's very handsome," Mary cut in. Followed by, "Well, he *is*."

Olivia blinked, trying to follow.

"I've never seen him," Philomena said.

"He wears only black," Mary said, rather confidentially.

"I saw him in dark blue," Anne contradicted.

"He wears only dark colors," Mary amended, shooting Anne an irritated glance. "And his eyes—oh, they could burn right through you."

"What color are they?" Olivia asked, imagining all sorts of interesting hues—red, yellow, orange . . .

"Blue."

"Gray," Anne said.

"Bluish gray. But they're quite piercing."

Anne nodded, having no correction to attach to that statement.

"What color is his hair?" Olivia asked. Surely this was an overlooked detail.

"Dark brown," the two girls answered in unison.

"As dark as mine?" Philomena asked, fingering her own locks.

"Darker," Mary said.

"But not black," Anne added. "Not quite."

"And he's tall," Mary said.

"They always are," Olivia murmured.

"But not too tall," Mary continued. "I don't like a gangly man, myself."

"Surely you've seen him," Anne said to Olivia, "what with his living right next door."

"I don't believe I have," Olivia murmured. "He only let the house at the beginning of the month, and I was at the Macclesfield house party for a week of that."

"When did you return to London?" Anne asked.

"Six days ago," Olivia replied, briskly returning to the topic at hand with: "I didn't even know there was a bachelor in residence." Which, it belatedly occurred to her, implied that if she *had* known, she would have tried to find out more about him.

Which was probably true, but she wasn't going to admit to it.

"Do you know what I heard?" Philomena suddenly asked. "He *thrashed* Julian Prentice."

"*What?*" This, from everyone.

"And you're only just mentioning this now?" Anne added, with great disbelief.

Philomena waved her off. "My brother told me. He and Julian are great friends."

"What happened?" Mary asked.

"That was the part I couldn't get very clearly," Philomena admitted. "Robert was somewhat vague."

"Men *never* recall the correct details," Olivia said, thinking of her own twin brother, Winston. He was worthless for gossip, just worthless.

Philomena nodded. "Robert came home, and he was in quite a state. Rather . . . er . . . disheveled."

They all nodded. They all had brothers.

"He could barely stand upright," Philomena continued. "And he stank to high heaven." She waved her hand in front of her nose. "I had to help him get past the drawing room so Mama wouldn't see him."

"Then he is now in your debt," Olivia said, always thinking.

Philomena nodded. "Apparently they were out and about, doing whatever it is men do, and Julian was a bit, er . . ."

"Soused?" Anne put in.

"He frequently is," Olivia added.

"Yes. Which stands to reason, given my brother's condition when he returned home." Philomena paused, her brow wrinkling as if she were considering something—but then, just as quickly, it was gone, and she continued, "He said that Julian did nothing out of the ordinary, and then there was Sir Harry, practically tearing him apart from limb to limb."

"Was there blood?" Olivia asked.

"Olivia!" Mary scolded.

"It's a pertinent question."

"I do not know if there was blood," Philomena said, a bit officiously.

"I would think so," Olivia mused. "What with limbs being torn off."

> *Limbs I would least mind doing without,*
> *in descending order*
> *By Olivia Bevelstoke*
> *(all limbs currently intact)*

No, forget that one. She wiggled her toes in her slippers reassuringly.

"He does have a blackened eye," Philomena continued.

"Sir Harry?" Anne asked.

"Julian Prentice. Sir Harry might have a blackened eye. I would not know. I've never seen him."

"I saw him two days ago," Mary said. "He did not have a blackened eye."

"Did he look at all impaired?"

"No. Lovely as ever. All in black, though. It's very curious."

"All?" Olivia pressed.

"Most. White shirt and cravat. But still—" Mary flipped a hand through the air, as if she just could not accept the possibility of it. "It's as if he's in mourning."

"Perhaps he is," Anne said, jumping on that. "For the fiancée!"

"The one he killed?" Philomena asked.

"He didn't kill anyone!" Olivia exclaimed.

"How do you know?" the other three said in unison.

Olivia would have answered, but it occurred to her that she *didn't* know. She'd never clapped eyes on the man, never even heard a whisper about him until this afternoon. But still, common sense was surely on her side. The killing of one's fiancée sounded far too much like one of those gothic novels Anne and Mary were always reading.

"Olivia?" someone said.

She blinked, realizing that she'd been silent for a beat too long. "It's nothing," she said, giving her head a little shake. "Just thinking."

"About Sir Harry," Anne said, a little smugly.

"It's not as if I've been given the opportunity to think of anything else," Olivia muttered.

"What would you rather be thinking about?" Philomena asked.

Olivia opened her mouth to speak, then realized she hadn't a clue how to answer. "Anything," she finally said. "Almost anything."

But her curiosity had been piqued. And Olivia Frances Bevelstoke's curiosity was a formidable thing indeed.

The girl in the house to the north was watching him again. She'd been doing it for the better part of a week now. At first Harry had thought nothing of it. She was the daughter of the Earl of Rudland, for God's sake, or if not that, then some sort of relation—if she were a servant she'd surely have been sacked by now for all the time she spent standing at the window.

And she wasn't the governess. The Earl of Rudland had a wife, or so Harry had been told. No wife allowed a governess who looked like *that* into her household.

So she was almost certainly the daughter. Which meant that he had no reason to suppose she was anything other than a typically nosy society miss, the sort who thought nothing of peering at one's new neighbors. Except that she had been watching him for *five days*. Surely if she were curious about only the cut of his coat and the color of his hair, she'd have completed her perusal by now.

He'd been tempted to wave. Plaster an enormous, cheerful smile on his face and wave. That would put a halt to her spying. Except then he would never know *why* she was so interested.

Which was unacceptable. Harry never could tolerate an unanswered "why."

Not to mention that he was not *quite* close enough to her window to see her answering expression. Which defeated the purpose of the wave. If she was going to be embarrassed, he wanted to see it. What was the fun in it, otherwise?

Harry sat back down at his desk, acting as if he hadn't a clue that she was peeking at him from behind her curtains. He had work to do, and he needed to stop wondering about the blonde up at the window. A messenger from the War Office had delivered a rather lengthy document earlier that morning, and it needed translating right away. Harry always followed the same routine when converting Russian to English—first a quick read, for the overall meaning, then a closer look, examining the document on a more word-by-word level. Only then, after this thorough perusal, did he pick up a pen and ink and begin his translation.

It was a tedious task. *He* liked it, but then again, he'd always liked puzzles. He could sit with a document for hours, and realize only when the sun went down that he had not eaten all day. But even he, who was so enamored of the task, could not imagine spending the day *watching* someone translate documents.

And yet there she was, once again at her window. Probably thinking she was so very good at concealment and he an absolute dunce.

He smirked. She had no idea. Harry might work for the dull branch of the War Office—the one that dealt with words and papers instead of guns, knives, and secret missions—but he was well trained. He'd spent ten years in the military, most of them on the Continent, where an observant eye and a keen sense for movement could make the difference between life and death.

He'd noticed, for example, that she had a habit of tucking loose strands of hair behind her ear. And because she sometimes watched him at night, he knew that when she let it down—the entire, unbelievably sunshiny mass of it—the ends hit right in the middle of her back.

He knew that her dressing gown was blue. And, regrettably, rather shapeless.

She had no talent for holding still. She probably thought she did; she wasn't a fidgeter, and her posture was straight and direct. But something always gave her away—a little flutter of her fingertips, or perhaps a tiny elevation of her shoulders as she drew breath.

And of course, by this point, Harry couldn't possibly *not* notice her.

It did make him wonder. What part of his being hunched over a sheaf of papers was so interesting to her? Because that was all he had been doing all week.

Perhaps he ought to liven up the spectacle. Really, it would be the kind thing to do. She had to be bored silly.

He could jump on his desk and sing.

Take a bite of food and pretend to choke. What would she do, then?

Now *that* would be an interesting moral dilemma. He set down his pen for a moment, thinking about the various society ladies he'd had cause to meet. He was not so very cynical; he fully believed that some of them, at least, would make an attempt to save him. But he rather doubted any possessed the necessary athletic skills to make it over in time.

He'd best chew his food carefully.

Harry let out a long breath and attempted to refocus his attention on his work. His eyes had been turned toward his papers the entire time he'd been thinking about the girl at the window, but he had not read a thing. He'd got *nothing* done in the past five days. He supposed he could draw the curtain, but that would be too obvious. Especially now, at half noon, with the sun high and bright.

He stared down at the words before him, but he could not concentrate. She was still there, still staring at him, imagining herself concealed behind the curtain.

Why the hell was she watching him?

Harry didn't like it. There was no way she could see what he was working on, and even if she could, he rather doubted she read Cyrillic. But still, the documents on his desk were often of a sensitive nature, occasionally even of national importance. If someone was spying on him . . .

He shook his head. If someone was spying on him, it wouldn't be the daughter of the Earl of Rudland, for God's sake.

And then, miraculously, she was gone. She turned first, her chin lifting perhaps an inch, and then she stepped away. She'd heard a noise; probably someone had called out to her. Harry didn't care. He was just glad she was gone. He needed to get to work.

He looked down, got halfway through the first page, and then:

"Good morning, Sir Harry!"

It was Sebastian, clearly in a jocular mood. He wouldn't be calling Harry Sir Anything, otherwise. Harry didn't look up. "It's afternoon."

"Not when one awakens at eleven."

Harry fought off a sigh. "You didn't knock."

"I never do." Sebastian flopped into a chair, apparently not noticing when his dark hair did its own flop—into his eyes. "What are you doing?"

"Working."

"You do that a lot."

"Some of us don't have earldoms to inherit," Harry remarked, trying to finish at least one more sentence before Sebastian would require his complete attention.

"Perhaps," Sebastian murmured. "Perhaps not."

This was true. Sebastian had always been second-in-line to inherit; his uncle the Earl of Newbury had sired only one son, Geoffrey. But the earl (who still thought Sebastian a complete wastrel, despite his decade of service to His Majesty's Empire) had not been concerned. After all, there had been little reason to suppose that Sebastian might inherit. Geoffrey had married while Sebastian was in the army, and his wife had borne two daughters, so clearly the man could produce a baby.

But then Geoffrey had taken a fever and died. As soon as it became apparent that his widow was not increasing and therefore no young heir was in the offing to save the earldom from the devastation that was Sebastian Grey, the long-widowed earl had taken it upon himself to produce a new heir to the title and to that end was now gadding about London, shopping for a wife.

Which meant that no one knew quite what to make of Sebastian. Either he was the devastatingly handsome and charming heir to an ancient and wealthy earldom, in which case he was without a doubt the biggest prize on the marriage mart, or he was the devastatingly handsome and charming heir to nothing, in which case he might be a society matron's worst nightmare.

Still, he was invited everywhere. And when it came to London society, he knew everything.

Which was why Harry knew he'd get an answer when he asked, "Does the Earl of Rudland have a daughter?"

Sebastian regarded him with an expression that

most would interpret as bored, but that Harry knew meant, *You nodcock.*

"Of course," Sebastian said.

The "nodcock" bit, Harry decided, was implied.

"Why?" Sebastian asked.

Harry glanced briefly toward the window, even though she wasn't there. "Is she blond?"

"Very much so."

"Quite pretty?"

Sebastian slid into a sly smile. "More than that, by most standards."

Harry frowned. What the devil was Rudland's daughter doing watching him so closely?

Sebastian yawned, not bothering to cover it, even when Harry shot him a disgusted look. "Any particular reason for the sudden interest?"

Harry stepped toward the window, regarding *her* window, which he now knew was on the second floor, third from the right. "She's watching me."

"Lady Olivia Bevelstoke is watching you," Sebastian repeated.

"Is that her name?" Harry murmured.

"She's not watching you."

Harry turned. "I beg your pardon."

Sebastian gave a rude shrug. "Lady Olivia Bevelstoke doesn't need you."

"I never said she did."

"She had five proposals of marriage last year, and the number would have been double that if she hadn't dissuaded several gentlemen before they made fools of themselves."

"You know a great deal about society for one who claims disinterest."

"Have I ever claimed disinterest?" Sebastian stroked his chin in an affectation of thoughtfulness. "How untruthful of me."

Harry gave him a bit of a stare, then rose to his feet and walked to the window, free to do so now that Lady Olivia was gone.

"Anything exciting?" Sebastian murmured.

Harry ignored him, moving his head slightly to the left, not that that did much to improve his vantage point. Still, she'd left the window scrim tied back farther than usual, and if the sun weren't glinting on the glass, he'd have had a good view into her room. Certainly the best yet.

"Is she there?" Sebastian asked, his voice dipping into a mocking quaver. "Is she watching you *right now*?"

Harry turned, then immediately rolled his eyes when he saw Sebastian moving his hands about, his fingers making odd flexing motions as if he were trying to fend off a ghost.

"You're an idiot," Harry said.

"But a handsome one," Sebastian returned, immediately resuming his slouch. "And terribly charming. It gets me out of so much trouble."

Harry turned, leaning lazily against the window frame. "To what do I owe the pleasure?"

"I pine for your company."

Harry waited patiently.

"I need money?" Sebastian tried.

"Far more likely, but I have it on the best authority that you lightened Winterhoe's purse by a hundred quid Tuesday last."

"And you say you don't follow gossip."

Harry shrugged. He paid attention when it suited him.

"It was two hundred, I'll have you know. Would have been more, too, if Winterhoe's brother hadn't shown up and hauled him off."

Harry did not comment. He had little affection for Winterhoe or his brother, but he could not help but sympathize.

"Sorry," Sebastian said, correctly interpreting Harry's silence. "How is the young whelp?"

Harry glanced toward the ceiling. His younger brother Edward was still abed, presumably sleeping off whatever excesses he'd got himself into the previous night. "Still detests me." He shrugged. The only reason Harry had moved to London was to keep an eye on his younger brother, and Edward hated that he'd been forced to bow to his authority. "He'll grow out of it."

"Are you evil these days, or just an old stick?"

Harry felt the stirrings of a smile. "An old stick, I think."

Sebastian slouched ever more into the chair and gave the impression of a shrug. "I'd rather be evil."

"There are some who would say you needn't worry on that score," Harry murmured.

"Now, now, Sir Harry," Sebastian admonished. "I've never debauched an innocent."

Harry acknowledged the statement with a nod. All appearances to the contrary, Sebastian did conduct his life according to a certain code of ethics. It was not a code that most would recognize, but it was there, nonetheless. And if he'd ever seduced a virgin, he'd certainly not done so on purpose.

"I heard you gave someone a beating last week," Sebastian said.

Harry shook his head in disgust. "He'll be fine."

"That's not what I asked."

Harry turned back from the window to face Sebastian directly. "Actually, you didn't ask anything."

"Very well," Sebastian said with exaggerated concession. "Why did you beat the young thing to a pulp?"

"It wasn't like that," Harry said irritably.

"I heard you knocked him unconscious."

"That he managed for himself." Harry shook his head with disgust. "He was completely sotted. I punched him once, in the face. At most, I hastened his blackout by ten minutes."

"It's not like you to strike another man unprovoked," Sebastian said quietly, "even if he has had too much to drink."

Harry's jaw clenched. He was not proud of the episode, but at the same time, he could not bring himself to regret it. "He was bothering someone," he said tightly. And that was all he was going to say. Sebastian knew him well enough to know what that meant.

Sebastian nodded thoughtfully, then let out a long sigh. Harry took that to mean that he would drop the subject, and he walked back over to his desk, surreptitiously glancing over at the window on his way.

"Is she there?" Sebastian asked suddenly.

Harry did not pretend to misunderstand. "No." He sat back down, finding his spot in the Russian document.

"Is she there *now*?"

It was remarkable how quickly this was growing tedious. "Seb—"

"Now?

"Why *are* you here?"

Sebastian sat up a bit. "I need you to go to the Smythe-Smith musicale on Thursday."

"Why?"

"I promised someone I'd go, and—"

"Whom did you promise?"

"It doesn't matter."

"It does to me, if I'm forced to attend."

Sebastian colored slightly, always an entertaining, if unusual, event. "Very well, it's my grandmother. She cornered me last week."

Harry groaned. Any other female, and he'd have been able to get out of it. But a promise to a grandmother—that had to be upheld.

"Then you'll go?" Sebastian asked.

"Yes," Harry said with a sigh. He hated these things, but at least at a musicale one didn't have to make polite conversation all evening. He could sit in his seat, say nothing, and if he looked bored, well, so would everyone else.

"Excellent. Shall I—"

"Wait a moment." Harry turned to him suspiciously. "Why do you need *me*?" Because really, Sebastian hardly lacked social confidence.

Sebastian shifted uncomfortably in his seat. "I suspect my uncle will be there."

"Since when has that scared you?"

"It doesn't." Seb shot him a look of pure disgust. "But Grandmama is likely to try to mend the rift and—Oh, for God's sake, does it matter? Will you go or won't you?"

"Of course." Because really, it hadn't been in any doubt. If Sebastian needed him, Harry would be there.

Sebastian stood, and whatever distress he'd been feeling was gone, replaced by his customary nonchalance. "I owe you."

"I've stopped counting."

Seb laughed at that. "I'll go wake the whelp for you. Even I think it's an unseemly hour to still be abed."

"Be my guest. You're the only thing about me Edward respects."

"Respects?"

"Admires," Harry amended. Edward had more than once expressed his disbelief that his brother—whom he found dull beyond measure—should be so close to Sebastian, whom he wished to emulate in every way.

Sebastian paused at the door. "Is breakfast still laid?"

"Get out of here," Harry said. "And shut the door, will you?"

Sebastian did so, but his chortling rang through the house nonetheless. Harry flexed his fingers and looked back at his desk, where the Russian documents still sat untouched. He had only two days to complete this assignment. Thank God the girl—Lady Olivia— had left her room.

At the thought of her, he looked up, but without his usual care, since he knew she was gone.

Except she wasn't.

And this time, she had to know that he'd seen her.

Chapter Two

Olivia dropped to all fours, her heart pounding. He'd seen her. He had definitely seen her. She'd seen it in his eyes, in the sharp twist of his head. Dear God, how would she explain herself? Genteel young ladies did not spy upon their neighbors. They gossiped about them, inspected the cuts of their coats and the quality of their carriages, but they did not, repeat *not*, spy on them through windows.

Even if said neighbor was a possible murderer.

Which Olivia still did not believe.

That said, however, Sir Harry Valentine was definitely up to something. His behavior this past week was not normal. Not that Olivia could claim knowledge as to what constituted normal for *him*, but she had two brothers. She knew what men did in their offices and studies.

She knew, for example, that most men did not *occupy*

their offices and studies, at least not for ten hours each day, as Sir Harry seemed to. And she knew that when they did happen to go into their offices, it was usually to avoid relations of the female persuasion, and not, as was the case with Sir Harry, to spend their time studiously examining papers and documents.

Olivia would have given her eyeteeth, and perhaps a molar or two, to have known what was in those papers. All day long, every day, he was there at his desk, poring over loose papers. Sometimes it almost looked as if he were copying them.

But that made no sense. Men like Sir Harry employed secretaries for that sort of thing.

Her heart still racing, Olivia glanced up, assessing her situation. Not that looking up was of any use; still, the window was above her, and really, it was only natural that she might—

"No, no, don't move."

Olivia let out a groan. Winston, her twin brother—or, as she liked to think of him, her younger brother, by precisely three minutes—was standing in the doorway. Or rather, he was leaning casually against the door frame, attempting to appear the devil-may-care charmer he was currently devoting his life attempting to be.

Which, admittedly, was not very good grammar, but it did seem to describe him precisely as he was. Winston's blond hair was artfully mussed, his cravat tied just so, and yes, his boots were made by Weston himself, but anyone with an ounce of sense could see he was still wet behind the ears. Why all of her friends went dreamy-eyed and downright stupid in his presence she'd never understand.

"Winston," she ground out, unwilling to offer any further acknowledgment.

"Stay," he said, holding a hand forward, palm toward her. "Just one more moment. I'm trying to burn the image into my memory."

Olivia gave him a surly bit of lip and carefully crawled along the wall, away from the window.

"Let me guess," he said. "Blisters on both feet."

She ignored him.

"You and Mary Cadogan are writing a new theatrical. You're playing the sheep."

Never had he been more deserving of a comeback, but sadly, never had Olivia been in less of a position to deliver one.

"Had I known," he added, "I'd have brought a riding crop."

She was *almost* close enough to bite his leg. "Winston?"

"Yes?"

"Shut up."

He laughed.

"I'm going to kill you," she announced, rising to her feet. She'd skirted half the length of the room. There was no way Sir Harry would be able to see her here.

"With your hooves?"

"Oh, stop it," she said disgustedly. And then she realized that he was ambling into the room. "Get away from the window!"

Winston froze, then twisted around to face her. His brows were arched in question.

"Step back," Olivia said. "That's it. Slowly, slowly . . ."

He feigned a motion forward.

Her heart lurched. "Winston!"

"Really, Olivia," he said, turning around and planting his hands on his hips. "What are you doing?"

She swallowed. There would be no avoiding telling him *some*thing. He'd seen her crawling about the room like an idiot. He would expect an explanation. Heaven knew she would, had their positions been reversed.

But she might not have to tell him the *truth*. Surely there was some other explanation for her actions.

Reasons Why I Might Be Crawling About
on the Floor
AND Need to Avoid the Window

No. She had nothing.

"It's our neighbor," Olivia said, resorting to the truth, since, given her position, she had no other choice.

Winston's head turned toward the window. Slowly, and with as much sarcasm as a lateral move of the head could convey.

Which, Olivia had to admit, was quite a bit when performed by a Bevelstoke.

"Our neighbor," he repeated. "Do we have one?"

"Sir Harry Valentine. He leased the house while you were in Gloucestershire."

Winston nodded slowly. "And his presence in Mayfair has you crawling on the floor . . . because . . ."

"I was watching him."

"Sir Harry."

"Yes."

"From your knees."

"Of course not. He saw me, and—"

"And now he thinks you're a lunatic."

"Yes. *No*! I don't know." She let out a furious exhale. "I'm hardly privy to his inner thoughts."

Winston quirked a brow. "As opposed to his inner bedchamber, which you are—"

"It's his *office*," she cut in heatedly.

"Which you feel the need to spy upon because . . ."

"Because Anne and Mary said—" Olivia cut herself off, well aware that if she said why she was spying on Sir Harry she'd look more of a fool than she did already.

"Oh no, don't stop now," he implored dryly. "If Anne and Mary said it, I *definitely* want to hear it."

Her mouth clamped into a businesslike frown. "Fine. But you mustn't repeat it."

"I try not to repeat anything they say," he said frankly.

"*Winston*."

"I won't say a word." He held up his hands, as if in surrender.

Olivia gave a curt nod of acknowledgment. "Because it isn't even true."

"That, I already knew, considering the source."

"Win—"

"Oh, come now, Olivia. You know better than to trust anything those two tell you."

She felt a reluctant need to defend them. "They're not that bad."

"Not at all," he agreed, "just lacking in any ability to discern truth from fiction."

He was correct, but still, they were her friends, and *he* was annoying, so it wasn't as if she was going to admit it. Instead, she ignored his statement altogether and continued with: "I mean it, Winston. You must keep this a secret."

"I give you my word," he said, sounding almost bored by the whole thing.

"What I say in this room . . ."

"Stays in this room," he finished. "Olivia . . ."

"Fine. Anne and Mary said they had heard that Sir Harry had killed his fiancée—no, don't interrupt, I don't believe it, either—but then I got to thinking, well, how does a rumor like that get started?"

"From Anne Buxton and Mary Cadogan," Winston answered.

"They never start rumors," Olivia said. "They only repeat them."

"A critical difference."

Olivia felt similarly, but this was neither the time nor place to agree with her brother. "We *know* he has a temper," she continued.

"We do? How?"

"You didn't hear about Julian Prentice?"

"Oh, that." Winston rolled his eyes.

"What do you mean?"

"He barely touched him. Julian was so far gone a gust of wind could have knocked him out."

"But Sir Harry *did* hit him."

Winston waved a hand. "I suppose."

"Why?"

He shrugged, then crossed his arms. "No one knows, really. Or at least, no one is telling. But stop for a moment—what does any of this have to do with you?"

"I was curious," she admitted. It sounded beyond foolish, but it was the truth. And she couldn't possibly embarrass herself any *more* this afternoon.

"Curious about what?"

"Him." She jerked her head toward the window. "I didn't even know what he looked like. And *yes*," she said pointedly, putting a halt to the interruption she could see forming on his lips, "I know that what he looks like has nothing at all to do with whether or not he's killed anyone, but I couldn't help myself. He lives right next door."

He crossed his arms. "And you're worried he's planning to steal over and slit your throat?"

"Winston!"

"I'm sorry, Olivia," he said, laughing, "but you must admit, it's the most ludicrous thing—"

"But it's not," she put in earnestly. "It *was*. That I agree. But then—I started watching him, and I tell you, Winston, there is something very peculiar about that man."

"Which you've discerned in the last—" Winston frowned. "How long have you been spying upon him?"

"Five days."

"Five *days*?" Gone was the bored-aristocrat expression, replaced by mouth-dropping disbelief. "Good Lord, Olivia, haven't you anything better to do with your time?"

She tried not to look embarrassed. "Apparently not."

"And he didn't see you? In all that time?"

"No," she lied, and quite smoothly, too. "And I don't want him to. That was why I was crawling away from the window."

He looked over at the window. Then back at her, his head moving slowly, and with great skepticism. "Very well. What have you discerned about our new neighbor?"

She plopped herself down into a chair at the back wall, surprised by how much she wanted to tell him her findings. "*Well*. Most of the time he seems quite ordinary."

"Shocking."

She scowled. "Do you want me to tell you or not? Because I won't continue if all you're going to do is mock me."

He motioned for her to continue with a patently sarcastic flick of his hand.

"He spends an inordinate amount of time at his desk."

Winston nodded. "A sure sign of murderous intent."

"When was the last time *you* spent any time at a desk?" she shot back.

"Point taken."

"And," she continued, with considerable emphasis "I also think he is given to disguises."

That got his attention. "Disguises?"

"Yes. Sometimes he wears spectacles and sometimes he does not. And twice he was worn an extremely peculiar hat. Inside."

"I can't believe I am listening to this," Winston stated.

"Who wears a hat inside?"

"You've gone mad. It's the only explanation."

"Furthermore, he wears only black." Olivia thought back to Anne's comments earlier in the week. "Or dark blue. Not that *that* is suspicious," she added, because the truth was, if she hadn't been the one uttering the words, she'd probably have thought her an idiot, too. The entire escapade did sound quite useless when put so plainly.

She sighed. "I know this sounds ridiculous, but I tell you, something is not right with that man."

Winston stared at her for several seconds before finally saying, "Olivia, you have too much time on your hands. Although . . ."

She knew he was letting his words trail of purposefully, but she also knew that she was not going to be able to resist the bait. "Although what?" she ground out.

"Well, I must say, it does demonstrate an uncharacteristic tenacity on your part."

"What do you mean by that?" she demanded.

The look he gave her was condescending in the way that only a sibling could manage. "You must admit, you don't possess a reputation for seeing things through to the end."

"That is not true!"

He crossed his arms. "What about that model of St. Paul's you were building?"

Her jaw dropped into an openmouthed gasp. She could not *believe* he was using that as an example. "The *dog* knocked it over!"

"Perhaps you recall a certain vow to write to Grandmother every week?"

"You're even worse at it than I am."

"Ah, but I never promised diligence. I also never took up oil painting or the violin."

Olivia's hands balled at her sides. So she hadn't taken more than six lessons at painting, or one at violin. It was because she had been dreadful at both. And who wanted to hammer endlessly at an endeavor for which one had no talent?

"We were speaking of Sir Harry," she ground out.

Winston smiled a little. "So we were."

She stared at him. Hard. He still had that look on his face—one part supercilious, two parts just plain annoying. He was taking far too much pleasure in having needled her.

"Very well," he said, suddenly solicitous. "Tell me, what is so 'not right' about Sir Harry Valentine?"

She waited a moment before speaking, then said, "Twice I have seen him throw masses of paper into the fire."

"Twice I have seen myself do the very same thing," Winston replied. "What else do you expect a man to do with paper that needs discarding? Olivia, you—"

"It was the *way* he was doing it."

Winston looked as if he'd like to respond but couldn't find words.

"He hurled it in," Olivia said. "Hurled it! In a mad rush."

Winston started shaking his head.

"Then he looked over his shoulder—"

"You really *have* been watching him for five days."

"Don't interrupt," she snapped, and then, without taking a breath: "He looked over his shoulder as if he could hear someone coming from down the hall."

"Let me guess. Someone *was* coming from down the hall."

"Yes!" she said excitedly. "His butler entered *exactly then*. At least I think it was his butler. It was someone, at any rate."

Winston looked at her hard. "And the other time?"

"The other time?"

"That he burned his papers."

"Oh," she said, "that. It was rather ordinary, actually."

Winston stared at her for several moments before saying, "Olivia, you must stop spying on the man."

"But—"

He held up a hand. "Whatever you think Sir Harry is, I promise you, you're wrong."

"I've also seen him stuffing money into a pouch."

"Olivia, I *know* Sir Harry Valentine. He's as normal as can be."

"You *know* him?" And he'd let her run on like an idiot? She was going to kill him.

How I Would Like to Kill My Brother, Version Sixteen By Olivia Bevelstoke

No, really, what was the point? She could hardly top Version Fifteen, which had featured both vivisection and wild boar.

"Well, I don't actually know him," Winston explained. "But I know his brother. We were at university together. And I know *of* Sir Harry. If he's burning papers it's merely to tidy his desk."

"And that hat?" Olivia demanded. "Winston, it has feathers." She threw her arms into the air and waved them about, trying to depict the hideousness of it. "Plumes of them!"

"That I cannot explain." Winston shrugged, then he grinned. "But I'd love to see it for myself."

She scowled, since it was the least infantile reaction she could think of.

"Furthermore," he continued with a cross of his arms, "he doesn't have a fiancée."

"Well, yes, but—"

"And he's never had one."

Which did support Olivia's opinion that the whole rumor was nothing but air, but it was galling that Winston was the one to prove it. If indeed he *had* proved it; Winston was hardly an authority on the man.

"Oh, by the by," Winston said, in what was far too casual a voice, "I assume that Mother and Father are not aware of your recent investigative activities."

Why, the little weasel. "You said you wouldn't say anything," Olivia said accusingly.

"I said I wouldn't say anything about that rot from Mary Cadogan and Anne Buxton. I didn't say anything about *your* brand of madness."

"What do you want, Winston?" Olivia ground out.

He looked her directly in the eye. "I'm taking ill on Thursday. Do *not* contradict."

Olivia mentally flipped through her social calendar. Thursday . . . Thursday . . . *the Smythe-Smith musicale*. "Oh, no you don't!" she cried, lurching toward him.

He fanned the air near his head. "My tender ears, you know . . ."

Olivia tried to think of a suitable retort and was viciously disappointed when all she came up with was: "You—you—"

"I wouldn't make threats, were I you."

"If I have to go, you have to go."

He gave her a sickly smile. "Funny how the world never seems to work that way."

"Winston!"

He was still laughing as he ducked out the door.

Olivia allowed herself just a moment to wallow in her irritation before deciding that she'd *rather* attend the Smythe-Smith musicale without her brother. The only reason she'd wanted him to go was to see him suffer, and she was sure she could come up with other ways to achieve that objective. Furthermore, if Winston were forced to sit still for the performance, he'd surely entertain himself by torturing *her* the entire time. The previous year he'd poked a hole in her right rib cage, and the year before that . . .

Well, suffice it to say that Olivia's revenge had included an aged egg *and* three of her friends, all convinced he'd fallen into desperate love, and she still didn't think the score had been made even.

So really, it was best that he'd not be there. She had far more pressing worries than her twin brother, anyway.

Frowning, she turned her attention back to her bedroom window. It was closed, of course; the day was not so fine as to encourage fresh air. But the curtains were tied back, and the clear pane of glass beckoned and taunted. From her vantage point at the far side of her room she could see only the brick of his outer wall, and maybe a sliver of glass from a different—not his study—window. If she twisted a bit. And if there weren't a glare.

She squinted.

She scooted her chair a bit to the right, trying to avoid the glare.

She craned her neck.

Then, before she had the chance to think the better of it, she dropped back to the floor, using her left foot to kick her bedroom door shut. The last thing she needed was Winston catching her on hands and knees again.

Slowly she inched forward, wondering what on earth she thought she was doing—really, was she just going to rise when she reached the window, as if to say, *I fell, and now I'm back up*?

Oh, that would make sense.

And then it occurred to her—in her panic, she'd quite forgotten that he must be wondering why she'd fallen to the floor. He'd seen her—of that she was certain—and then she'd dropped.

Dropped. Not turned, not walked away, but dropped. Like a stone.

Was he staring up at her window right now, wondering what had become of her? Did he think she was ill? Might he even come to her house to inquire after her welfare?

Olivia's heart began to race. The embarrassment would be unfathomable. Winston would not stop laughing for a week.

No, no, she assured herself, he wouldn't think she was ill. Just clumsy. Surely just clumsy. Which meant that she needed to stand, get up and about, and show herself walking around the room in perfect health.

And maybe she should wave, since she knew he knew she knew he'd seen her.

She paused, going over that last bit in her head. Was that the right number of *knews*?

But more to the point, this was the first time he'd spotted her at the window. He had no idea she'd been watching him for five days. Of that she was certain. So really, he would have no reason to be suspicious.

They were in London, for heaven's sake. The most populous city in Britain. People saw one another in windows all the time. The only dodgy thing about the encounter was that she'd acted like an utter fool and failed to acknowledge him.

She needed to wave. She needed to smile and wave as if to say—*Isn't this all so very amusing?*

She could do that. Sometimes it felt like her whole life was smiling and waving and pretending it was all so very amusing. She knew how to behave in any social situation, and what was this if not an—albeit unusual—social situation?

This was where Olivia Bevelstoke shone.

She scrambled to the side of the room so that she could rise to her feet out of his line of sight. Then, as if nothing were amiss, she strolled toward the window, parallel to the outer wall, clearly focused on something ahead of her, because that was what she would be doing while minding her own business in her bedchamber.

Then, just at the correct moment, she would glance to the side, as if she'd heard a bird chirping, or maybe a squirrel, and she would happen to see out the window, because that was what *would* happen in such a situation, and then, when she caught a glimpse of her neighbor, she would smile ever so slightly with recognition. Her eyes would show the faintest spark of surprise, and she would wave.

Which she did. Perfectly. At the wrong person.

And now Sir Harry's butler must think her an absolute moron.

Chapter Three

Mozart, Mozart, Bach (the elder), more Mozart.

Olivia looked down at the program for the annual Smythe-Smith musicale, idly fingering the corner until it grew soft and ragged. It all looked the same as last year, except that there seemed to be a new girl at the cello. Curious. Olivia chewed on the inside of her lip as she considered this. How many Smythe-Smith cousins of the female variety could there be? According to Philomena, who had got it from her elder sister, the Smythe-Smiths had played as a string quartet every year since 1807. And yet the girls performing never managed to age past twenty. There was always another waiting in the wings, it seemed.

Poor things. Olivia supposed they were all forced to be musical whether they liked it or not. It wouldn't do to run out of cellists, and heaven knew, two of the girls hardly looked strong enough to hoist their violins.

Musical Instruments I Might Like To Play,
Had I Talent
By Lady Olivia Bevelstoke

Flute
Piccolo
Tuba

It was good to choose the unexpected from time to time. And the tuba might double as a weapon.

Musical instruments she was fairly certain she would *not* wish to play would include anything of the stringed variety, because even if she managed to exceed the accomplishments of the Smythe-Smith cousins (legendary for their musicales for all the wrong reasons), she would still likely sound like a dying cow.

She'd tried the violin once. Her mother had had it removed from the house.

Come to think of it, Olivia was rarely invited to sing, either.

Ah well, she had other talents, she supposed. She could produce a better-than-average watercolor, and she was rarely at a loss in conversation. And if she wasn't musical, at least no one was forcing her on a stage once a year to bludgeon the ears of the unwary.

Or not so unwary. Olivia looked about the room. She recognized almost everyone—surely they all knew what to expect. The Smythe-Smith musicale had become a rite of passage. One had to do it because . . .

Well now, that was a good question. Possibly unanswerable.

Olivia looked back down at her program, even though she'd already read through it three times. The card was a creamy color, and the hue seemed to melt into the yellow silk of her skirts. She'd wanted to wear her new blue velvet, but then she'd thought a cheerful color might be more useful. Cheerful and distracting. Although, she thought, frowning down at her attire, the yellow wasn't proving all that distracting, and she was no longer so sure she liked the cut of the lace on the border, and—

"He's here."

Olivia looked up from her program. Mary Cadogan was standing above her—no, now she was sitting down, taking the seat Olivia was supposed to have reserved for her mother.

Olivia was about to ask who, but then the Smythe-Smiths began to warm up their instruments.

She flinched, then winced, then made the mistake of looking toward the makeshift stage to see what could have made so wretched a sound. She was not able to determine the origin, but the wretched *expression* on the face of the violist was enough to make her avert her eyes.

"Did you hear me?" Mary said urgently, poking her in the side. "He's here. Your neighbor." At Olivia's blank stare, she practically hissed, "Sir Harry Valentine!"

"Here?" Olivia instantly twisted in her seat.

"Don't look!"

And twisted back. "Why is he here?" she whispered.

Mary fussed with her dress, a lavender muslin which was apparently every bit as uncomfortable as it looked. "I don't know. He was probably invited."

That *had* to be true. No one in their right mind would attend the annual Smythe-Smith musicale uninvited. It was, in the most delicate of descriptions, an assault on the senses.

One of the senses, anyway. It was probably a good night to be deaf.

What was Sir Harry Valentine doing here? Olivia had spent the past three days with curtains drawn, assiduously avoiding all windows on the south side of Rudland House. But she hadn't expected to see him *out*, since as she well knew, Sir Harry Valentine didn't go out.

And surely anyone who spent as much time with pen, ink, and paper as he did possessed sufficient intelligence to know that if he *did* decide to go out, there were better options than the Smythe-Smith musicale.

"Has he ever attended anything like this before?" Olivia asked through the corner of her mouth, keeping her head facing forward.

"I don't think so," Mary whispered back, also staring straight ahead. She leaned in toward Olivia slightly, until their shoulders almost touched. "He has been to two balls since his arrival in town."

"Almacks?"

"Never."

"That horse race in the park that everyone went to last month?"

She felt, rather than saw, Mary shake her head. "I don't think so. But I can't be certain. I wasn't allowed to go."

"Neither was I," Olivia murmured. Winston had told her all about it, of course, but (also of course) he had not given as detailed an accounting as she would have liked.

"He spends a great deal of time with Mr. Grey," Mary continued.

Olivia's chin drew back with surprise. "*Sebastian* Grey?"

"They are cousins. First, I believe."

At that Olivia gave up all pretense of not carrying on a conversation and looked straight at Mary. "Sir Harry Valentine is cousin to Sebastian Grey?"

Mary gave a little shrug. "By all accounts."

"Are you certain?"

"Why is it so difficult to believe?"

Olivia paused. "I have no idea." But it was. She knew Sebastian Grey. Everyone did. Which was why he seemed such a peculiar match for Sir Harry, who, as far as Olivia could tell, left his office only to eat, sleep, and knock Julian Prentice unconscious.

Julian Prentice! She'd forgotten all about him. Olivia straightened and looked about the room with practiced discretion.

But of course Mary instantly knew what she was doing. "Who are you looking for?" she whispered.

"Julian Prentice."

Mary gasped with delighted horror. "Is he here?"

"I don't think so. But Winston said that it was not such a vicious thing as we thought. Apparently Julian was so sotted Sir Harry could have knocked him down by blowing on him."

"Except for the blackened eye," Mary reminded her, ever the stickler for detail.

"The point is, I don't think he *thrashed* him."

Mary paused for a second, then must have decided

it was time to move on. She looked this way and that, then scratched at the spot where the stiff lace of her gown bent up against her collarbone. "Er, speaking of your brother, is he attending?"

"Heavens, no." Olivia managed not to roll her eyes, but it was a close thing. Winston had given a rather convincing show of a head cold and bundled himself off to bed. Their mother had been so well fooled that she had asked the butler to check in on him at hourly intervals and send for her if he worsened.

Which had provided a bright spot in the evening. Olivia had it on the best of authority that there would be a gathering at White's later that evening. Ah well, it would have to proceed without Winston Bevelstoke.

Which very well might have been her mother's intention.

"Do you know," Olivia murmured, "the older I get, the more I admire my mother."

Mary looked at her as if she'd gone eccentric. "What are you talking about?"

"It's nothing." Olivia gave a little wave. It would be far too difficult to explain. She stretched her neck a bit, trying to make it look as if she weren't perusing the crowd. "I don't see him."

"Who?" Mary asked.

Olivia fought off the urge to bat her. "Sir Harry."

"Oh, he's here," Mary said confidently. "I saw him."

"He's not here now."

Mary—who had just moments earlier admonished Olivia for her lack of discretion—displayed astonishing flexibility as she twisted herself nearly backward. "Hmmm."

Olivia waited for more.

"I don't see him," Mary finally said.

"Is it possible you were wrong?" Olivia asked hopefully.

Mary gave her an irritated look. "Of course not. Perhaps he's in the garden."

Olivia turned, even though one couldn't see the garden from the ballroom, where the musicale was being held. It was a reflex, she supposed. If you knew someone was somewhere, you couldn't *not* turn in that direction, even if you couldn't possibly see them.

Of course she didn't *know* that Sir Harry was in the garden. She didn't even know for certain that he was at the musicale. She had only Mary's claim, and while Mary was quite dependable on matters of party attendance, she had, by her own admission, only seen the man a few times. She could easily have been mistaken.

Olivia decided to cling to that thought.

"Look what I brought," Mary said, digging into her sovereign purse.

"Oh, that's lovely," Olivia said, peering down at the beadwork.

"Isn't it? Mama got it in Bath. Oh, here we are." Mary pulled out two little tufts of cotton. "For my ears," she explained.

Olivia's lips parted with admiration. And envy. "You don't have two more, do you?"

"Sorry," Mary said with a shrug. "It's a very small purse." She turned forward. "I think they're ready to begin."

One of the Smythe-Smith mothers called out for everyone to sit down. Olivia's mother looked over at her, saw that Mary had taken her seat, and gave a little wave before finding a spot next to Mary's mother.

Olivia took a deep breath, mentally preparing for her third encounter with the Smythe-Smith string quartet. She'd perfected her technique the year before; it involved breathing deeply, finding a spot on the wall behind the girls from which she must not avert her eyes, and pondering various traveling opportunities, no matter how plebian or routine:

Places I Would Rather Be, Edition 1821
By Lady Olivia Bevelstoke

France
With Miranda
With Miranda in France
In bed with a cup of chocolate and a newspaper
Anywhere with a cup of chocolate and a newspaper
Anywhere with either a cup of chocolate
or a newspaper

She looked over at Mary, who appeared on the verge of nodding off. The cotton was sticking partway out of her ears, and Olivia very nearly had to sit on her hands just to keep from yanking it out.

If it had been Winston or Miranda, she would definitely have done so.

The strains of Bach, recognizable only by its Baroque . . . well, she wouldn't call it melody, precisely, but it did have something to do with notes moving up and down a scale. Whatever it was, it slapped her ears, and Olivia snapped her head back toward the front.

Eyes on the spot, eyes on the spot.
She'd rather be:

> *Swimming*
> *On horseback*
> *Not swimming on horseback*
> *Asleep*
> *Eating an ice*

Did that qualify as a place? It was more of an experience, really, as was "asleep," but then again, "asleep" implied being in bed, which *was* a place. Although, technically speaking, one could fall asleep sitting up. Olivia never did so, but her father frequently nodded off during her mother's prescribed "family time" in the sitting room, and Mary, apparently, could even do so during *this* cacophony.

Traitor. Olivia would never have brought only one set of cotton.

Eyes on the spot, Olivia.

Olivia sighed—a bit too loudly, not that anyone could hear—and went back to her deep breaths. She focused on a sconce behind the violist's miserable head—no, make that the miserable violist's head . . .

Really, that one girl did *not* look happy. Did she know how dreadful the quartet was? Because the other three clearly had no clue. But the viola player, she was different, she was . . .

Making Olivia actually hear the music.

Not good! Not good! Her brain rebelled, and she started back with those blasted breaths again, and . . .

And then, somehow, it was done, and the musicians were standing and making rather pretty curtsies.

Olivia found herself blinking excessively; her eyes didn't seem to be working properly after so much time on one spot. "You fell asleep," she said to Mary, giving her a betrayed sort of look.

"I did not."

"Oh, you did."

"Well, these worked, at any rate," Mary said, yanking the cotton from her ears. "I could hardly hear a thing. Where are you going?"

Olivia was already halfway down the aisle. "To the washroom. Really must . . ." And that, she decided, would have to suffice. She had not forgotten the possibility that Sir Harry Valentine was somewhere in the room, and if ever a situation called for making haste, this was it.

It wasn't that she was a coward—not at all. She wasn't trying to avoid the man, she was merely trying to avoid his having the opportunity to surprise her.

Be prepared. If it hadn't been her motto before, then she was adopting it now.

Wouldn't her mother be impressed? She was always telling her to be more improving. No, that wasn't proper English. What did her mother say? Didn't matter; she was almost to the door. She need only push past Sir Robert Stoat, and—

"Lady Olivia."

Drat. Who—

She turned. And felt her stomach drop. *And* realized that Sir Harry Valentine was much taller than he'd seemed in his office.

"I'm sorry," she said serenely, because she had always been rather good at playacting. "Have we been introduced?"

But from the mocking curve of his smile, she was fairly certain she'd not been able to mask her first flash of surprise.

"Forgive me," he said smoothly, and she shivered, because his voice—it wasn't what she'd thought it would be. It sounded like the smell of brandy, and it felt like the taste of chocolate. And she wasn't so certain why she'd shivered, because now she felt rather warm.

"Sir Harry Valentine," he murmured, executing a elegantly polite bow. "You are Lady Olivia Bevelstoke, are you not?"

Olivia thought very regal thoughts as she lifted her chin half an inch. "I am."

"Then I am very pleased to make your acquaintance."

She nodded. She probably ought to speak; it would certainly be more polite. But she felt in danger of losing her poise, and it was wiser to remain silent.

"I am your new neighbor," he added, looking vaguely amused at her reaction.

"Of course," she replied. She kept her face even. He would not get the best of her. "To the south?" she asked, pleased by the slightly bored note in her voice. "I had heard it was to be let."

He didn't say anything. Not right away. But his eyes fixed on hers, and it took every ounce of her fortitude to maintain her expression. Placid, composed, and with just a hint of curiosity. She thought the last necessary—if she hadn't been spying on him for nearly a week, she would certainly have found the encounter somewhat curious.

A strange man, acting as if they'd met.

A strange, handsome man.

A strange, handsome man who looked as if he might . . .

Why was he looking at her lips?

Why was she *licking* her lips?

"I welcome you to Mayfair," she said quickly. Anything to break the silence. Silence was not her friend, not with this man, not anymore. "We shall have to have you over."

"I would enjoy that," he said, and to her rapidly growing panic, he sounded as if he meant it. Not just the part about enjoying, but that he actually meant to accept the offer, which any fool could have seen was made out of sheer politeness.

"Of course," she said, and she was *sure* she wasn't stammering, except that it sounded a bit as if she was. Or as if she had something in her throat. "If you'll excuse me . . ." She motioned to the door, because surely he'd noticed that she had been moving toward the exit when he'd intercepted her.

"Until next time, Lady Olivia."

She searched for a witty rejoinder, or even one sarcastic and sly, but her mind was a hazy blank. He was gazing upon her with an expression that seemed to say nothing of him, and yet everything of *her*. She had to remind herself that he didn't know all of her secrets. He didn't know *her*.

Good heavens, apart from this spying nonsense, she didn't *have* any secrets.

And he didn't know that, either.

Somewhat rejuvenated by her indignation, she

gave him a nod—small and polite, utterly correct for dismissals. And then, reminding herself that she was Lady Olivia Bevelstoke, and she was comfortable in any social situation, she turned, and she left.

And gave utmost thanks that when she tripped over her own feet, she was already in the hall, where he could not see.

Chapter Four

That had gone well.

Harry congratulated himself as he watched Lady Olivia hurry from the room. She wasn't moving with any great speed, but her shoulders were a bit raised, and she was holding her dress with her hand, lifting the hem. Not by any huge number of inches—the way women did when they needed to run. But she was holding it nonetheless, surely an unconscious gesture, as if her fingers thought they needed to prepare for a race, even if the rest of her was determined to remain calm.

She knew he'd seen her spying on him. He'd known that already, of course. If he hadn't been certain the moment their eyes had met three days earlier, he'd have known shortly thereafter; she had pulled her curtains tight and hadn't peeked out once since she'd been found out.

A clear admission of guilt. A mistake that no professional would ever have made. If Harry had been in her position . . .

Of course, Harry never *would* have been in her position. He did not enjoy espionage—never had, and the War Office was well aware of it. But still, all things considered, he wouldn't have got caught.

Her misstep had reaffirmed his suspicions. She was just what she seemed—a typical, most probably spoiled, society miss. Perhaps a bit nosier than average. Certainly more attractive than average. The distance—not to mention the two panes of glass between them—had not done her justice. He'd not been able to see her face, not really. He'd known the shape, a bit like a heart, a bit like an oval. But he hadn't known the features, that her eyes were spaced the tiniest bit wider than was usual, or that her eyelashes were three shades darker than her brows.

Her hair he'd seen quite well—soft, buttery blond, with more than a hint of curl. It ought not have seemed more seductive than it had loose around her shoulders, but somehow, in the candlelight, with one curl resting along the side of her neck . . .

He'd wanted to touch her. He'd wanted to tug gently on the curl, just to see if it would bounce right back into place when he let go, and then he'd wanted to pull out the hairpins, one by one, and watch each lock fall from her coiffure, slowly transforming her from icy perfection to tumultuous goddess.

Dear God.

And now he was officially disgusted with himself. He knew he shouldn't have read that book of poetry before he'd gone out for the evening. And in French, too. Damn language always made him randy.

He couldn't recall the last time he'd had such a reaction to a woman. In his defense, he'd been holed up in his office so much lately that he had met precious few women to whom he might react. He'd been in London for several months now, but it seemed the War Office was always dropping off some document or another, and the translations were *always* needed with all possible haste. And if by some miracle he managed to clear his desk of work, that was when Edward decided to get himself in a bloody heap of trouble—debts, drunkenness, unsuitable women—Edward was not picky about his vices, and Harry could not summon enough heartlessness to let his brother wallow in his own mistakes.

Which meant that Harry rarely had time to make mistakes of his own—mistakes of the female persuasion, that was. Harry was not in the habit of living like a monk, but really, how long had it been . . . ?

Having never been in love, he had no idea if absence made the heart grow fonder, but after tonight, he was quite certain that abstinence made the rest of a man rather surly indeed.

He needed to find Sebastian. His cousin's social agenda was never limited to one event per evening. Wherever he was going after this, it would surely include women of questionable morals. And Harry was going with him.

Harry headed toward the far side of the room, intending to find something to drink, but as he stepped forth, he heard about half a dozen gasps, followed by, "This wasn't on the program!"

Harry glanced this way and that, then followed the general direction of stares toward the stage. One of the Smythe-Smith girls had retaken her position and appeared to be preparing an impromptu (but please, God, not improvised) solo.

"Sweet merciful Jesus," Harry heard, and there was Sebastian, standing next to him, regarding the stage with something that was definitely more dread than amusement.

"You owe me," Harry said, murmuring the words malevolently in Sebastian's ear.

"I thought you'd stopped counting."

"This is a debt that can never be repaid."

The girl started her solo.

"You may be right," Sebastian admitted.

Harry looked at the door. It was a lovely door, perfectly proportioned and leading out of the room. "Can we leave?"

"Not yet," Sebastian said ruefully. "My grandmother."

Harry looked over at the elderly Countess of Newbury, who sat with the other dowagers, smiling broadly and clapping her hands. He turned back to Sebastian, remembering. "Isn't she deaf?"

"Nearly so," Sebastian confirmed. "But not stupid. You'll notice she put her cone away for the performance." He turned to Harry with a gleam in his eye. "By the by, I saw you made the acquaintance of the lovely Lady Olivia Bevelstoke."

Harry didn't bother to respond, at least not with anything more than a slight tilt of his head.

Sebastian leaned toward him, his voice dropping into annoying registers. "Did she admit to everything? Her insatiable curiosity? Her overwhelming lust for you?"

Harry turned and regarded him squarely. "You're an ass."

"You tell me that a lot."

"It never grows old."

"And neither do I," Sebastian said with a half smile. "I find it so convenient to be immature."

The violin solo reached what seemed to be a crescendo, and the crowd held a collective breath, waiting for the ensuing flourish, followed by what *had* to be the finish.

Except it wasn't.

"That was cruel," Sebastian said.

Harry winced as the violin scraped into a higher octave. "I didn't see your uncle," he pointed out.

Sebastian's lips tightened, and tiny white lines formed at the corners of his mouth. "He sent his regrets just this afternoon. It almost makes me wonder if he set me up. Except he's just not that clever."

"Did you know?"

"About the music?"

"It's a brutal use of the word."

"I'd heard rumors," Sebastian admitted. "But nothing could have prepared me for . . ."

"This?" Harry murmured, somehow unable to take his eyes off the girl on the stage. She held her violin lovingly, and her absorption in the music was unfeigned. She looked as if she was enjoying herself, as if she were hearing something quite different than everyone else in the room. And maybe she was, lucky girl.

What must it be like, to live in one's own world? To

see things as they ought to be, and not as they were? Certainly the violin player *ought* to be good. She had the passion, and if what the Smythe-Smith matrons had said earlier in the evening was true, she practiced every day.

What ought his life be?

He ought not have had a father who drank more than he breathed.

He ought not have a brother who was determined to follow the same path.

He ought . . .

He grit his teeth. He ought not fall into fits of self-pity. He was a better man than that. A stronger man, and—

A sudden shiver of awareness tingled through him, and, as was his habit whenever something did not feel right, he looked to the door.

Lady Olivia Bevelstoke. She was standing alone, watching the Smythe-Smith girl with an inscrutably blank expression. Except . . .

Harry's eyes narrowed. He couldn't be positive, but from this angle, it almost looked as if she were staring at the Grecian urn behind the Smythe-Smith girl.

What was she *doing*?

"You're staring," came Sebastian's ever-grating voice in his ear.

Harry ignored him.

"She *is* beautiful."

Harry ignored him.

"Engaging, as well. But not engaged."

Harry ignored him.

"It's not for a lack of trying on the part of the good bachelors of Great Britain," Sebastian continued, unperturbed as always by Harry's lack of response. "They keep asking. Alas, she keeps refusing. I heard that the elder Winterhoe even—"

"She's cold," Harry cut in, with a bit more bite to his voice than he'd intended.

Sebastian's voice was filled with delighted amusement as he said, "I beg your pardon?"

"She's cold," Harry repeated, recalling their brief exchange. She'd held herself like a bloody queen. Every word had crackled with frost, and now she did not even deign to look at the poor girl playing the violin.

He was surprised she'd come tonight, to be honest. It did not seem the most likely venue for icy diamonds of the first water. Someone had most likely forced her to attend.

"And here I had such high hopes for your future together," Sebastian murmured.

Harry turned to offer a scathing retort, or at least one with all the sarcasm he could muster, but the music took a turn, and the violinist once again reached a crescendo. This time it *had* to be the end, but the crowd was taking no chances, and a rousing round of applause erupted before she'd even completed the final note.

Harry walked alongside Sebastian as he made his way toward his grandmother. She'd come in her own carriage, Sebastian had told him, and therefore they need not wait until she was ready to depart. Still, he did need to say good-bye, and although Harry was no direct relation, he ought to make his greeting as well.

But before they could make it across the room, they

were accosted by one of the Smythe-Smith mothers, calling, "Mr. Grey! Mr. Grey!"

From the intensity in her voice, Harry judged, the Earl of Newbury must be meeting with difficulties in his quest for a fertile wife.

Sebastian, to his credit, showed none of his haste to depart as he turned and said, "Mrs. Smythe-Smith, it has been such a delightful evening."

"I am so pleased you were able to attend," she gushed.

Sebastian smiled in return, the sort that said he couldn't imagine being anywhere else. And then he did what he always did when he wanted to get out of a conversation. He said:

"May I present my cousin, Sir Harry Valentine."

Harry nodded politely, murmuring her name. That Mrs. Smythe-Smith thought Sebastian the bigger prize was evident; she looked directly at him as she asked, "What did you think of my Viola? Wasn't she just splendid?"

Harry was not quite able to mask his surprise. Her daughter was named Viola?

"She plays the violin," Mrs. Smythe-Smith explained.

"What is the violist called?" Harry could not help asking.

Mrs. Smythe-Smith glanced at him with some impatience. "Marianne." Then back to Sebastian: "Viola was the soloist."

"Ah," Sebastian replied. "It was a rare treat."

"Indeed. We are so very proud of her. We shall have to plan for solos for next year."

Harry began to plan for his trip to the Arctic, to correspond.

"I am so glad you were able to attend, Mr. Grey," Mrs. Smythe-Smith continued, apparently unaware that she'd said this already. "We have another surprise for the evening."

"Did I mention my cousin is a baronet?" Sebastian put in. "Lovely estate back in Hampshire. The hunting is divine."

"Really?" Mrs. Smythe-Smith turned to Harry with new interest and a broad smile. "I am so grateful for your attendance, Sir Harry."

Sir Harry would have responded with more than a nod except that he was plotting the imminent demise of Mr. Grey.

"I must tell you both about our surprise," Mrs. Smythe-Smith said excitedly. "I want you to be the first to know. We shall have dancing! This evening!"

"Dancing?" Harry echoed, struck nearly into incoherence. "Er, will Viola be playing?"

"Of course not. I shouldn't want her to miss out. But it just so happens that we have a number of other amateur musicians in the audience, and it is such great fun to be spontaneous, don't you think?"

Harry rated spontaneity up with trips to the dentist. What he did rate highly, however, was petty revenge. "My cousin," he said with great feeling, "adores dancing."

"He does?" Mrs. Smythe-Smith turned back to Sebastian with delight. "You do?"

"I do," Sebastian said, perhaps a bit more tightly than was necessary, given that it was not a lie; he did like to dance, far more than Harry ever had.

Mrs. Smythe-Smith looked at Sebastian with beatific expectancy. Harry looked at them both with self-satisfied expectancy; he did love when everything wrapped up neatly. In his favor, specifically.

Sebastian, aware that he'd been outmaneuvered, said to Mrs. Smythe-Smith, "I hope your daughter will save the first dance for me."

"It would be her honor to do so," Mrs. Smythe-Smith said, clasping her hands together with joy. "If you will excuse me, I must make arrangements to begin the music."

Sebastian waited until she'd wended through the crowd, then said, "You will pay for this."

"Oh, I think we're even now."

"Well, you're stuck here, too, at any rate," Sebastian replied. "Unless you wish to walk home."

Harry would have considered it, were it not pouring rain. "I'm happy to wait for you," he said, with all the good cheer in the world.

"Oh, look!" Sebastian said, with patently false surprise. "Lady Olivia. Right there. I'd wager *she* likes to dance."

Harry considered saying, *You wouldn't*, but really, what was the point? He knew Sebastian would.

"Lady Olivia!" Sebastian called out.

The lady in question turned, and there was no way she could avoid them, what with Sebastian plowing through the crowd to her side. Harry, too, could find no way to avoid the encounter; not that he would give her the satisfaction of doing so.

"Lady Olivia," Sebastian said again, once they were at speaking range. "How lovely to see you."

She gave a faint impression of a nod. "Mr. Grey."

"Taciturn this evening, are we, Olivia?" Sebastian murmured, but before Harry could wonder at the familiarity of such a statement, he continued with: "Have you met my cousin, Sir Harry Valentine?"

"Er . . . yes," she stammered.

"I made Lady Olivia's acquaintance this very evening," Harry cut in, wondering what Seb was up to. He knew very well that the two of them had already spoken.

"Yes," Lady Olivia said.

"Ah, poor me," Sebastian said, changing the subject with startling speed. "I see Mrs. Smythe-Smith signaling to me. I must find her Viola."

"Does she play as well?" Lady Olivia asked, her eyes clouding with confusion. And perhaps a little worry.

"I do not know," Sebastian replied, "but she clearly anticipated the future of her progeny. Viola is her darling daughter."

"She plays the violin," Harry put in.

"Oh." She seemed amused by the irony. Or maybe just puzzled. "Of course."

"Enjoy the dancing, you two," Sebastian said, giving Harry a quick glance of positively evil intent.

"There is dancing?" Lady Olivia asked, looking somewhat panicked.

Harry took pity on her. "It is my understanding that the Smythe-Smith quartet will not be playing."

"How . . . nice." She cleared her throat. "For them. So they can dance, of course. I'm sure they would like to."

Harry felt a little spark of mischief (or was it menace?) wiggling through him. "Your eyes are blue," he commented.

She threw him a startled glance. "I beg your pardon?"

"Your eyes," he murmured. "They're blue. I thought they might be, given your coloring, but it was difficult to tell from so far away."

She froze, but he had to admire her adherence to purpose as she said, "I'm sure I don't know what you are talking about."

He leaned in just enough so that she would notice. "Mine are brown."

She looked as if she were about to make a retort, but instead she blinked, and almost appeared to be peering at him more closely. "They *are*," she murmured. "How odd."

He wasn't sure whether her reaction was amusing or disturbing. Either way, he wasn't through provoking her. "I think the music is starting," he said.

"I should find my mother," she blurted out.

She was getting desperate. He liked that.

Perhaps the evening would turn out to be enjoyable, after all.

Chapter Five

There had to be a way to force the evening to a close. She was a much better actor than Winston. If he could feign a plausible head cold, Olivia decided, surely she could manage plague.

Ode to Plague
By Olivia Bevelstoke

Biblical
Bubonic
Better than leprosy

Well it *was*. In these circumstances, at least. She needed something not just disgusting; it had to be violently transmissible as well. With history. Hadn't the plague killed half of Europe a few hundred years ago? Leprosy had never been so efficient.

Briefly she considered the ramifications of putting her hand to her neck and murmuring, "Are these boils?"

It was tempting. It really was.

And Sir Harry, drat the man, looked pleased as punch, as if there were nowhere he'd rather be.

But here. Torturing her.

"Look at that," he said conversationally. "Sebastian is dancing with Miss Smythe-Smith."

Olivia searched the room, determinedly not looking at the man next to her, "I am sure she is delighted."

There was a pause, and then Sir Harry inquired, "Are you looking for someone?"

"My mother," she practically snapped. Hadn't he heard her the first time?

"Ah." He was blessedly silent for a moment, and then: "Does she resemble you?"

"What?"

"Your mother."

Olivia swung her gaze over to him. Why was he asking this? Why was he even talking to her? He'd made his point, hadn't he?

He was an awful man. It might not explain the paper and fires and the funny hat, but it explained *this*. Right here, right now. He was, quite simply, awful.

Arrogant.

Annoying.

And quite a bit more, she was sure, except that she was too flustered to think properly. Synonym retrieval required a far clearer head than she could achieve in his presence.

"I thought to help you look for her," Sir Harry said. "But alas, we have not met."

"She looks a bit like me," Olivia said distractedly. And then, for no reason that she could identify, she added, "Or rather, I look like her."

He smiled at that, just a little one, and Olivia had the oddest sense that for once he wasn't laughing at her. He wasn't trying to be provoking. He was just . . . smiling.

It was disconcerting.

She couldn't look away.

"I have always valued precision in language," he said softly.

She stared at him. "You are a very strange man."

She *would* have been mortified, because that was not the sort of thing she normally said aloud, except that he deserved it. And now he was laughing. Presumably at her.

She touched her neck. Maybe if she pinched herself the welt would pass for a boil.

Diseases I Know How To Feign
By Olivia Bevelstoke

Head cold
Lung Ailment
Megrim
Sprained Ankle

The last wasn't strictly a disease, but it certainly had its useful moments.

"Shall we dance, Lady Olivia?"

Like right now. Only she'd thought of it too late. "You wish to dance," she echoed. It seemed inconceivable that he'd want to, even more inconceivable that he might think she would.

"I do," he said.

"With me?"

He looked amused—condescendingly so—by the question. "I had thought to ask my cousin, as he is the only person in the room with whom I can claim any familiarity, but that would cause a bit of a sensation, wouldn't you agree?"

"I believe the song has ended," Olivia said. If it wasn't true, it would be soon.

"Then we shall dance the next one."

"I have not agreed to dance with you!" She bit her lip. She sounded like an idiot. A petulant idiot, which was the worst kind.

"You will," he said confidently.

Not since Winston had told Neville Berbrooke that she was "interested" had she so badly wanted to strike another human being. She would have done so, too, if she'd thought she could get away with it.

"You don't really have a choice," he continued.

His jaw or the side of his head? Which would cause more pain?

"And who knows?" He leaned in, his eyes glittering hot in the candlelight. "You might enjoy yourself."

The side of his head. Definitely. If she came at him with a wide, arcing swing, she might knock him off balance. She'd like to see him sprawled on the floor. It would be a *gorgeous* sight. He might strike his head on a table, or even better, grasp the tablecloth on the way down, taking the punchbowl and all of Mrs. Smythe-Smith's cut crystal with him.

"Lady Olivia?"

Shards everywhere. Maybe blood, too.

"Lady Olivia?"

If she couldn't actually *do* it, she could fantasize about it.

"Lady Olivia?" He was holding out his hand.

She looked over. He was still upright, not a speck of blood or broken glass in sight. Pity. And he quite clearly expected her to accept his invitation to dance.

He was, unfortunately, right. She didn't have a choice. She could—and probably would—continue to insist she'd never laid eyes on him before this evening, but they both knew the truth.

Olivia wasn't quite certain what would happen if Sir Harry announced to the *ton* that she'd spied on him from her bedroom window for five days, but it would not be good. The speculation would be vicious. At best she'd have to hide at home for a week to avoid gossip. At worst, she could find herself engaged to marry the boor.

Good *God*.

"I would love to dance," she said quickly, taking his outstretched hand.

"Enthusiasm as well as precision," he murmured.

He really was a strange man.

They reached the dance floor a few moments before the musicians lifted their instruments.

"A waltz," Sir Harry said, upon hearing the first two notes. Olivia gave him a curious, startled look. How did he *know* such a thing so quickly? Was he musical? She hoped so. It meant the evening would have been even more of a torture to him than it was to her.

Sir Harry took her right hand and held it in its proper position in the air. The contact would have been shocking enough, but his other hand—at the small of her back—it was different. Warm. No, hot. And it made her feel ticklish in very odd places.

She'd danced dozens of waltzes. Maybe even hundreds. But no one's hand at the small of her back had ever felt quite like this.

It was because she was still rattled. Nervous in his presence. That had to be it.

His grip was firm, but still quite gentle, and he was a good dancer. No, he was a splendid dancer, far better than she was. Olivia faked it well, but she would never be a superb dancer. People said she was, but that was only because she was pretty.

It wasn't fair, she would be the first to admit it. But one could get away with quite a lot in London, simply by being pretty.

Of course it also meant that one was never presumed to be clever. All of her life it had been that way. People had always expected her to be some sort of china doll, there to look lovely, and be displayed, and *do* absolutely nothing.

Sometimes Olivia wondered if this might be why she occasionally misbehaved. Never anything on a grand scale; she was far too conventional for that. But she had been known to speak too freely, express an opinion too strongly. Miranda had once said that she would never wish to be that pretty, and Olivia hadn't understood, not really. Not until Miranda had moved away, and there was no one left with whom to have a truly excellent conversation.

She looked up at Sir Harry, trying to study his face without being obvious about it. Was he handsome? She supposed. He had a small scar, barely noticeable really, near his left ear, and his cheekbones were a bit more prominent than was classically handsome, but still, he had something. Intelligence? Intensity?

He had a touch of gray at his temples, too, she noticed. She wondered how old he was.

"You're a very graceful dancer," he said.

She rolled her eyes. She couldn't help it.

"Have you become immune to compliments, Lady Olivia?"

She gave him a sharp look. It was no less than he deserved. His tone had been equally sharp. Close to insulting.

"I have heard," he said, expertly turning her to the right, "that you have left shattered hearts all across town."

She stiffened. It was just the sort of thing people liked to say to her, thinking she'd be proud of it. But she wasn't proud. And what's more, it *hurt* that everyone thought she would be. "That is hardly a kind, or an appropriate, thing to say."

"Are you always appropriate, Lady Olivia?"

She glared at him, but only for a second. His eyes met hers, and there it was again—the intelligence. The intensity. She had to look away.

She was a coward. A pathetic, spineless, miserable excuse for . . . for . . . well, for herself. She'd never backed down from a battle of wills. And she hated herself for doing so now.

When she heard his voice again, it was closer to her ear, his breath hot and moist. "And are you always kind?"

She clenched her teeth. He was goading her. And while she would love to deliver a setdown, she refused to do so. It was what he was trying for, after all. He wanted her to respond, just so that he could do the same.

Besides, she couldn't think of anything suitably blistering.

His hand moved against her back—subtle, expert pressure that guided her in the dance. They turned, and then again, and she caught a glimpse of Mary Cadogan, eyes wide, mouth in a perfect little oval.

Wonderful. This would be all over town by tomorrow afternoon. One dance with a gentleman ought not cause a scandal, but Mary was sufficiently intrigued by Sir Harry—she would find a way to make it sound breathless and terribly *au courant*.

"What are your interests, Lady Olivia?" he asked.

"My interests?" she echoed, wondering if anyone had ever asked her this before. Certainly not so directly.

"Do you sing? Paint watercolors? Stab a needle in that fabric that goes in that hoop?"

"It's called embroidery," she said, somewhat testily; his tone was almost mocking, as if he didn't expect her to have interests.

"Do you do it?"

"No." She hated embroidery. She always had. And she wasn't good at it, either.

"Do you play an instrument?"

"I like to shoot," she said bluntly, hoping to put

a stop to the conversation. It wasn't exactly true, but it wasn't really a lie, either. She didn't not like shooting.

"A woman who likes guns," he said softly.

Good Lord, the evening would never end. She let out a frustrated exhale. "Is this an exceptionally long waltz?"

"I don't think so."

Something about his tone caught her attention, and she looked up, just in time to see his lips curve as he said, "It only seems long. Because you don't like me."

She gasped. It was true, of course, but he wasn't supposed to say it.

"I have a secret, Lady Olivia," he whispered, leaning down just as far as he could without breaking the bounds of propriety. "I don't like you, either."

Olivia was still not liking Sir Harry several days later. It didn't matter that she hadn't spoken to him, hadn't even seen him. She knew he existed, and that seemed to be enough.

Every morning one of the maids entered her bed-chamber and opened the curtains, and every morning, as soon as the maid left, Olivia leaped to her feet and yanked them back closed. She refused to give him any reason to accuse her of spying on him again.

Plus, what was to stop him from spying on *her*?

She hadn't even left the house since the night of the musicale. She'd feigned a head cold (so easy to claim she'd caught it from Winston) and stayed inside. It wasn't that she was worried about crossing paths with Sir Harry. Really, what was the likelihood that they would be coming down their front steps at the same time? Or returning from an outing? Or seeing each other on Bond Street? Or at Gunther's? Or at a party?

She wasn't going to run into him. She rarely even thought about it.

No, the bigger issue was avoiding her friends. Mary Cadogan had called the day after the musicale and then the day after that and then the day after that. Finally, Lady Rudland had told her that she would send a note when Olivia was feeling better.

She could not imagine having to tell Mary Cadogan about her conversation with Sir Harry. It was bad enough remembering it—which she seemed to do, on a minute-ly basis. To have to recount it to another human being . . .

It was almost enough to make a head cold devolve into plague.

What I Detest About Sir Harry Valentine
By the normally benevolent
Lady Olivia Bevelstoke

I think he thinks I'm unintelligent.
I know he thinks I am unkind.
He blackmailed me into dancing with him.
He's a better dancer than I am.

After three days of self-imposed isolation, however, Olivia was itching to move past the boundaries of her house and garden. Deciding that the early morning was the best time to avoid other people, she donned her bonnet and gloves, grabbed the freshly delivered morning newspaper, and headed out to her favorite bench in Hyde Park. Her maid, who unlike Olivia did enjoy needlework, followed along, clutching her embroidery and complaining about the hour.

It was a glorious morning—blue sky, puffy clouds, light breeze. Perfect weather, really, and no one out and about. "Come along, Sally," she called out to her maid, who was lagging at least a dozen steps behind.

"It's *early*," Sally moaned.

"It's half seven," Olivia told her, holding steady for a few moments to allow Sally to catch up.

"That's early."

"Normally, I would agree with you, but as it happens I believe I am turning over a new leaf. Just see how lovely it is outside. The sun is shining, there is music in the air . . ."

"I hear no music," Sally grumbled.

"Birds, Sally. The birds are singing."

Sally remained unconvinced. "That leaf of yours— I don't suppose you'd consider turning it back over again?"

Olivia grinned. "It won't be so bad. As soon as we get to the park, we shall sit and enjoy the sunshine. I will have my newspaper and you your embroidery and no one will bother us."

Except that after a mere fifteen minutes, Mary Cadogan came positively running up.

"Your mother told me you were here," she said breathlessly. "You're feeling better, then?"

"You spoke to my mother?" Olivia asked, unable to believe her bad fortune.

"She told me on Saturday that she would send me a note as soon as you were feeling better."

"My mother," Olivia muttered, "is remarkably prompt."

"Isn't she, though?"

Sally moved over on the bench, barely even looking up from her needlework. Mary settled in between the two of them, scooting this way and that until an inch of bench could be seen between her pink skirts and Olivia's green.

"I want to know *everything*," Mary said to Olivia, her voice low and thrilled.

Olivia briefly considered feigning ignorance but really, what was the point? They both knew exactly what Mary was talking about. "There's not much to say," she said, crinkling her newspaper in an attempt to remind Mary that she had come to the park to read. "He recognized me as his neighbor and asked me to dance. It was all very civilized."

"Did he say anything about his fiancée?"

"Of course not."

"What about Julian Prentice?"

Olivia rolled her eyes. "Do you really think he would tell a complete stranger, and a lady at that, about his giving another gentleman a blackened eye?"

"No," Mary said glumly. "It was really too much to hope for. I vow, I cannot get the details from *anyone*."

Olivia did her best to appear bored by the entire affair.

"Very well," Mary continued, undaunted by her companion's lack of response. "Tell me about the dance."

"*Mary.*" It was a bit of a groan, a bit of a snap. Certainly rude, but Olivia desperately did not want to tell Mary anything.

"You must," Mary insisted.

"Surely there is something else in London of interest besides my one, very short, very dull dance with Sir Harry Valentine."

"Not really," Mary answered. She shrugged, then stifled a yawn. "Philomena's mother dragged her off to Brighton, and Anne is ill. She probably has the same head cold you had."

Probably not, Olivia thought.

"No one has seen Sir Harry since the musicale," Mary added. "He has not attended *anything.*"

This did not surprise Olivia. He was most likely at his desk, furiously scribbling away. Possibly wearing that ridiculous hat.

Not that she would know. She had not looked out the window in days. She hadn't even looked *at* the window. Well, not more than six or eight times, anyway.

Each day.

"What did you talk about, then?" Mary asked. "I know you spoke to him. I saw your lips moving."

Olivia turned on her, eyes flaring with irritation. "You were watching my lips?"

"Oh, please. It's not as if you've never done the same thing."

Not only true, but irrefutable, since she'd done it *with* Mary. But a response—no, a retort—was definitely in order, so Olivia gave a little snort and said, "I've never done it to *you.*"

"But you would," Mary said with certainty.

Also true, but not something Olivia intended to admit.

"What *did* you talk about?" Mary asked again.

"Nothing out of the ordinary," Olivia lied, crinkling her newspaper again—more loudly this time. She'd got through the society pages—she always started at the back of the paper—but she wanted to read the parliamentary report. She always read the parliamentary report. Every day. Even her father didn't read it every day, and he was a member of the House of Lords.

"You looked angry," Mary persisted.

I am now, she wanted to grumble.

"Were you?"

Olivia grit her teeth. "I'm sure you were mistaken."

"I don't *think* so," Mary said, in that excruciating singsong voice she employed when she thought she was in the know.

Olivia looked over at Sally, who was pulling her needle through the fabric, pretending she wasn't listening. Then she looked back at Mary, giving her an urgent sort of look, as if to say—*Not in front of the servants.*

It was not a permanent solution to the Mary problem, but it would put her off for a little while, at least.

She crinkled her newspaper again, then looked down at her hands in dismay. She'd got it before the butler had had a chance to iron the paper, and now the ink was coming off on her skin.

"That's disgusting," Mary said.

Olivia could think of no response, except, "Where is *your* maid?"

"Oh, over there," Mary replied, waving her hand in

the general vicinity of behind them. And then Olivia realized she'd made a terrible miscalculation, because Mary immediately turned to Sally and said, "You know my Genevieve, don't you? Why don't you go talk to her?"

Sally did know Mary's Genevieve, and she also knew that Genevieve's English skills were limited at best, but as Olivia couldn't very well jump in and insist that Sally *not* speak to Genevieve, Sally was forced to set down her embroidery and head off to find her.

"There," Mary announced proudly. "That was neatly done. Now tell me, what was he like? Was he handsome?"

"You've seen him."

"No, was he handsome up close? Those *eyes*." Mary shivered.

"Oh!" Olivia exclaimed, suddenly remembering. "They were *brown*, not bluish gray."

"That can't be. I'm quite certain—"

"You got it wrong."

"No. I never get things like that wrong."

"Mary, I was this close to his face," Olivia said, motioning to the distance between them on the bench. "I assure you, his eyes are brown."

Mary looked horrified. Finally, she shook her head and said, "It must be the way he looks at a person. So piercing. I just assumed his eyes were blue." She blinked. "Or gray."

Olivia rolled her eyes and looked straight ahead, hoping that would be the end of it, but Mary was not to be deterred. "You still didn't tell me about him," she pointed out.

"Mary, there is nothing to say," Olivia insisted. She looked down at her lap in dismay. Her newspaper was now a crumpled, unreadable heap. "He asked me to dance. I accepted."

"But—" And then Mary gasped.

"But what?" Really, Olivia was losing patience with this.

Mary grabbed her arm, actually grabbed it. Hard.

"What is it now?"

Mary pointed a finger in the direction of the Serpentine. "Over there."

Olivia saw nothing.

"On the *horse*," Mary hissed.

Olivia shifted her gaze to the left and then—

Oh, no. It couldn't be.

"Is that him?"

Olivia didn't answer.

"Sir Harry," Mary clarified.

"I know who you're talking about," Olivia snapped.

Mary craned her neck. "I think it *is* Sir Harry."

Olivia *knew* it was, not so much because it looked like the gentleman in question, but rather because how could her luck be anything but?

"He rides well," Mary murmured admiringly.

Olivia decided it was time to think religiously and pray. Maybe he wouldn't see them. Maybe he would but decide to ignore them. Maybe lightning—

"I think he saw us," Mary said, all glee and delight. "You should wave. *I* would, but we haven't been introduced."

"Don't give him any encouragement," Olivia ground out.

Mary turned on her in an instant. "I *knew* you didn't like him."

Olivia closed her eyes in misery. This was supposed to have been a peaceful, solitary outing. She wondered how long it would be until Mary caught Anne's head cold.

Then she wondered if there was anything she could do to hasten the infection.

"Olivia," Mary hissed, jabbing her in the ribs.

Olivia opened her eyes. Sir Harry was now quite a bit closer, clearly riding in their direction.

"I wonder if Mr. Grey is here as well," Mary said hopefully. "He might be Lord Newbury's heir, you know."

Olivia pasted a tight smile onto her face as Sir Harry approached, apparently without his might-be-an-heir cousin. He did ride well, she noticed, and his mount was very fine—a gorgeous brown gelding with white socks. He was dressed for a ride—a real one, not a stately trot on the park path. His dark hair was wind-blown, and his cheeks had a bit of color in them, and it *should* have made him look more approachable and friendly, but, Olivia thought with some disdain, he'd need to smile for that.

Sir Harry Valentine did not *do* smiles. Certainly not in her direction.

"Ladies," he said, coming to a halt in front of them.

"Sir Harry." It was all Olivia could manage, given that she was loath to unclench her teeth.

Mary kicked her.

"May I introduce Miss Cadogan," Olivia said.

He tilted his head graciously. "I am pleased to make your acquaintance."

"Sir Harry," Mary said, giving him a nod of greeting in return. "It is a pleasant morning, is it not?"

"Very much so," he replied. "Wouldn't you agree, Lady Olivia?"

"Indeed," she said tightly. She turned toward Mary, hoping he would follow suit and direct his questions at *her*.

But of course he did not. "I have not seen you in Hyde Park before, Lady Olivia," he said.

"I don't normally venture forth this early."

"No," he murmured, "I would imagine you have very important things to do at home at this time of the morning."

Mary gave her a curious look. It was a cryptic statement.

"Things to do," he went on, "people to watch . . ."

"Is your cousin riding as well?" Olivia asked quickly.

His brows rose mockingly. "Sebastian is rarely seen before noon," he replied.

"But you are an early riser?"

"Always."

Another thing to detest about him. Olivia didn't mind getting up early, but she hated people who were cheerful about it.

Olivia made no further comment, purposefully trying to extend the moment into awkwardness. Perhaps he would take the hint and leave. Anybody with sense knew that conversation was impossible between two ladies on a bench and a gentleman on horseback. Her neck was already beginning to cramp from looking so far up.

She reached up and rubbed the side of her neck, hoping he would take the hint. But then—because clearly everyone was against her, even herself—she had an extremely ill-timed burst of memory. About her imaginary boils. And the plague. Of the bubonic variety. And heaven help her, she laughed.

Except she couldn't laugh, not with Mary sitting right next her and Sir Harry looking down his arrogant nose, so she clamped her mouth shut. Except *that* sent the air through her nose, and she snorted. Most inelegantly. And that tickled.

Which made her laugh for real.

"Olivia?" Mary asked.

"It's nothing," she said, waving her hand at Mary as she turned the other way, trying to cover her face. "Really."

Sir Harry said nothing, thank God. Although it was probably only because he thought her insane.

But Mary—now she was a different story, and she never knew when to let go. "Are you sure, Olivia, because—"

Olivia still looked down into her shoulder, because somehow she knew she'd laugh anew if she didn't. "I just thought of something, that is all."

"But—"

Amazingly, Mary stopped pestering her.

Olivia would have been relieved, except that it seemed highly unlikely that Mary might suddenly develop tact and sense. And indeed, she was proved correct, because Mary hadn't cut herself off out of any sympathy for Olivia. She'd cut herself off because—

"Oh, look, Olivia! It's your brother."

Chapter Six

*H*arry *had* been planning to head home. It was his custom to take an early-morning ride, even in town, and he'd been just about ready to exit the park when he spied Lady Olivia sitting on a bench. He found this sufficiently intriguing to stop and be introduced to her friend, but after a few moments of idle chatter, he decided he didn't find either one of *them* sufficiently intriguing to keep him from his work.

Especially since Lady Olivia Bevelstoke was the reason he'd fallen so far behind in the first place.

She'd ceased spying upon him, that was true, but the damage was done. Every time he sat at his desk, he could feel her eyes upon him, even though he knew very well she'd shut her curtains tight. But clearly, reality had very little to do with the matter, because all he had to do, it seemed, was glance at her window, and he lost an entire hour's work.

It happened thus: He looked at the window, because it was *there*, and he couldn't very well never happen to glance upon it unless he also shut his curtains tight, which he was not willing to do, given the amount of time he spent in his office. So he saw the window, and he thought of her, because, really, what else would he think of upon seeing her bedroom window? At that point, annoyance set in, because A) she wasn't worth the energy, B) she wasn't even there, and C) he wasn't getting any work done because of her.

C always led into a bout of even deeper irritation, this time directed at himself, because D) he really ought to have better powers of concentration, E) it was just a stupid window, and F) if he was going to get agitated about a female, it ought to be one he at least *liked*.

F was where he generally let out a loud growl and forced himself to get back to his translation. It usually worked for a minute or two, and then he'd look back up, and happen to see the window, and the whole bloody nonsense cycled back to the beginning.

Which was why, when he saw the look of utter dread cross Lady Olivia Bevelstoke's face at the mention of her brother, he decided that no, he did not need to get back to work just yet. After all the annoyance she had caused him, he was looking forward to watching her experience similar pain.

"Have you met Olivia's brother, Sir Harry?" Miss Cadogan asked.

Harry swung himself down from his mount; it seemed he would be here for a while. "I have not had the pleasure."

Lady Olivia's face assumed a decidedly sour mien at his use of the word "pleasure."

"He is her twin brother," Miss Cadogan continued, "recently down from university."

Harry turned to Lady Olivia and said, "I did not realize you were a twin."

She shrugged.

"Has your brother completed his studies?" he asked.

She nodded curtly.

He almost shook his head at her attitude. She really was quite an unfriendly female. It was a shame she was so pretty. She did not deserve the good fortune of her looks. Harry rather thought she ought to have a large wart on her nose.

"He might be acquainted with my brother, then," Harry commented. "They would be of an age."

"Who is your brother?" Miss Cadogan asked.

Harry told them a bit about Edward, stopping a moment before Lady Olivia's brother arrived. He was on foot, walking by himself, with the loose-limbed gait of a young man. He looked rather like his sister, Harry noticed. His blond hair was several shades darker, but the bright eyes were precisely the same, both in color and shape.

Harry bowed; so did Mr. Bevelstoke.

"Sir Harry Valentine, my brother, Mr. Winston Bevelstoke; Winston, Sir Harry."

Said by Lady Olivia with a stunning lack of interest or inflection.

"Sir Harry," Winston said politely. "I am acquainted with your brother."

Harry didn't recognize him, but he supposed young

Bevelstoke was one of Edward's many acquaintances. He'd met most of them here and there; most were entirely unmemorable.

"You are our new neighbor, I understand," Winston said.

Harry acknowledged this with a murmur and nod.

"To the south."

"Indeed."

"I've always liked that house," Winston said. Or rather, pontificated. It certainly sounded as if he were about to take the statement on a grand journey. "Brick, is it not?"

"Winston," Olivia said impatiently, "you know very well it's brick."

"Well, yes," he said, with an offhanded wave, "or at least I was moderately certain. I don't often pay attention to those things, and, as you know, my bedroom faces the other direction."

Harry felt a smile creeping along his lips. This could only get better.

Winston turned to Harry and said, for no apparent reason other than to torture his sister, "Olivia's room faces the south."

"Does it now?"

Olivia looked as if she might—

"It does," Winston confirmed, putting a halt to Harry's speculation on what Lady Olivia might or might not do. But he was thinking that spontaneous combustion was not outside the realm of possibility.

"You've probably seen her window," Winston went on. "You really couldn't miss it. It's—"

"*Winston.*"

Harry actually stepped back an inch or two. It looked

as if there might be violence. And despite Winston's greater height and weight, he rather thought he'd put his money on his sister.

"I am sure Sir Harry is not interested in a floor plan of our home," Olivia bit off.

Winston stroked his chin thoughtfully. "I wasn't thinking of a floor plan so much as an elevation."

Harry turned back to Olivia. He was not sure he had ever seen such well-controlled fury. It was impressive.

"It's so nice to see you this morning, Winston," Miss Cadogan put in, quite possibly oblivious to the familial tension. "Are you often out and about this early?"

"No," he replied. "Mother sent me to fetch Olivia."

Miss Cadogan smiled brightly and returned her attention to Harry. "Then it seems you are the only regular morning visitor here in the park. I, too, came looking for Olivia. We haven't had a chance to chat for ages. She has been ill, you know."

"I did not know," Harry said. "I hope you are feeling better."

"Winston was also ill," Olivia said. She offered a frightening smile. "Much sicker than I."

"Oh, no!" Miss Cadogan gushed. "I am so sorry to hear that." She turned to Winston with great concern. "Had I known, I would have brought you a tincture."

"I shall be sure to inform you next time he falls ill," Olivia told her. She turned to Harry, lowered her voice, and said, "It happens more often that we would like. It's very distressing." And then, down to a whisper: "He was born that way."

Miss Cadogan rose to her feet, all of her attention

on Winston. "Are you feeling better now? I must say, you look a bit peaked."

Harry thought he looked the picture of health.

"I'm fine," Winston bit off, his ire clearly directed at his sister, who was still sitting on the bench, looking extremely satisfied with her recent accomplishments.

Miss Cadogan looked past him to Olivia, who was shaking her head, mouthing, *"He's not."*

"I will definitely bring you that tincture," Miss Cadogan said. "It tastes a bit foul, but our housekeeper swears by it. *And* I insist that you return home at once. It's chilly out."

"It's really not necessary," Winston protested.

"I was planning to return soon, anyway," Miss Cadogan put in, proving that young Bevelstoke was no match for the combined might of two determined women. "You may escort me."

"Do inform Mother that I shall be back momentarily," Olivia said sweetly.

Her brother glared at her, but he had clearly been outmaneuvered, and so he took Miss Cadogan's arm and led her away.

"Well played, Lady Olivia," Harry said admiringly, once the others were out of earshot.

She gave him a bored look. "You are not the only gentleman I find irritating."

There was no way he could ignore a comment like that, so he sat beside her, plopping right down into the spot recently vacated by Miss Cadogan. "Anything interesting?" he asked, motioning toward her newspaper.

"I would not know," she replied. "I am besieged by interruptions."

He chuckled. "My cue to apologize, I am sure, but I shan't indulge you."

Her lips pressed together, presumably pinching back a retort.

He sat back, crossing his right ankle over his left knee, letting his lazy pose signal that he was settling in beside her. "After all," he mused, "it is not as if I am invading your privacy. We are sitting on a bench in Hyde Park. Open air, public place, et cetera, et cetera."

He paused, giving her the chance to comment. She did not. So he continued on with: "If you'd wanted privacy, you might have taken your newspaper to your bedchamber, or perhaps to your office. Those are places, would you not agree, where one might operate under the assumption of privacy?"

Again he waited. Again, she refused to engage. So he lowered his voice to a murmur and asked, "Do you have an office, Lady Olivia?"

He did not think she would answer, as she was staring straight ahead, quite determinedly not looking at him, but much to his surprise, she ground out, "I do not."

He admired her for that, but not enough to change tack. "Pity, that," he murmured. "I find it most beneficial to have a place that is my own that is not used for sleeping. You should consider an office, Lady Olivia, if you wish for a place to read your newspaper away from the prying eyes of others."

She turned to him with an impressively indifferent expression. "You're sitting on my maid's embroidery."

"My apologies." He looked down, pulled the fabric

out from beneath him—he was barely on the hem, but he decided to be magnanimous and decline to comment—and set it aside. "Where *is* your maid?"

She waved her hand in an unspecific direction. "She went off to join Mary's maid. I'm sure she will return at any moment."

He had no response to that, so instead he said, "You and your brother have an interesting relationship."

She shrugged, clearly trying to be rid of him.

"Mine detests me."

That caught her interest. She turned, smiled too sweetly, and said, "I would like to meet him."

"I'm sure you would," he replied. "He is not often in my office, but when he gets up at a reasonable hour, he breakfasts in the small dining room. The windows are just two past my office toward the front of the house. You might try looking for him there."

She gave him a hard look. He smiled blandly in return.

"Why are you here?" she asked.

He motioned to his mount. "Out for a ride."

"No, why *here*?" she ground out. "On this bench. Sitting next to me."

He thought about that for a moment. "You vex me."

Her lips pursed. "Well," she said, somewhat briskly. "I suppose that's only fair."

The sentiment was rather sporting of her, even if the tone was not. She had, after all, just minutes earlier said that she found him irritating.

Her maid arrived then. Harry heard her before he saw her, stomping over the damp grass with great irritation, traces of a Cockney accent evident in her voice.

"Why does that woman seem to think I should learn French? She's the one in England, I say. Oh." She paused, looking at Harry with some surprise. When she continued, her voice and accent were considerably more cultured. "I am sorry, my lady. I did not realize you had company."

"He was just leaving," Lady Olivia said, all sweetness and light. She turned to him with a smile so dazzlingly sunny he finally understood all those broken hearts he kept hearing about. "Thank you so much for your company, Sir Harry," she said.

His breath caught, and it occurred to him that she was an exceedingly good liar. If he hadn't just spent the past ten minutes with the lady he was now referring to in his head as "Surly Girl," he might have fallen in love with her himself.

"As you indicated, Lady Olivia," he said quietly, "I was just leaving."

And so he did, with every intention of never seeing her again.

At least not on purpose.

Thoughts of Lady Olivia firmly behind him, Harry got back to work later that morning, and by afternoon was lost in a sea of Russian idioms.

Kogda rak na goryeh svistnyet = When the crawfish whistles on a mountain = When pigs fly.

Sdelatz slona iz mukha = Make an elephant out of a fly = Make a mountain out of a molehill.

S dokhlogo kozla i shersti klok = Even from the dead goat, even a piece of wool is worth something =

Equals . . .

Equals . . .

He pondered this for several minutes, idly tapping his pen against his blotter, and was just about to give up and move on when he heard a knock at the door.

"Enter." He didn't look up. It had been so long since he'd been able to maintain his focus for an entire paragraph; he wasn't going to break the rhythm now.

"Harry."

Harry's pen stilled. He'd been expecting the butler with the afternoon's post, but this voice belonged to his younger brother. "Edward," he said, making sure he knew exactly where he'd left off before looking up. "This is a pleasant surprise."

"This came for you." Edward crossed the room and placed an envelope on his desk. "It came by courier."

The outside of the envelope did not indicate the sender, but the markings were familiar. It was from the War Office, and it was almost certainly of some importance; they rarely sent communication of this sort directly to his home. Harry set it aside, intending to read it when he was alone. Edward knew that he translated documents, but he did not know for whom. Thus far Harry had not seen any indication that he could be trusted with the knowledge.

The missive could wait a few minutes, however. Right now Harry was curious as to his brother's presence in his office. It was not Edward's habit to deliver items about the house. Even if he had been the one to receive the letter, he most likely would have tossed it on the tray in the front hall for the butler to deal with.

Edward did not interact with Harry unless forced to do so, by outside influence or by necessity. Necessity usually being of the financial variety.

"How are you today, Edward?"

Edward shrugged. He looked tired, his eyes red and puffy. Harry wondered how late he'd been out the night before.

"Sebastian will be joining us for supper this evening," Harry said. Edward rarely ate at home, but Harry thought he might, if he knew Seb would be there.

"I have plans," Edward said, but then he added, "but perhaps I could delay them."

"I would appreciate that."

Edward stood in the center of the office, the very image of a sulky, sullen boy. He was two and twenty now, and Harry supposed he thought himself a man, but his bearing was callow and his eyes still young.

Young, but not youthful. Harry was disturbed by how haggard his brother appeared. Edward drank too much, and probably slept too little. He was not like their father, though. Harry couldn't quite put his finger on the difference, except that Sir Lionel had always been jolly.

Except when he was sad and apologetic. But he generally forgot about that by the next morning.

But Edward was different. Overindulgence did not make him effusive. Harry could not imagine him getting up on a chair and waxing poetic about the *thplendidneth* of a *thchool*. Edward did not attempt to be charming and debonair during the rare occasions that they shared a meal. Instead, he sat in stony silence, answering nothing but direct queries, and then with only the bare minimum of words.

Harry was painfully aware that he did not know his brother, knew nothing of his thoughts or interests. He had been gone the bulk of Edward's formative years, off on the Continent, fighting alongside Seb in the 18th Hussars. When he returned, he'd tried to rekindle the relationship, but Edward had wanted nothing to do with him. He was only here, in Harry's home, because he could not afford rooms of his own. He was the quintessential younger brother, with no inheritance to speak of, and no apparent skills. He'd scoffed at Harry's suggestion that he, too, join the military, accusing him of wanting only to be rid of him.

Harry hadn't bothered to suggest the clergy. It was difficult to imagine Edward leading anyone toward moral rectitude, and besides that, Harry *didn't* want to be rid of him.

"I received a letter from Anne earlier in the week," Harry mentioned. Their sister, who had married William Forbush at the age of seventeen and never looked back, had ended up in Cornwall, of all places. She sent Harry a letter each month, filled with news of her brood. Harry wrote back in Russian, insisting that if she did not use the language, she'd lose it altogether.

Anne's reply had been his warning, clipped from his letter and pasted onto a new sheet of paper, followed by, in English: "That is my intention, dear brother."

Harry had laughed, but he hadn't stopped with the Russian. And she must have taken the time to read and translate, because when she replied, she often had questions about the things he'd written.

It was an entertaining correspondence; Harry always looked forward to her letters.

She did not write to Edward. She used to, but she'd stopped when she realized that he would never return the gesture.

"The children are well," Harry continued. Anne had five of them, all boys save the last. Harry wondered what she looked like now. He hadn't seen her since he left for the army.

Harry sat back in his chair, waiting. For anything. For Edward to speak, to move, to kick the wall. Most of all, he was waiting for him to ask for an advance on his allowance, for surely that was the reason for his appearance. But Edward said nothing, just stubbed his toe along the floor, catching the edge of the dark-hued carpet and flipping it over before kicking it back down with his heel.

"Edward?"

"You'd best read the letter," Edward said gruffly as he moved to leave. "They said it was important."

Harry waited for him to depart, then picked up the directive from the War Office. It was unusual for them to contact him in this manner; they usually just sent over someone with documents in hand. He flipped over the note, used his forefinger to break the seal, and then opened it.

It was short, just two sentences long, but it was clear. Harry was to report to the offices at Horse Guards in Whitehall immediately.

He groaned. Anything that required his actual presence could not be good. The last time they'd hauled him in, it was to order him to play nursemaid to an elderly Russian countess. He'd had to remain glued to her side for three weeks. She'd complained about the heat, the food, the music . . . The only thing she hadn't complained about was the vodka, and that was because she'd brought her own.

She'd insisted on sharing, too. Anyone who spoke

Russian as well as Harry did could not drink British swill, she'd announced. She actually reminded him a bit of his grandmother for that.

But Harry did not drink, not even a drop, and he spent night after night dumping his glass into a potted plant.

Strangely, the plant had thrived. Quite possibly, the finest moment of the assignment was when the butler frowned down at the botanical wonder and said, "I didn't think that *made* flowers."

Still, Harry had no desire to repeat the experience. Unfortunately, he was rarely given the luxury of refusing. Funny, that. *They* needed *him*, as Russian translators weren't exactly thick on the ground. And yet he was expected to jump to their bidding.

Harry briefly considered finishing the page he was working on before departing, then decided against it. Best to get it over with.

And besides, the countess was back in St. Petersburg, presumably complaining about the cold, the sun, and the lack of English gentlemen forced to wait on her hand and foot.

Whatever it was they wanted of him, it couldn't be as bad as that, could it?

Chapter Seven

It was worse.

"Prince Who?" Harry asked.

"Prince Alexei Ivanovich Gomarovsky," replied Mr. Winthrop, who was Harry's frequent liaison with the War Office. Winthrop might have had a Christian name, but if so, Harry had not been made aware of it. He was simply Mr. Winthrop, of medium height and medium build, with medium brown hair, and a face that was unremarkable in every way. As far as Harry knew, he never left the War Office building.

"We don't like him," Winthrop said, with very little inflection. "He makes us nervous."

"What do *we* think he might do?"

"We're not sure," he replied, seemingly oblivious to Harry's sarcasm. "But there are a number of aspects to his visit that place him under suspicion. Foremost of which is his father."

"His father?"

"Ivan Alexandrovich Gomarovsky. Now deceased. He was a supporter of Napoleon."

"And the prince still has a position in Russian society?" Harry found that difficult to believe. It had been nine years since the French had marched on Moscow, but Franco-Russian relations were still frosty at best. The tsar and his people had not appreciated Napoleon's invasion. And the French had long memories; the humiliation and devastation of the retreat would stay with them for many years to come.

"His father's treasonous activities were never discovered," Winthrop explained. "He died last year of natural causes, still believed to be a loyal servant of the tsar."

"How do we know that he was a traitor?"

Winthrop brushed off his question with a vague wave. "We have information."

Harry decided to accept that at face value, since he wasn't likely to be told anything more.

"We also wonder at the timing of the prince's visit. Three known sympathizers of Napoleon—two of them British subjects—arrived in town yesterday."

"You allow traitors to remain free?"

"It is often in our best interests to allow the opposition to believe that they are undetected." Winthrop leaned forward, resting his forearms on his desk. "Bonaparte is sick, probably dying. He is wasting away."

"Bonaparte?" Harry asked doubtfully. He'd seen the fellow once. From afar, of course. He was short, yes, but with a remarkable belly. It was difficult to imagine him thin and gaunt.

"We have learned"—Winthrop shuffled some papers on his desk until he found what he was looking for—"that his trousers have had to be taken in by nearly five inches."

Harry was impressed despite himself. No one could accuse the War Office of a lack of attention to detail.

"He won't escape St. Helena," Winthrop continued. "But we must remain vigilant. There will always be those who plot in his name. We believe Prince Alexei might be one of those people."

Harry exhaled. Irritably, because he wanted Winthrop to know just how much he did not wish to be involved in this sort of business. He was a translator, for God's sake. He liked words. Paper. Ink. He did not like Russian princes, and he had no wish to spend the next three weeks pretending he did. "What do you require of me?" he asked. "You know that I do not engage in espionage activities."

"Nor would we want you to," Winthrop said. "Your language skills are far too valuable for us to have you lurking in some dark corner, hoping you don't get shot."

"It's hard to believe you have difficulty recruiting spies," Harry murmured.

Once again, sarcasm was lost on Winthrop. "Your command of the Russian language, along with your position in society, makes you ideal to keep an eye on Prince Alexei."

"I don't go out much in society," Harry reminded him.

"Yes, but you could."

Winthrop's words hung over the room like a sword. Harry knew very well that there was only one other man at the War Department whose Russian fluency rivaled his own. He also knew that George Fox was the son of an innkeeper who had married a Russian girl who'd come to England as a servant to a diplomat. Fox was a good man, sharp and brave, but he would never gain entrée to the same functions as a prince. Frankly, Harry wasn't so sure that he could, either.

But Sebastian, with his possible earldom, might. And it wasn't as if Harry had never tagged along before.

"We won't ask you to take any direct action," Winthrop said, "although, with your background at Waterloo, we are confident that you would be more than capable."

"I'm done with fighting," Harry warned him. And he was. Seven years on the Continent was enough. He had no plans to pick up a saber again.

"We know. That is why all we are asking is that you keep an eye on him. Listen to his conversations when you are able. Report to us anything you find suspicious."

"Suspicious." Harry echoed. Did they think the prince was going to spill secrets at Almacks? Russian speakers were rare in London, but surely the prince would not be so foolish as to assume that no one would understand what he was saying.

"This comes from Fitzwilliam," Winthrop said in a quiet voice.

Harry looked up sharply. Fitzwilliam ran the War Office. Not officially, of course. Officially, he did not even exist. Harry didn't know his real name, and he was not sure he knew what he looked like; the two times they had met, his appearance had been so altered that Harry could not discern what was truth and what was disguise.

But he knew that if Fitzwilliam ordered something, it must be done.

Winthrop took a folder from his desk and held it out to Harry. "Read this. It's our dossier on the prince."

Harry took the document and started to rise, but Winthrop stopped him with a gruff, "That cannot leave the premises."

Harry felt himself pause, the sort of annoyed, over-played cessation of movement one did when one is being ordered about. He sat back down, opened the folder, pulled out four sheets of paper, and began to read.

Prince Alexei Ivanovich Gomarovsky, son of Ivan Alexandrovich Gomarovsky, grandson of Alexei Pav-lovich Gomarovsky, et cetera, et cetera, unmarried, no betrothal on record. In London visiting the ambas-sador, who was his sixth cousin.

"They're all related," Harry muttered. "Hell, he's probably related to me."

"Pardon?"

Harry gave Winthrop a brief glance. "Sorry."

Traveling with a retinue of eight, including a diplo-matic consort of astonishing menace and hulk. Liked vodka (of course), English tea (how open-minded of him), and the opera.

Harry nodded as he read. Perhaps this wouldn't be so bad. He enjoyed the opera himself, but he never seemed to find the time to go. Now it would be a re-quirement. Excellent.

He turned a page. There was a sketch of the prince. He held it up. "Does this resemble him?"

"Not very much," Winthrop admitted.

Harry shuffled the sketch to the back. Why did they even bother? He continued reading, gathering bits and pieces of the prince's personal history. His father had died at the age of sixty-three of a heart ailment. Poison was not suspected. His mother was still living, dividing her time between St. Petersburg and Nizhny Novgorod.

He flipped to the last page. The prince appeared to be on the prowl for women, showing a particular preference for blondes. He had visited the most exclusive brothel in London six times during the two weeks he'd been in London. He had also attended numerous social functions, possibly even searching for a British wife. It was rumored that his fortunes in Russia had diminished and that he might need a bride with a sizable dowry. He had shown particular attention to the daughter of—

"Oh. *No.*"

"Is there a problem?" Winthrop inquired.

Harry held up the paper, not that Winthrop could read the writing from across the desk. "Lady Olivia Bevelstoke," he said, his voice laden with grim disbelief.

"Yes." That was all. Just yes.

"I know her."

"We know."

"I don't like her."

"We're sorry to hear that." Winthrop cleared his throat. "We were not sorry, however, to learn that Rudland House is directly to the north of your newly rented residence."

Harry ground his teeth together.

"We were not mistaken in this, were we?"

"No," Harry said grudgingly.

"Good. Because it is essential that you keep an eye on her, too."

Harry was not able to hide his displeasure.

"Will that be a problem?"

"Of course not, sir," Harry said, since they both knew the question had been purely rhetorical.

"We do not suspect Lady Olivia of collusion with the prince, but we do think, given his well-documented talent for seduction, that she might succumb to bad judgment."

"You have documented his talent for seduction," Harry stated. He didn't even want to know how that had been achieved.

Again, the vague dismissive wave. "We have our ways."

Harry was of half a mind to say that if the prince managed to seduce Lady Olivia, it was good riddance for Britain, but something stopped him. A fleeting flash of memory, something in her eyes perhaps . . .

Whatever her sins, she didn't deserve this.

Except . . .

"We are counting on you to keep Lady Olivia out of trouble," Winthrop was saying.

She *had* been spying on him.

"Her father is an important man."

She'd said she liked guns. And hadn't her maid said something about speaking in French?

"She is well known and well liked in society. Should anything happen to her, the scandal would be irreparable."

But she couldn't have known that Harry worked for

the War Office. No one knew that he worked for the War Office. He was just a translator.

"It would be impossible for us to conduct our investigations under the scrutiny such a disaster would bring." Winthrop paused, finally. "Do you understand what I am saying?"

Harry nodded. He still didn't think that Lady Olivia was a spy, but his curiosity had been more than piqued. And wouldn't he feel like a fool if he turned out to be wrong?

"My lady."

Olivia looked up from the letter she was writing to Miranda. She had been debating whether to tell her about Sir Harry. Olivia couldn't imagine anyone else she could—or would—tell, but then again, it wasn't the sort of escapade that made sense on paper.

She wasn't so sure it made sense at all.

She looked up. The butler stood in the doorway, holding a silver tray with a calling card upon it.

"A guest, my lady."

She glanced up at the clock on the sitting-room mantel. It was a bit early for visitors, and her mother was still out shopping for hats. "Who is it, Huntley?"

"Sir Harry Valentine, my lady. I believe he has let the house to the south."

Slowly, Olivia set down her pen. Sir Harry? Here? *Why?*

"Shall I show him in?"

Olivia didn't know why he was asking. If Sir Harry was in the front hall, he could practically see Huntley talking to her. There would be no pretending she was unavailable. She nodded, straightened the pages of the letter and tucked them into a drawer, and then stood, feeling as if she needed to be on her feet when he arrived.

Within moments he appeared in the doorway, clad in his customary dark hues. He carried a small package under his arm.

"Sir Harry," she said lightly, rising to her feet. "What a surprise."

He nodded his greeting. "I always strive to be a good neighbor."

She nodded in return, watching warily as he entered the room.

She could not imagine why he might have chosen to call. He had been most unpleasant toward her the day before in the park, and the truth was, she had not behaved any better. She could not remember the last time she had treated anyone so poorly, but in her defense, she was terrified that he would attempt to blackmail her again, this time for something far more dangerous than a dance.

"I hope I am not interrupting," he said.

"Not at all." She motioned to the desk. "I was writing a letter to my sister."

"I did not realize you had one."

"My sister-in-law," she amended. "But she is as a sister to me. I have known her all of my life."

He waited until she took a seat on the sofa, then sat in the Egyptian-style chair directly across from her. He did not appear to be uncomfortable, which Olivia found interesting. She hated sitting in that chair.

"I brought you this," he said, handing her the parcel.

"Oh. Thank you." She took it with some awkwardness. She did not want gifts from this man, and she certainly did not trust his motivations for presenting her with one.

"Open it," he urged.

It was wrapped plainly, and her fingers were shaking—hopefully not so much that he could see. It took her a few tries to undo the knot in the string, but eventually she was able to peel back the paper.

"A book," she said with a touch of surprise. She'd known that was what it had to be, from the weight and the shape of the package, but still, it was a very odd choice.

"Anyone can bring flowers," he remarked.

She turned it over—it had been upside down when she'd unwrapped it—and looked at the title. *Miss Butterworth and the Mad Baron.* Now she was *really* surprised. "You brought me a gothic novel?"

"A *lurid* gothic novel," he corrected. "It seemed the sort of thing you might enjoy."

She looked up at him, assessing that comment.

He looked back, as if daring her to question him.

"I don't really read," she murmured.

His brows rose.

"I mean I *can*," she said quickly, irritation rising within her, as much at herself as at him. "I just don't much enjoy it."

His brows remained up.

"Am I not supposed to admit that?" she asked pertly.

He smiled slowly, and an agonizingly long moment passed before he said, "You don't think before you speak, do you?"

"Not very often," she admitted.

"Try it," he said, motioning toward the book. "I thought you might find it more entertaining than the newspaper."

It was just the sort of thing a man would say. No one ever seemed to understand that she preferred the news of the day to silly figments of someone else's imagination.

"Have *you* read it?" she asked, looking down as she opened to a random page.

"Gad, no. But my sister recommended it highly."

She looked up sharply. "You have a sister?"

"You seem to find that surprising."

She did. She wasn't sure why, except that her friends had seen fit to tell her *everything* about him, and somehow that had been left off.

"She lives in Cornwall," he said, "surrounded by cliffs, legend, and a gaggle of small children."

"What a lovely description." And she meant it, too. "Are you a devoted uncle?"

"No."

Her surprise must have shown, because he said, "Am I not supposed to admit that?"

She laughed without meaning to. "Touché, Sir Harry."

"I would like to be a devoted uncle," he told her, his smile growing warm and true, "but I have not had the opportunity to meet any of them."

"Of course," she murmured. "You were on the Continent for so many years."

His head tilted ever so slightly to the side. She wondered if he always did that when he was curious. "You know quite a bit about me," he said.

"Everyone knows that much about you." Really, the man should not be surprised.

"There is not much privacy in London, is there?"

"Almost none at all." The words were out of her mouth before she realized what she'd said, what she might have just admitted to. "Would you care for tea?" she asked, deftly changing the topic.

"I would love some, thank you."

Once she'd rung for Huntley and given him instructions, Sir Harry said, quite conversationally, "When I was in the army, that was what I missed the most."

"Tea?" That seemed difficult to believe.

He nodded. "I *longed* for it."

"It wasn't provided for you?" For some reason Olivia found this simply unacceptable.

"Sometimes. Other times we had to make do."

Something about his voice—wistful and young—made her smile. "I do hope ours meets with your approval."

"I'm not picky."

"Really? I would think that with such a love for it, you would be a connoisseur."

"Rather, I went without so many times that I appreciate every drop."

She laughed. "It was tea you missed, really? Most gentlemen of my acquaintance would say brandy. Or port."

"Tea," he said firmly.

"Do you drink coffee?"

He shook his head. "Too bitter."

"Chocolate?"

"Only with heaps of sugar."

"You are a very interesting man, Sir Harry."

"I am certainly aware that *you* find me interesting."

Her cheeks burned. And here she was starting to actually like the man. The worst part of it all was, he had a point. She *had* been spying on him, and it *had* been rude. But still, he didn't need to go out of his way to make her uncomfortable.

The tea arrived, giving her respite from meaningful conversation. "Milk?" she asked.

"Please."

"Sugar?"

"No. Thank you."

She didn't bother to look up as she remarked, "Really? No sugar? Even though you sweeten your chocolate?"

"And my coffee, if I'm forced to drink it. Tea is a different beast altogether."

Olivia handed him his cup and set to work preparing her own. There was a certain comfort to be found in familiar tasks. Her hands knew just what to do, the memories of the motions long since etched into her muscles. The conversation, too, was bolstering. Simple and meaningless, and yet it restored her equilibrium. So much so that as he took his second sip, she was finally able to upset *his* equilibrium, smiling sweetly as she said:

"They say you killed your fiancée."

He choked, which gave her great pleasure (his shock, not his choking; she hoped she'd not become *that* ruthless), but he recovered quickly, and his voice was smooth and even when he responded, "Do they?"

"They do."

"Do they say how I killed her?"

"They do not."

"Do they say when?"

"They might have done," she lied, "but I wasn't listening."

"Hmmm." He appeared to be considering this. It was a disconcerting sight, this tall, utterly masculine man, sitting in her mother's mauve sitting room with a dainty teacup in his hand. Apparently pondering murder.

He took a sip. "Did anyone happen to mention her name?"

"Your fiancée's?"

"Yes." It was a silky, utterly urbane "yes," as if they were discussing the weather, or perhaps the likelihood of Bucket of Roses winning the Ascot Cup on Ladies' Day.

Olivia gave her head a little shake and lifted her own cup to her lips.

He closed his eyes for just a moment, then looked at her directly, his head moving sadly from side to side. "She rests in peace now, that is all that is important."

Olivia didn't just choke on her tea, she spit it nearly across the room. And he laughed, the wretch.

"Good God, that was the most fun I've had in years," he said, trying to catch his breath.

"You're despicable."

"You accused me of murder!"

"I did not. I only said that someone else did."

"Oh, yes," he said mockingly, "*there's* a really big difference."

"For your information, I didn't *believe* it."

"I am warmed to the core by your support."

"Don't be," she said sharply. "It was nothing more than common sense."

He laughed again. "Is that why you were spying on me?"

"I wasn't—" Oh, for heaven's sake, why was she still denying it? "Yes," she practically spat. "Wouldn't you do the same?"

"I might call for a constable first."

"I might call for a constable first," she mimicked, using a voice she usually reserved for her siblings.

"You *are* testy."

She glared at him.

"Very well, did you at least discover something interesting?"

"Yes," she said, narrowing her eyes. "Yes, I did."

He waited, then finally said, with no small amount of sarcasm, "Do tell."

She leaned forward. "Explain the hat."

He looked at her as if she'd gone mad. "What are you talking about?"

"The hat!" she exclaimed, waving her hands alongside her head, her wrists flicking up as if to indicate the silhouette of a headpiece. "It was ridiculous! It had feathers. And you were wearing it inside."

"Oh. That." Harry fought a chuckle. "That was for your benefit, really."

"You didn't know I was there!"

"Excuse me, yes I did."

Her lips parted, and she looked a trifle queasy as she asked, "When did you see me?"

"The first time you stepped in front of the window." Harry shrugged, raising his eyebrows as if to say— *Just try to contradict me.* "You're not as good at concealment as you think."

She drew back in a huff. It was ludicrous, but he suspected she thought she'd been insulted. "And the papers in the fire?" she demanded.

"Don't you ever toss papers in the fire?"

"Not in a mad rush, I don't."

"Well, that was for your benefit, too. You were going to such trouble. I thought I had best make it worth your while."

"You . . ."

She didn't look able to complete the sentence, so he added, almost offhandedly, "I was near to jumping on the desk and dancing a jig, but I thought that would be too obvious."

"You were making fun of me the whole time."

"Well . . ." He thought about that. "Yes."

Her lips parted. She looked outraged, and he almost felt apologetic—really, it had to be a male reflex, to feel ashamed when a female had that look on her face. But she had not a leg to stand on, not even a toe. "Might I remind you," he pointed out, "that *you* were spying on *me*. If anyone is the wronged party, it is I."

"Well, I do think you've had your revenge," she responded primly, her chin poking up in the air.

"Oh, I don't know about that, Lady Olivia. It will be a long time before we are even."

"What are you planning?" she asked suspiciously.

"Nothing." He grinned. "Yet."

She made a funny little huffing sound—it was quite endearing, really—and he decided to go in for the winning blow with, "Oh, and by the way, I have never been betrothed."

She blinked, looking somewhat confused by his sudden change of topic.

"The dead fiancée?" he supplied helpfully.

"Not so dead, then?"

"Never even alive to begin with."

She nodded slowly, then asked, "Why did you come here today?"

Harry certainly wasn't going to tell her the truth, that she was now his assignment, and he was supposed to make sure that she didn't unwittingly commit treason. So he just said, "It seemed polite."

He was going to have to spend a great deal of time with her in the next few weeks, or if not with her, then at least in her vicinity. He no longer suspected that there had been any nefarious purpose to her spying on him. He never had, really, but it would have been foolish not to be careful. Still, her story about the dead fiancée was so ludicrous it had to be true. It did seem exactly the reason a bored debutante would spy on a neighbor.

Not that he knew much of bored debutantes.

But he supposed he would soon.

He smiled at her. He was enjoying himself far more than he'd expected to.

She looked as if she might roll her eyes, and for some reason he wanted her to. He liked her much more when her face was in motion, replete with emotion. At the Smythe-Smith musicale, she had been cool and uncompromisingly reserved. Except for a few unharnessed flashes of ire, she had been devoid of expression.

It had grated. It had got under his fingernails, like an itch that could never be satisfied.

She offered more tea, and he took it, strangely content to prolong the visit. As she was pouring, however, the butler entered the room again, bearing a silver tray.

"Lady Olivia," he intoned. "This arrived for you."

The butler bent down so that Lady Olivia could remove a card from the tray. It looked like an invitation of sorts, festive and grand, with a ribbon and a seal.

A seal?

Harry shifted his position ever so slightly, trying to get a better view. Was it a royal seal? The Russians did like their royal trappings. He supposed the British did, too, but that was neither here nor there. She wasn't being pursued by King George.

She glanced at the card in her hands, then moved to set it down on the table beside her.

"Don't you want to open it?"

"I'm sure it can wait. I wouldn't wish to be rude."

"Do not mind me," he assured her. He motioned toward the card. "It does look interesting."

She blinked a few times, looking first at the card and then up at him with a curious expression.

"Grand," Harry clarified, thinking his first choice of adjectives had not been well thought.

"I know who it's from," she said, apparently unaffected by the knowledge.

He cocked his head, hoping the motion would serve as the question it would be impolite to voice aloud.

"Oh, very well," she said, sliding her finger under the seal. "If you insist."

He hadn't insisted in the least, but he wasn't about to say anything that might make her change her mind.

And so he waited patiently while she read, enjoying the play of emotion across her face. She rolled her eyes once, let out a small but beleaguered exhalation, and then finally groaned.

"Unpleasant news?" Harry inquired politely.

"No," she said. "Just an invitation I'd rather not accept."

"Then don't."

She smiled tightly. Or maybe it was ruefully. He couldn't be sure.

"This is more of a summons," she told him.

"Oh, come now. Who has the authority to issue a summons to the illustrious Lady Olivia Bevelstoke?"

Wordlessly, she handed him the card.

Chapter Eight

Reasons Why a Prince Might
Pay Attention to Me
By Lady Olivia Bevelstoke

Ruination
Marriage

*N*either option was particularly appealing. Ruination, for obvious reasons, and marriage for . . . well,
a whole host of reasons.

Reasons Why I Would Not Care
to Marry a Russian Prince
By Lady Olivia Bevelstoke

I don't speak Russian.
I can't even manage French.

I don't want to move to Russia.
I hear it's quite cold there.
I would miss my family.
And tea.

Did they drink tea in Russia? She looked over at Sir Harry, who was still examining the card she'd handed to him. For some reason she thought he would know. He'd traveled widely, or at least as widely as the army would have needed him to, and he did like tea.

And her list hadn't even begun to touch upon the *royal* aspects of marriage to a prince. The protocol. The formality. It sounded an absolute nightmare.

A nightmare in a very cold climate.

Quite honestly, she was beginning to think that ruination was the lesser of the two evils.

"I did not realize you moved in such rarefied circles," Sir Harry said, once he was done with his perusal of the invitation.

"I don't. I've met him twice. No" —she thought back over the past few weeks— "three times. That's all."

"You must have made quite an impression."

Olivia sighed wearily. She'd known that the prince had found her attractive. She'd had enough men pursue her in the past that she could recognize the signs. She'd tried to dissuade him as politely as she could, but she couldn't very well rebuff him completely. He was a prince, for heaven's sake. If there was going to be tension between their two nations, *she* wasn't going to be the cause of it.

"Will you go?" Sir Harry asked.

Olivia grimaced. The prince, who was apparently

unaware of the English custom that gentlemen called upon ladies, had requested that she pay him a visit. He had gone so far as to specify a time, two days hence, at three in the afternoon, which led Olivia to feel that he had taken a rather liberal view of the word "request."

"I don't see how I can refuse," she replied.

"No." He looked down again at the invitation, shaking his head. "You can't."

She groaned.

"Most women would find it flattering."

"I suppose it is. I mean, yes, of course it is. He *is* a prince." She tried to put a little excitement into her voice. She didn't think she succeeded.

"But you still don't wish to go?"

"It's a nuisance, is what it is." She gave him a direct look. "Have you ever been presented at court? No? It's dreadful."

He laughed, but she was too worked up to do anything but continue. "The dress has to be just so, with hoops and panniers even though no one has worn that nonsense for years. Your curtsy must be exactly the right depth, and heaven forbid you smile at the wrong moment."

"Somehow I don't think Prince Alexei expects you to don hoops and panniers."

"I know he doesn't, but it's still going to be grotesquely formal, and I don't know the first thing about Russian protocol. Which means my mother will insist upon finding someone to teach me, although where she will find a tutor at this late date, I don't know. And then I will have to spend the next two days learning how deep a Russian curtsy must be, and are there any topics it would be considered impolite to discuss, and oh!"

She left off with the *oh*, because honestly, the entire topic was giving her a stomachache. Nerves. It was nerves. She hated nerves.

She looked over at Sir Harry. He was sitting very still, with an inscrutable expression on his face.

"Aren't you going to tell me it won't be so terrible?" she asked.

He shook his head. "No. It will be terrible."

She slumped. Her mother would have a fit of the vapors if she saw her like this, all slouchy in the presence of a gentleman. But really, couldn't he have lied and said she was going to have a marvelous time? If he'd lied, she would still be sitting straight.

And if it made her feel better to affix blame upon someone else, so be it.

"At least you have a few days until you have to present yourself," he offered.

"Only two," she said gloomily. "And I'll probably see him tonight, as well."

"Tonight?"

"The Mottram ball. Are you going?" She flapped her hand in front of her face. "No, of course you're not."

"I beg your pardon?"

"Oh, I'm sorry." She felt herself blush. That had been terribly thoughtless of her. "I simply meant that you don't go out. Not that you couldn't. You just do not choose to. Or at least I assume that's the reason."

He stared at her, so long and so level, that she was compelled to continue. "I watched you for five days, remember."

"It is something I'm unlikely to forget." He must have taken pity on her, because he did not pursue the topic further, instead saying, "As it happens I do plan to attend the Mottram ball."

She smiled, more than a little surprised by the flutters of delight in her midsection. "Then I will see you there."

"I would not miss it for the world."

As it happened, Harry *hadn't* planned to attend the Mottram ball. He wasn't even sure if he had received an invitation, but it was easy enough to attach himself to Sebastian, who would certainly be going. This meant he was forced to endure Seb's interrogation—*why* did he suddenly wish to go out and *who* might be responsible for the change of heart? But Harry had plenty of experience dodging Sebastian's questions, and once they arrived, it was such a crush that he was able to lose his cousin immediately.

Harry remained at the perimeter of the ballroom, casting an appraising eye over the crowd. It was difficult to estimate how many were in attendance. Three hundred? Four? It would be easy to pass along a note without being detected, or to conduct a furtive conversation, all the while appearing as if nothing were amiss.

Harry gave himself a mental shake. He was starting to think like a bloody spy, for God's sake. Which he did not have to do. His orders had been to keep an eye on Lady Olivia and the prince, together or separately. He wasn't supposed to attempt to prevent anything or stop anything or really, *anything*.

Watch and report, that was all.

He didn't see Olivia or anyone who looked vaguely royal, for that matter, so he got himself a glass of punch and sipped at it for several minutes, entertaining himself by watching Sebastian move about the room, charming everyone in his path.

It was a talent, that. One he most definitely did not possess.

After about thirty minutes of watching and waiting (no reporting to be done, whatsoever), there was a small stir near the east entrance, so Harry began to wend his way over. He got himself as close as he was able, then leaned toward the gentleman next to him and asked, "Do you know what all the fuss is about?"

"Some Russian prince." The man shrugged, unimpressed. "Been in town for a couple of weeks."

"Causing quite a stir," Harry commented.

The man—Harry didn't know him, but he seemed like the sort who spent his evenings at events such as these—snorted. "The ladies have gone stupid for him."

Harry returned his attention to the small knot of people near the door. There was the usual movement of bodies, and every now and then he caught a glimpse of the man at the center of it all, but not for long enough to get a good look at him.

The prince was quite blond, that much he'd been able to see, and taller than average, although probably not, Harry noted with some satisfaction, as tall as he was.

There was no reason Harry should be introduced to the prince, and no one who would think to do so, so he hung back, trying to take measure of the man as he moved through the crowd.

He was arrogant, that was for certain. At least ten young ladies were presented to him, and each time, he did not even so much as nod. His chin remained high, and he acknowledged each of them with nothing more than a sharp, downward glance.

He treated the gentlemen with similar disdain, speaking only to three.

Harry wondered if there was *anyone* in attendance the prince did not consider beneath his notice.

"You look very serious this evening, Sir Harry."

He turned and smiled before he could think the better of it. Lady Olivia had somehow sneaked up to his side, heartbreakingly beautiful in midnight-blue velvet.

"Aren't unmarried ladies supposed to wear pastels?" he asked her.

Her brows rose at his impertinence, but her eyes sparkled with humor. "Yes, but I'm no longer so new. It's my third year out, you know. Practically on the shelf."

"Somehow I find it difficult to believe that that is anyone's fault but your own."

"Ouch."

He grinned at her. "And how have you been faring this evening?"

"I have nothing to report. We've only just arrived."

He knew that, of course. But he couldn't very well let on that he'd been watching for her, so he said, "Your prince is here."

She looked as if she wanted to groan. "I know."

He leaned in with a conspiratorial smile. "Shall I help you to avoid him?"

Her eyes lit up. "Do you think you can?"

"I am a man of many talents, Lady Olivia."

"Funny hats notwithstanding?"

"Funny hats notwithstanding."

And then, just like that, they both laughed. Together. The sound came together like a perfect chord, clear and true. And then, at quite the same time, they both seemed to realize that moment was significant, although neither had any idea why.

"Why do you wear such dark colors?" she asked.

He looked down at his evening kit. "You don't like my coat?"

"I do," she assured him. "It's very elegant. It's just that it has been commented upon."

"My taste in clothing?"

She nodded. "It was a slow week for gossip. Besides, you commented on *my* gown."

"True enough. Very well, I wear dark colors because it makes my life easier."

She said nothing, just waited with an expectant look on her face, as if to say—*surely there's more.*

"I shall let you in on a grave secret, Lady Olivia."

He leaned forward, and so did she, and it was another one of those moments. Perfect accord.

"I am daft when it comes to colors," he said in a low, grave voice. "Can't tell red and green apart to save my life."

"Really?" Her voice was a bit loud, and she glanced about self-consciously before continuing in a quieter tone. "I have never heard of such a thing."

"I'm not the only one, I'm told, but I've never met anyone else so afflicted."

"But surely there is no need for dark colors all the time." She sounded—and looked—utterly fascinated. Her eyes were sparkling with it, and her voice was full of interest.

If Harry had known that his difficulties seeing colors would be such a boon with the ladies, he'd have trotted it out years ago.

"Can't your valet pick out your attire?" she said.

"Yes, but then I'd have to trust him."

"You don't?" She looked intrigued. Amused. Perhaps a combination of both.

"He has a rather dry sense of humor, and he knows I can't sack him." He gave her a helpless shrug. "He saved my life once. And perhaps more importantly, my horse's as well."

"Oh, then you definitely cannot sack him. Your horse is lovely."

"I'm quite fond of him," Harry said. "The horse. And the valet, I suppose."

She nodded approvingly. "You should be thankful that dark colors suit you. Not everyone wears black well."

"Why, Lady Olivia, is that a compliment?"

"Not so much a compliment to you as an insult to everyone else," she assured him.

"Thank heavens for that. I don't think I would know how to conduct myself in a world in which you offered compliments."

She touched him lightly on the shoulder—flirtatious, daring, and utterly ironic. "I feel *exactly* the same way."

"Very well. Now that we are in accord, what shall we do about your prince?"

She gave him a sideways sort of look. "I know that you are just dying for me to say that he's not my prince."

"I expected you would, yes," he murmured.

"In the interest of disappointing you, I shall have to say that he is as much my prince as he is anyone else's here." She pressed her lips together as she glanced about the room. "Except for the Russians, I suppose."

At any other time, Harry would have said that he was Russian, or at least one quarter so. He'd have made a splendid remark, maybe something about not wanting to claim the prince, regardless, and then dazzled her with his command of the language.

But he couldn't. And truth be told, it was disconcerting how much he wanted to.

"Can you see him?" she asked. She was craning her neck, standing on her tiptoes, but although she was of slightly above average height, there was no way she could see over the crowd.

Harry, however, could. "Over there," he said with a nod toward the doors leading out to the garden. The prince was standing in the center of a small group of people, looking utterly bored by their attentions, and yet at the same time as if he expected it as his due.

"What is he doing?" Olivia asked.

"He is being presented to . . ." Well, hell. He had no idea to whom he was being presented. " . . . someone."

"Male or female?"

"Female."

"Young or old?"

"Is this an interrogation?"

"Young or old?" she repeated. "I know everyone here. It is my *vocation* to know everyone at these events."

He cocked his head to the side. "Is this something you take special pride in?"

"Not particularly, no."

"She's of middling age," he said.

"What is she wearing?"

"A dress," he retorted.

"Can you describe it?" she asked impatiently. Then: "You're as bad as my brother."

"I quite like your brother," he said, mostly just to annoy her.

She rolled her eyes. "Don't worry, you'll get to know him better and change your mind."

He smiled at that. He couldn't help it. He wasn't sure how he could have thought her cold and remote. If anything, she was brimming with mischief and humor. All it seemed she needed was to be in the company of a friend.

"Well?" she demanded. "What sort of dress is she wearing?"

He shifted his weight from foot to foot to get a better look. "Something puffy, with . . ." He motioned toward his shoulders, as if he had any hope of describing female attire. He shook his head. "I can't tell the color."

"Interesting." Her brow wrinkled. "Does that mean it must be either red or green?"

"Or any one of a thousand shades thereof."

Her posture changed completely. "That's really fascinating, did you know?"

"Actually, I've always found it more of a nuisance."

"I suppose you would," she acknowledged. Then she asked, "The woman he's talking to—"

"Oh, he's not talking to her," Harry said, with a bit more feeling than he'd intended.

She stood on her tiptoes again, not that that would improve her view. "What do you mean?"

"He doesn't talk to anyone. Hardly anyone, at least. Mostly he does a lot of looking down his nose."

"That's very strange. He talked a great deal to me."

Harry shrugged. He didn't know what to say to that, other than the obvious, which was that the prince wanted to get her into his bed. Which didn't seem appropriate for the moment.

Although he had to give the prince credit for good taste.

"Very well," Olivia said. "The woman he's not talking to. Is she wearing a rather vulgar diamond?"

"On her neck?"

"No, through her nose. Of course on her neck."

He gave her a rather assessing stare. "You are not the person I thought you were."

"Considering your initial impression of me, that's probably a good thing. Is she wearing a diamond?"

"Yes."

"Then it's Lady Mottram," she said firmly. "Our hostess. Which means he'll be busy for several minutes. It would be impolite to ignore her."

"I would not count on his going out of his way to be polite."

"Don't worry. He won't get away. Lady M has *tentacles*. And two unmarried daughters."

"Shall we head in the opposite direction?"

Her brows rose impishly. "Let's."

She took off, wending her way expertly through the crowd. He followed the sound of her laughter, and, every few seconds when she turned back to make sure he was there, the dazzling flash of her smile.

Eventually they reached an alcove, and she flopped into a seat, breathless and giddy. He stood beside her, his mien considerably more sedate. He didn't want to sit. Not yet. He needed to keep an eye out for the prince.

"He won't find us here!" she said gaily.

Nor would anyone else, Harry could not help but notice. There was nothing risqué about the alcove; it was quite properly open to the ballroom. But the way it was angled—off the corner, with its walls curling round like a womb—one had to be at just the right angle to see in.

It could never be a scene of seduction, or any kind of mischief for that matter, but it was remarkably private. Well buffered, too, from the noise of the party.

"That was fun," Olivia announced.

He was surprised to find himself agreeing with her. "It was, wasn't it?"

She let out a deflating little sigh. "I suppose I won't be able to avoid him all night."

"You can try."

She shook her head. "My mother will find me out."

"Is she trying to marry you off to him?" he asked, coming to sit beside her on the curved wooden bench.

"No, she'd not want me to move so far away. But he's a prince." She looked up at him with a fatalistic sort of expression. "It's an honor. His attentions, I mean."

Harry nodded. Not in agreement, just in sympathy.

"And what's more—" She broke off, then opened her lips as if to begin again. But she didn't.

"What's more?" he gently prodded.

"Can I trust you?"

"You can," he told her, "but I'm sure you're already aware that you should never trust a gentleman who says you can trust him."

That brought out a tiny smile. "Truer words, and all that. Still . . ."

"Go ahead," he said gently.

"Well . . ." Her eyes had a faraway look to them, as if she were searching for words, or maybe she'd found them, but the sentences sounded wrong. And when she finally spoke, she wasn't looking at him.

But she wasn't quite avoiding him either.

"I have . . . rejected the advances of a number of gentlemen."

He wondered at her careful use of the word "rejected," but did not interrupt.

"It's not that I considered myself above them. Well, some of them, I suppose." She turned and gave him a direct look. "Some of them were just awful."

"Understood."

"But most of them . . . There was nothing *wrong*. They just weren't right." She let out a sigh, and it sounded a little sad.

He hated that.

"No one will say it to my face, of course," she went on.

"But you have gained a reputation as being overly particular?"

She gave him a rueful glance. " 'Picky' was the word

I heard. Well, one of them." Her eyes grew clouded. "The only one I care to repeat."

Harry looked down at his left hand. It had flexed out, hard, and was now balled into a fist. Olivia was doing her best to minimize, but she had been hurt by the gossip.

She leaned back against the wall behind her, her wistful breath wafting through the air. "And this . . . oh, this really takes the prize, because—" She shook her head, and her eyes looked heavenward, as if seeking guidance, or forgiveness. Or maybe just understanding.

She looked out over the crowd, and she was smiling, but it was a sad, bewildered sort of smile. And she said, "Some of them even said, 'Who does she think she's waiting for? A prince?'"

"Ah."

She turned toward him, her brows arched, her expression utterly frank. "You see my dilemma?"

"Indeed."

"If I am seen to reject him, I'll be . . ." She chewed on her lip, searching for the correct word. " . . . not a laughingstock . . . I don't know what I'll be. But it won't be nice."

He didn't seem to move a muscle, and yet his face was achingly kind as he said, "Surely you don't need to marry him just to prove your niceness to society."

"No, of course not. But I must be seen to at least give him all due courtesies. If I reject him out of hand . . ." Olivia sighed. She hated this. She hated all of this, and she'd never really spoken to anyone about it, because they would only say something awful and snide like— *Don't we all wish we had your problems.*

And she *knew* she was lucky, and she *knew* she was blessed, and she knew she had no right to complain about anything in her life, and she wasn't complaining, not really.

Except sometimes she did.

And sometimes she just wanted the gentlemen to stop paying attention, to stop calling her beautiful and lovely and graceful (which she was not). She wanted them to stop paying calls, and stop asking her father for permission to court her, because none of them was ever right, and blast it all, she didn't want to settle for the best of the acceptables.

"Have you always been pretty?" he asked, very quietly.

It was a strange question. Strange, and powerful, and not the sort of thing she'd ever consider answering, except, somehow . . .

"Yes."

Somehow, with him, it seemed all right.

He nodded. "I thought so. Yours is that kind of face."

She turned to him with an oddly renewed sense of energy. "Have I told you about Miranda?"

"I don't believe so."

"My friend. Who married my brother."

"Ah, yes. You were writing a letter to her this afternoon."

Olivia nodded. "She was a bit of an ugly duckling. She was so thin, and her legs so long. We used to joke that they went all the way to her neck. But I never saw her that way. She was just my friend. My dearest, funniest, loveliest friend. We took our lessons together. We did everything together."

She looked over at him, trying to gauge his interest.

Most men would have run for the trees by now—a young woman blithering on about childhood friendship. Good heavens.

But he just nodded. And she knew that he understood.

"When I was eleven—it was my birthday, actually—I had a party—Winston, too—and all of the local children came. I suppose it was considered a coveted invitation. Anyway, there was a girl there—I can't even remember her name—but she said some horrid things to Miranda. I don't think it had ever even occurred to Miranda that she wasn't considered pretty before that day. I know it hadn't occurred to me."

"Children can be unkind," he murmured.

"Yes, well, so can adults," she said briskly. "Anyway, it's all neither here nor there. It's just one of those memories that has stayed with me."

They sat in silence for a few moments, and then he said, "You didn't finish the story."

She turned, surprised. "What do you mean?"

"You didn't finish the story," he said again. "What did you do?"

Her lips parted.

"I can't imagine you did nothing. Even at eleven, you would *not* have done nothing."

A slow smile spread across her face, growing . . . growing . . . until she could feel it in her cheeks, and then her lips, and then her heart. "I believe I had words with that girl."

His eyes caught hers in an odd sort of kinship. "Was she ever invited to your birthday parties again?"

Still, she was smiling. Grinning. "I don't think she was."

"I'd bet she hasn't forgotten *your* name."

Olivia felt joy bubbling up from within. "I reckon she hasn't."

"And your friend Miranda had the last laugh," he said. "Marrying the future Earl of Rudland. Was there a bigger catch in the district?"

"No. There wasn't."

"Sometimes," he said thoughtfully, "we do get what we deserve."

Olivia sat beside him, quietly, happy in her thoughts. Then, out of nowhere, she turned to him and said, "I *am* a devoted aunt."

"Your brother and Miranda have children?"

"A daughter. Caroline. She is my absolute most favorite thing in the entire world. Sometimes I think I could just eat her up." She looked over at him. "What are you smiling about?"

"The tone of your voice."

"What about it?"

He shook his head. "I have no idea. You sound like . . . like . . . I don't know, almost like you are waiting for dessert."

She let out a laugh. "I shall have to learn how to divide my attentions. They are expecting another."

"My congratulations."

"I didn't think I liked children," Olivia mused, "but I *adore* my niece."

She was quiet again, thinking how nice it was to be with someone she didn't have to talk to every moment. But then of course she did speak, because she never stayed silent for long.

"You should visit your sister in Cornwall," she told him. "Meet your nieces and nephews."

"I should," he agreed.

"Family is important."

He was quiet for a little bit longer than she would have expected before he said, "Yes, it is."

It wasn't quite right. Something in his voice rang hollow. Or maybe not. She hoped not. It would be such a disappointment if he turned out to be one of those men who had no care for his family.

But she didn't want to think about this. Not right now. If he had faults, or secrets, or anything, really, beyond what she saw right at this moment, she didn't want to know about them.

Not tonight.

Definitely not tonight.

Chapter Nine

They couldn't remain in the alcove all night, and so with much regret Olivia stood, perfected her posture, then looked over her shoulder at Harry and said, "Once more into the breach, dear friend."

He rose to his feet as well, regarding her with a warm, quizzical expression. "I thought you didn't like to read."

"I don't, but for heaven's sake, it's *Henry the Fifth*. Even I couldn't escape that." Olivia nearly shuddered, remembering Governess Four, the one who had insisted on doing all the *Henrys*. Inexplicably, in reverse order. "And I tried. Believe me, I tried."

"Why do I have the feeling that you were not a model student?" he wondered.

"I was only trying to make Miranda look good by comparison." It wasn't strictly true, but Olivia had not minded that it had been the result of her bad behavior. It wasn't that she didn't like learning, she just disliked being told *what* to learn. Miranda, who had always had her nose in a book, was happy to soak in whatever knowledge the governess *du jour* chose to impart. Olivia was always happiest when they were between governesses, when the two of them were left to their own devices. Instead of being forced to learn by rote and memorization, they had come up with all sorts of games and pneumonics. Olivia had never been so good at maths as when she had no one to teach her.

"I am beginning to think your Miranda must be a saint," Sir Harry said.

"Oh, she has her moments," Olivia returned. "You will never meet anyone so stubborn."

"More than you?"

"Much more." She looked at him in surprise. She wasn't stubborn. Impulsive, yes, and more than occasionally foolhardy, but not stubborn. She had always known when to give in. Or to give up.

She cocked her head to the side, regarding him as he looked out over the crowd. What an interesting man he had turned out to be. Who would have dreamed he would have such a devilish sense of humor? Or be so disarmingly perceptive. Talking with him was like finding a friend she'd known all of her life. Which was astonishing. Friends with a gentleman—who would have thought it possible?

She tried to imagine admitting to Mary or Anne or Philomena that she knew she was pretty. She could never. It would be seen as the worst kind of conceit.

With Miranda it would have been different. Miranda would have understood. But Miranda wasn't often in London anymore, and Olivia was only just now coming to realize what a great big gaping hole this had left in her life.

"You look very serious," Harry said, and she realized that at some point she had become so lost in her thoughts that she hadn't noticed he'd turned back to her. He was looking at her most intently, his eyes so warm, so focused . . . on her.

She wondered what he saw there.

And she wondered if she measured up.

And most of all, she wondered why it mattered so much that she did.

"It's nothing," she said, because she could see that he was expecting some kind of response.

"Well, then." He moved his head, then looked back over the crowd, and the intensity of the moment vanished. "Shall we go find your prince?"

She gave him a pert look, grateful for the opportunity to bring her thoughts back to safer spheres. "Shall I finally indulge you and protest that he is not *my* prince?"

"I would be most grateful."

"Very well, he is not my prince," she recited dutifully.

He almost looked disappointed. "Is that all?"

"You were perhaps expecting great drama?"

"At the very least," he murmured.

She chuckled to herself and stepped into the ballroom proper, gazing out over the crowd. It was an exceptionally beautiful evening; she wasn't sure why she had not noticed it earlier. The ballroom was crowded, as all ballrooms were, but something about the air was different. The candles, perhaps? Maybe there were more of them, or maybe they burned brighter. But everyone was bathed in a warm, flattering glow. Everyone looked pretty tonight, Olivia realized, everyone.

What a lovely thing that was. And how happy they all appeared.

"He's off in the far corner," she heard Harry say from behind her. "To the right."

His voice in her ear was warm and soothing, sliding through her with a strange, shivery caress. It made her want to lean back, to feel the air that was next to his body, and then—

She stepped forward. Those were not safe thoughts. Not in the middle of a crowded room. Definitely not about Sir Harry Valentine.

"I think you should wait here," Harry said. "Let him come to you."

She nodded. "I don't think he sees me."

"He will soon."

Somehow his words felt like a compliment, and she wanted to turn and smile. But she didn't, and she didn't know why.

"I should stand with my parents," she said. "It would be more proper than—Well, than anything else I've done this evening." She looked up at him—at Sir Harry Valentine, her new neighbor, and unbelievably, her new friend. "Thank you for a wonderful adventure."

He bowed. "It was my pleasure."

But their farewells felt far too formal, and Olivia couldn't bear to depart on such a tone. So she grinned at him—her real smile, not the one she kept on her face for social niceties, and asked, "Would you mind terribly if I opened my curtains again at home? It's getting beastly dark in my bedroom."

He laughed aloud, with enough volume to attract glances. "Will you be spying on me?"

"Only when you wear funny hats."

"There is only the one, and I only wear it on Tuesdays."

And somehow that seemed the perfect way to end their encounter. She bobbed a little curtsy, said farewell, and then slipped off into the crowd before either of them could say anything more.

Not five minutes after Olivia located her parents, Prince Alexei Gomarovsky of Russia located her.

He was, she had to admit, an extremely arresting man. Very handsome, in a cool, Slavic way, with icy blue eyes and hair that was the exact color of her own. Which was rather remarkable, really; one didn't often see hair quite that blond on a grown man. It did make him stand out in a crowd.

Well, that and the enormous attendant who followed him everywhere. The palaces of Europe could be dangerous places, the prince had told her. A man of his renown could not travel without guards.

Olivia stood between her parents and watched as the crowds fell away to make room for the prince. He stopped directly in front of her, his heels clicking together in an odd military fashion. His posture was amazingly straight, and she had the strangest notion that years from now, when she could not recall the details of his face, she would remember the way he held himself, tall and proud and correct.

She wondered if he had served in the war. Harry had, but he would have been across the Continent from the Russian army, wouldn't he?

Not that that mattered.

The prince tilted his head ever so slightly to the side and smiled, a close-lipped affair that wasn't so much unfriendly as it was condescending.

Or maybe it was just a cultural difference. She knew she shouldn't rush to judgment. Perhaps people smiled differently in Russia. And even if they didn't—he was royalty. She could not imagine that a prince could reveal his inner self to many people. He was probably a perfectly nice, perpetually misunderstood man. What an isolated life he must lead.

She would hate it.

"Lady Olivia," he said, his English accented but not excessively so. "I am deeply pleased to see you again this evening."

She swept into a middling curtsy—lower than she would normally do at such an event, but not so deep as to appear obsequious and out of place. "Your Highness," she said softly.

When she rose, he took her hand and laid a feather-light kiss on her knuckles. The air crackled with whispers around them, and Olivia was uncomfortably aware of being at the very center of attention. It felt as if everyone in the room had taken a step back, leaving a moat of emptiness around them—the better to see the drama unfolding.

He relinquished her hand slowly, then said, his voice a low murmur, "You are, as you must know, the loveliest woman in attendance."

"Thank you, Your Highness. You do me a great honor."

"I speak only the truth. You are a vision of beauty."

Olivia smiled and tried to be the pretty statue he seemed to want her to be. She wasn't really certain how she was meant to respond to his repeated compliments. She tried to imagine Sir Harry using such effusive language. He probably would burst out laughing, just trying to get the first sentence out.

"You smile at me, Lady Olivia," the prince said.

She thought quickly—very quickly. "It is simply the joy from your compliments, Your Highness."

Dear heavens, if Winston could hear her, he'd be rolling on the ground laughing. Miranda, too.

But the prince obviously approved, for his eyes lit with heat, and he held out his arm. "Come take a walk about the ballroom with me, *milaya*. Perhaps we shall dance."

Olivia had no choice but to lay her hand on his arm. He was wearing a formal state uniform of deep crimson, with four gold buttons on each sleeve. The wool was scratchy, and she could only think that he must be dreadfully hot in the crowded ballroom. But he showed no sign of discomfort. If anything, he seemed to radiate a certain coolness, as if he were there to be admired but not touched.

He knew that everyone was watching him. He must be accustomed to such attention. She wondered if he realized how uncomfortable she felt in this tableau. And she was used to having eyes upon her. She knew she was popular, she knew that other young ladies looked to her as an arbiter of fashion and style. But this—this was something else altogether.

"I have been enjoying your English weather," the prince said, as they turned a corner. Olivia found that she had to focus on her gait to remain in the correct position at his side. Each step was carefully measured, each footfall utterly precise, heel to toe in the exact same motion, every time.

"Tell me," he added, "is it usually so warm at this time of year?"

"We have had more sun than is usual," she replied. "Is it very cold in Russia?"

"Yes. It is . . . how do you say it . . ." He paused, and for the briefest of moments she saw a flash of struggle in his face as he tried to think of the correct words. His lips pressed together with irritation, then he asked her, "Do you speak French?"

"Very badly, I'm afraid."

"That is a pity." He sounded vaguely annoyed by her deficiency. "I am more, er . . ."

"Fluent?" she supplied.

"Yes. It is much spoken in Russia. More even than Russian among many."

Olivia found that most intriguing, but it seemed impolite to comment upon it.

"Did you receive my invitation this afternoon?"

"Yes, I did," she replied. "I am honored to accept."

She wasn't honored. Well, maybe honored, but certainly not pleased. As expected, her mother had insisted that they accept, and Olivia had already spent three hours in emergency fittings for a new gown. It was to be ice-blue silk, the exact color, Olivia suddenly realized, of Prince Alexei's eyes.

She hoped he would not think she had planned it on purpose.

"How long do you intend to stay in London?" she asked him, hoping she sounded more eager than desperate.

"It is not certain. It depends on . . . many things."

He did not seem inclined to expand upon that cryptic comment, so she smiled—not the real one, she was far too tense to summon that. But he did not know her well enough to see through her society smile. "I do hope you enjoy your stay," she said prettily, "however long you choose to visit us."

He nodded regally, declining to comment.

They rounded another corner. Olivia could see her parents now, still across the room. They were watching her, as was everyone else. Even the dancing had stopped. People were talking, but their voices were low. They sounded like insects, buzzing about.

Lord, how she wanted to go home. The prince might be a perfectly nice man. In fact, she hoped he was. It would make the story so much better—if he were a lovely person, trapped in a prison of formality and tradition. And if he *was* perfectly nice, then she would be perfectly happy to make his acquaintance and talk with him, but not, dear heavens, like this, in front of all the *ton*, with hundreds of pairs of eyes watching her every movement.

What would happen if she tripped? Stumbled over her feet as they turned the next corner. She could do it up small—with just the tiniest bob. Or she could play it for all it was worth, tumbling to the ground in a mad heap.

It would be spectacular.

Or spectacularly awful. And it didn't matter which, because she didn't have the courage to do it, anyway.

Just a few more minutes, she told herself. They were in the final stretch. She would be returned to her parents. Or maybe she would have to dance, but even that would not be so awful. Surely they would not be alone on the dance floor. That would be far too obvious, even for this crowd.

Just a few more minutes, and then it would all be over.

Harry watched the golden couple as closely as he was able, but the prince's decision to take a turn about the room made his job that much more difficult. It wasn't imperative that he remain close; the prince wasn't likely to do or say anything the War Office would find relevant. But Harry was loath to let Olivia out of his sight.

It was probably only because he knew that Winthrop was suspicious of him, but Harry had disliked the prince immediately. He didn't like his proud stance, never mind that his own years in the military had left him with remarkably straight shoulders of his own. He didn't like the prince's eyes, nor the way they seemed to narrow upon everyone he met. And he did not like the way his mouth moved when he spoke, his upper lip curled into a perpetual snarl.

Harry had met people like the prince. Not royalty, that was true, but grand dukes and the like, preening about Europe as if they owned the place.

Which they did, he supposed, but they were still a bunch of asses, in his opinion.

"Ah, there you are." It was Sebastian, holding an almost empty champagne flute. "Bored yet?"

Harry kept one eye on Olivia. "No."

"Interesting," Seb murmured. He finished his champagne, set the glass down on a nearby table, then leaned in so that Harry could hear him. "Who are we looking for?"

"No one."

"No, never mind. My mistake. Who are we looking *at*?"

"No one," Harry said, taking a half step to the right, trying to see past the extremely portly earl who had just blocked his view.

"Ah. We are just ignoring me for . . . what reason?"

"I'm not."

"And yet you are still not looking at me."

Harry had to admit defeat. Sebastian was fiendishly tenacious, and twice that annoying. He looked his cousin squarely in the eye. "I have seen you before."

"And yet I remain ever delightful to gaze upon. One misses a great deal, not looking at me." Sebastian offered a sickly sort of smile. "Are you ready to leave?"

"Not yet."

Seb's brows went up. "Are you serious?"

"I'm enjoying myself," Harry said.

"Enjoying yourself. At a ball."

"You manage it."

"Yes, but I'm me. You're you. You don't like these things."

Harry caught a glimpse of Olivia out of the corner of his eye. She caught his attention, and then he caught her eye, and then, simultaneously, they both looked away. She had the prince to keep busy, and he had Sebastian, who was proving himself more of a nuisance than usual.

"Were you just exchanging glances with Lady Olivia?" Sebastian inquired.

"No." Harry wasn't the best liar, but he could do quite a good job when he kept it to monosyllables.

Sebastian rubbed his hands together. "The evening grows interesting."

Harry ignored him. Or tried to.

"They're already calling her Princess Olivia," Sebastian said.

"Who are 'they,' anyway?" Harry demanded, swinging around to face Sebastian. "*They* say I killed my fiancée."

Sebastian blinked. "When did you get engaged?"

"My point precisely," Harry practically spat. "And she's not going to marry that idiot."

"You almost sound jealous."

"Don't be ridiculous."

Sebastian smiled knowingly. "I thought I saw you with her earlier this evening."

Harry didn't bother to deny it. "Polite conversation. She's my neighbor. Aren't you always telling me to be more sociable?"

"So you got that whole spying-on-you-from-her-bedroom-window matter settled?"

"A misunderstanding," Harry said.

"Hmmmm."

Harry was instantly on alert. Anytime Sebastian appeared thoughtful—the devious I'm-thinking-of-an-evil-plan thoughtful, not the kind and considerate thoughtful—it was time to tread carefully.

"I'd like to meet that prince," Sebastian said.

"Good God." Harry was exhausted, just standing next to him. "What are you going to do?"

Sebastian stroked his chin. "I'm not quite certain. But I'm confident the correct course of action will make itself known to me at the proper time."

"You're going to make it up as you go along?"

"It usually works rather well."

There would be no stopping him, this Harry knew. "Listen to me," he hissed, grabbing his cousin's arm with enough urgency to obtain his instant attention. Harry could not tell him about his assignment, but Seb would have to know that there was more to this than an infatuation with Lady Olivia. Otherwise, he could ruin the whole thing, with a single reference to Grandmère Olga.

Harry kept his voice low. "This evening, with the prince, I do *not* speak Russian. And neither do you." Sebastian wasn't even close to being fluent, but he could certainly stumble through a conversation.

Harry looked at him intently. "Do you understand?"

Seb's eyes fixed on his, and then he nodded—once, with a gravity he rarely allowed others to see. And then, in the blink of an eye, it was gone, and his loose-limbed posture returned, along with his lopsided smile.

Harry stepped back, quietly watching. Olivia and the prince had completed three-fourths of their stately promenade and were now walking directly toward them. The crowds of partygoers swept out of their path, like beads of oil on water, and Sebastian was standing still, his only movement the fingers of his left hand, idly rubbing together, thumb against the rest.

He was thinking. Seb always did that when he was thinking.

And then, with timing so perfect no one could ever believe it wasn't an accident, Sebastian plucked a new champagne glass from a roving footman's tray, tilted his head back for a sip, and then—

Harry didn't know how he managed it, but it was all over the floor—a splintering crash, shards of glass, and champagne, bubbling furiously on the parquet.

Olivia jumped back; the hem of her gown had been splashed.

The prince looked furious.

Harry said nothing.

And then Sebastian smiled.

Chapter Ten

$\mathcal{L}$ady Olivia!" Sebastian exclaimed. "I am so sorry. Please accept my apologies. Terribly clumsy of me."

"Of course," she said, discreetly shaking out one foot, then the next. "It is nothing. Just a spot of champagne." She smiled up at him, a reassuring it's-no-trouble-at-all sort of smile. "I've heard it is good for the skin."

She'd heard nothing of the sort, but what else could she say? It wasn't like Sebastian Grey to be so clumsy, and really, it was just a few drops on her slippers. Beside her, however, the prince was seething with anger. She could feel it in his stance. He'd received more of a splashing than she had, although in all fairness, it had all landed on his boots, and hadn't she heard that some men cleaned their boots with champagne, anyway?

Still, whatever Prince Alexei had grunted in Russian, she had a feeling it was not complimentary.

"For the skin? Really?" Sebastian asked, giving every appearance of an interest she was quite sure he did not possess. "I'd not heard that. How fascinating."

"It was in a ladies' magazine," she lied.

"Which would explain why I did not know of it," Sebastian replied smoothly.

"Lady Olivia, will you introduce me to your friend?" Prince Alexei said sharply.

"Of–of course," Olivia stammered, surprised by his request. He had not seemed interested in meeting very many people in London, with the exception of dukes, royals, and, well, her. Perhaps he wasn't as arch and proud as she thought. "Your Highness, may I present Mr. Sebastian Grey. Mr. Grey, Prince Alexei Gomarovsky of Russia."

The two men made their bows, Sebastian's considerably deeper than the prince's, which was so shallow as to be almost impolite.

"Lady Olivia," Sebastian said, once he was through bowing to the prince, "have you met my cousin, Sir Harry Valentine?"

Olivia's lips parted in surprise. What was he up to? He knew very well that—

"Lady Olivia," Harry said, suddenly right in front of her. His eyes met hers, and they flared with something she could not quite identify. It sparked through her, made her want to shiver. And then it was gone, as if they were nothing more than mere acquaintances. He gave her a gracious nod, then said to his cousin, "We are already acquainted."

"Oh, yes, of course," Sebastian said. "I keep forgetting. You are neighbors."

"Your Highness," Olivia said to the prince, "may I

present Sir Harry Valentine. He lives directly to the south of me."

"Indeed," the prince said, and then, while Harry was bowing, he said something in rapid Russian to his attendant, who gave a curt nod.

"You were speaking with each other earlier in the evening," the prince said.

Olivia stiffened. She had not realized that he had been watching her. And she wasn't quite certain why this bothered her so much. "Yes," she said, for there could be no good reason to deny it. "I count Sir Harry among my many acquaintances."

"For which I am most grateful," Harry said. His voice had an edge to it, at odds with the gentle sentiment of the words. Stranger still, he was looking at the prince the entire time he spoke.

"Yes," the prince replied, his eyes never leaving Harry's. "You would be, wouldn't you?"

Olivia looked at Harry, then at the prince, then back at Harry, who held the prince's eye as he said, "I would."

"It's a lovely party, isn't it?" Sebastian put in. "Lady Mottram has quite outdone herself this year."

Olivia nearly burst out with an inappropriate giggle. There was something about his demeanor—so excessively jolly—it should have cut through the tension like a knife. But it didn't. Harry was watching the prince with cool reserve, and the prince—he was watching Harry with icy disdain.

"Is it chilly in here?" she asked, to no one in particular.

"A bit," Sebastian replied, since they seemed to be

the only ones actually speaking. "I have long thought it must be difficult to be a woman, with all your wispy, unsubstantial garments."

Olivia's gown was velvet, but with short capped sleeves, and her arms were prickling with goose bumps. "Yes," she replied, because no one else was speaking. Then she realized she had nothing more to say beyond that, so she cleared her throat and smiled, first at Harry and the prince, who still were not looking at her, and then at the people behind them, all of whom *were* looking at her, although they were pretending not to.

"Are you one of Lady Olivia's many admirers?" Prince Alexei asked Harry.

Olivia turned to Harry with widened eyes. What on earth could he say to so direct a question?

"All of London admires Lady Olivia," Harry replied deftly.

"She is one of our most admired ladies," Sebastian added.

Olivia ought to have said something quiet and modest in the wake of such praise, but it was all too strange—too utterly bizarre—to say a thing.

They weren't talking about her. They were saying her name, and paying her compliments, but it was all a part of some strange and stupid male dance for domination.

It would have been flattering if it hadn't made her so uneasy.

"Is that music I hear?" Sebastian said. "Perhaps the dancing will recommence soon. Do you dance in Russia?"

The prince gave him a cold stare. "I beg your pardon."

"Your Highness," Sebastian corrected, although he didn't sound particularly penitent, "do you dance in Russia?"

"Of course," the prince bit off.

"Not all societies do," Sebastian mused.

Olivia had no idea if that was true. She rather suspected it was not.

"What brings you to London, Your Highness?" Harry asked, entering the conversation for the first time. He had answered queries, but only that. Otherwise, he had remained an observer.

The prince looked at him sharply, but it was difficult to discern whether he found the question impertinent. "I visit my cousin," he replied. "He is your ambassador."

"Ah," Harry said graciously. "I have not made his acquaintance."

"Of course not."

It was an insult, clear and direct, but Harry did not look the least bit put out. "I met many Russians while serving in His Majesty's army. Your countrymen are most honorable."

The prince acknowledged the compliment with a curt nod.

"We could not have defeated Napoleon if not for your tsar," Harry continued. "And your land."

Prince Alexei finally looked him in the eye.

"I wonder if Napoleon would have fared better if winter had not come so early that year," Harry continued. "Brutal, it was."

"For the weak, perhaps," the prince responded.

"How many of the French perished in the retreat?" Harry wondered aloud. "I can't recall." He turned to Sebastian. "Do you remember?"

"Over ninety percent," Olivia said, before it occurred to her that perhaps she should not.

All three men looked at her. There were no varying degrees of their surprise; they were all close to stunned.

"I enjoy reading the newspaper," she said simply. The ensuing silence told her that this was not enough of an explanation, so she added, "I am sure that the majority of the details were not reported, but it was fascinating, nonetheless. And really quite sad." She turned to Prince Alexei and asked, "Were you there?"

"No," he said brusquely. "The march was on Moscow. My home is to the east, in Nizhny. And I was not old enough to serve in the army."

Olivia turned to Harry. "Were you yet in the army?"

He nodded, tilting his head toward Sebastian. "We had both just gained our commissions. We were in Spain, under Wellington."

"I had not realized you served together," Olivia said.

"The 18th Hussars," Sebastian told her, quiet pride in his voice.

There was an awkward silence, and so she said, "How very dashing." It seemed like the sort of thing they would expect her to say, and Olivia had long since realized that at times like these, it made a great deal of sense to do the expected.

"Did not Napoleon say that he was surprised when

a hussar reached his thirtieth birthday?" the prince murmured. He turned to Olivia and said, "They have a reputation for . . . how do you say it . . ." He moved his fingers in a circular motion near his face, as if that would jog his memory. "Recklessness," he said suddenly. "Yes, that is it."

"It is a pity," he continued. "They are thought to be quite brave, but most often"—he made a slitting motion across his throat—"they are cut down."

He looked up at Harry and Sebastian (but mostly at Harry) and gave them a bland smile. "Did you find that to be true, Sir Harry?" he asked—softly, stingingly.

"No," Harry replied. Nothing more, just *no*.

Olivia's eyes darted back and forth between the two men. Nothing Harry could have said—no protest, no sarcastic remark—could have irritated the prince more.

"Do I hear music?" she asked. But no one was paying her any attention.

"How old are you, Sir Harry?" the prince asked.

"How old are *you*?"

Olivia swallowed nervously. That could not be an appropriate question to ask of a prince. And she *knew* he had not used an appropriate tone. She tried to exchange a wary glance with Sebastian, but he was watching the other two men.

"You have not answered my question," Alexei said dangerously, and indeed, beside him his guard made an ominous shift of position.

"I am twenty-eight," Harry said, and then, with a pause just long enough to indicate that it had been an afterthought, he added, "Your Highness."

Prince Alexei's mouth slid into a very small smile. "We have two more years to make good on Napoleon's prediction, then, do we not?"

"Only if you plan to declare war on England," Harry said lightly. "Otherwise, I have retired from the cavalry."

The two men stared each other down for what seemed an eternity, and then, abruptly, Prince Alexei burst out laughing. "You amuse me, Sir Harry," he said, but the bite in his voice contradicted his words. "We shall spar again, you and I."

Harry nodded graciously, with all due deference.

The prince placed his hand over Olivia's, still resting in the crook of his arm. "But it will have to be later," he said, giving him a victorious smile. "After I have danced with Lady Olivia."

And then he turned so that their backs were to Harry and Sebastian, and led her away.

Twenty-four hours later, Olivia was exhausted. She hadn't got home from the Mottram ball until nearly four in the morning, then her mother had refused to allow her to sleep late, instead dragging her to Bond Street for final fittings for her presentation gown for the prince. Then, of course, there were no naps for the weary because she had to go and be presented, which seemed like a bit of nonsense to her, as she'd spent the better part of the prior evening in the prince's company.

Didn't one get "presented" to people one *didn't* already know?

She and her parents had gone to Prince Alexei's residence, a set of apartments in the home of the ambassador. It had been terribly grand, terribly formal, and frankly, terribly dull. Her dress, which had required a corset that would have been far more at home in the previous century, was uncomfortable and hot—except for her arms, which were bare and freezing.

Apparently the Russians did not believe in heating their homes.

The entire ordeal lasted three hours, during which her father drank several cups of a clear spirit that had left him extremely sleepy. The prince had offered her a glass as well, but her father, who had already taken his first taste, immediately whisked it from her hands.

Olivia was supposed to go out again that evening— Lady Bridgerton was hosting a small soirée—but she pleaded exhaustion, and much to her surprise, her mother relented. Olivia suspected that she was tired as well. And her father was in no state to go anywhere.

She took supper in her room (after a nap, a bath, and another, shorter, nap), and was planning to read the newspaper in bed, but just as she was reaching for it, she saw *Miss Butterworth and the Mad Baron* lying on her bedside table.

It was so odd, she thought, picking up the slim volume. Why would Sir Harry give her such a book? What did it say about her that he thought she would enjoy such a thing?

She thumbed through it, taking in passages here and there. It seemed a little frivolous. Did this mean he had thought *she* was frivolous?

She looked over at her window, shielded by her heavy curtains, pulled tight against the night. Did he still think she was frivolous? Now that he actually knew her?

She turned back to the book in her hands. Would he choose it as a gift for her now? A lurid, gothic novel, that was what he'd called it.

Was that what he thought of her?

She snapped the book shut, then positioned it on her lap, spine down. "One, two, *three*," she proclaimed, swiftly pulling her hands away to let *Miss Butterworth* fall open to whichever page she liked.

It plopped to one side.

"Stupid book," she muttered, trying it all over again. Because really, she did not possess enough interest to choose a page herself.

It fell over again, to the same side.

"Oh, this is ridiculous." Even more ridiculous: she climbed out of bed, sat herself on the floor, and prepared to repeat the experiment for a third time, because surely it would work if the book was on a properly flat surface.

"One, two, thr—" She snapped her hands back into place; the bloody thing was falling over to the side again.

Now she *really* felt like a fool. Which was impressive, considering the degree of idiocy required to actually remove herself from bed in the first place. But she was not going to let the bloody little book win, so for her fourth attempt, she let the pages fan open just a bit before she let go. A little encouragement, that's what it needed.

"One, two, three!"

And finally, it fell open. She looked down. To page 193, to be precise.

She slid down to her belly, propped herself up on her elbows, and began to read:

> *She could hear him behind her. He was closing the distance between them, and soon she would be caught. But for what purpose? Good or evil?*

"Evil receives my vote," she murmured.

> *How would she know? How would she know? How would she know?*

Oh, for heaven's sake. This was why she read the newspaper. Just imagine: *Parliament was called to order. To order. To order.*

Olivia shook her head and continued reading.

> *And then she recalled the advice given to her by her mother, before the blessed lady had gone to her reward, pecked to death by pigeons—*

"What?"

She looked over her shoulder at her door, aware that she'd practically shrieked the word. But really—*pigeons*?

She scrambled to her feet, grasping *Miss Butterworth* in her right hand, her index finger sliding between the pages to mark her spot.

"Pigeons," she repeated. "Seriously?"

She opened the book again. She couldn't help it.

She had been only twelve, far too young for such a conversation, but perhaps her mother had—

"Boring." She chose another page, mostly at random. It did seem to make some sense, however, to head closer to the beginning.

Priscilla grasped the window ledge, her ungloved hands clutching at the stone with every ounce of her might. When she'd heard the baron jiggling the doorknob, she'd known she had but seconds to act. If he found her there, in his inner sanctum, who knew what he might do? He was a violent man, or so she'd been told.

Olivia wandered over to her bed and half leaned, half perched herself on the edge, reading all the while.

No one knew how his fiancée had died. Some said illness, but most claimed poison. Murder!

"Really?" She looked up, blinking, then turned toward her window. A dead fiancée? Gossip and rumors? Did Sir Harry know about this? The parallels were amazing.

She could hear him entering the room. Would he notice that the window was open? What would she do? What could she do?

Olivia sucked in her breath. She was on the edge of her seat. Not figuratively, that would never do. She was *literally* sitting on the edge of the bed. Which accounted for any and all breathlessness.

> *Priscilla whispered a prayer, and then, with eyes closed tight, she let go.*

End of chapter. Olivia flipped the page eagerly.

> *It was only a few feet to the cold, hard ground.*

What? Priscilla was on the ground floor? Olivia's eagerness quickly gave way to irritation. What sort of pea brain dangled from a ground-floor window? She'd allow for a bit of elevation for the building's foundation, but *really*. One would be hard-pressed even to sprain an ankle in such a mild fall.

"That's rather manipulative," she said, narrowing her eyes. Who was this author, anyway, trying to scare her readers over nothing? Did Harry have any idea what he'd given her, or had he just been going blindly on a recommendation from his sister?

She looked over at her window. It was still the same size, with the same curtains—unchanged in every way. She wasn't sure why this surprised her.

What time was it, anyway? Almost half nine. He probably wouldn't be in his office. Well, he might. He did tend to work late, although come to think of it, he never had told her just what it was he did there with such diligence.

She pushed herself up and away from the edge of

the bed and walked toward the window. Slowly, with cautious feet, which was ridiculous, since he couldn't possibly see her through the curtains.

Miss Butterworth still in her left hand, she reached out with her right and pulled the curtains open . . .

Chapter Eleven

All things considered, Harry was ready to call it a decent day's work.

On a normal day, he'd have translated twice what he'd managed for today, possibly more, but he'd been distracted.

He'd found himself staring up at Olivia's window, even though he knew she wasn't there. This was the day she was supposed to visit the prince. At three in the afternoon. Which meant she'd probably have left home shortly before two. The Russian ambassador's residence was not very far away, but the earl and countess would not want to risk being late. There was always traffic, or they could break a wheel, or a street urchin might dash into the road . . . No one with any prudence left their home without allotting extra time for unforeseen delays.

Olivia would probably be stuck there for two hours,

possibly three; no one knew how to drag these things out like the Russians. Then a half hour to get home, and—

Well, she'd be home now, that was for certain. Unless she'd gone back out again, but he hadn't noticed the Rudland carriage departing.

Not that he'd been looking. But his curtains were open. And when he was angled just so, he could see a small strip of light shining through from the street. And of course any carriages that happened to roll by.

He stood and stretched, lifting his hands above his head and rolling his head down and around. He planned to do one more page tonight—the clock on the mantel proclaimed the time to be only half nine— but just now he needed to shake some blood back into his legs. He walked out from behind his desk, and then over to the window.

And there she was.

For a split second they stood frozen, caught in the moment of wondering—*Should I pretend I don't see?*

And then Harry thought—*of course not.*

He waved.

She smiled. And waved back. And then—

He found himself staring with surprise. She was opening the window.

So of course he did the same.

"I know you said you hadn't read this," she said without preamble, "but did you even peek?"

"Good evening to you," he called. "How was the prince?"

She shook her head impatiently. "The book, Sir Harry, the book. Did you read *any* of it?"

"I'm afraid not. Why?"

She held it up with two hands, right in front of her face, then moved it to the side so that she could see him. "It is ridiculous!"

He nodded agreeably. "I thought it might be."

"Miss Butterworth's mother gets pecked to death by pigeons!"

He fought a chuckle. "Do you know, I think that might make it considerably more interesting to me."

"Pigeons, Sir Harry! Pigeons!"

He grinned up at her. He felt a bit like Romeo to her Juliet, minus the feuding families and poison.

And with pigeons.

"I wouldn't mind hearing that part," he told her. "It sounds quite suspenseful."

She scowled at him, batting away a piece of hair that the breeze had blown into her face. "It happened before the book began. If we're lucky, Miss Butterworth will get her own pecking before I reach the end."

"So you've been reading it, then?"

"Bits and pieces," she admitted. "That's all. The opening of chapter four and"—she looked down, leafing quickly through the pages before glancing back up—"page one hundred ninety-three."

"Have you ever considered starting at the beginning?"

There was a pause. A rather long one. And then, with disdain: "I wasn't planning to read it."

"It just swept you in, eh?"

"No! That's not it at all." She crossed her arms, which caused her to drop the book. For a moment she disappeared from view, then up she popped again,

Miss Butterworth in hand. "It was so irritating I couldn't stop."

He leaned against the ledge, grinning up at her. "It sounds gripping."

"It's nonsense, is what it is. Between Miss Butterworth and the mad baron, I'm cheering for the baron."

"Oh, come now. It's a romance. Surely you must side with your fellow lady."

"She's an idiot." She looked back down at the book for a moment, flipping through the pages with remarkable speed. "I can't tell yet if the baron is murderous as well as mad, but if so, I do hope he succeeds."

"It'll never happen," Harry told her.

"What makes you think that?" She swiped a hand at her hair again, trying to get it off her nose. The breeze was picking up, and he was finding the whole thing rather entertaining.

"Isn't the author a woman?" he asked.

Olivia nodded. "Sarah Gorely. I've never heard of her."

"And it's meant to be a romance?"

She nodded again.

He shook his head. "She'll never kill off the heroine."

Olivia stared at him for a long moment, then immediately turned to the end of the book.

"Oh, don't do that," he scolded. "You'll spoil it."

"I'm not going to read it," she retorted. "How can it be spoiled?"

"Trust me," he said. "When a man writes a romance, the woman dies. When a woman writes one, it ends all tidy and sweet."

Her lips parted, as if she weren't sure whether to take offense at the generalization. Harry bit back a grin. He liked her befuddled.

"How is it romantic if the woman dies?" she asked suspiciously.

He shrugged. "I didn't say it made sense, just that it was true."

She didn't seem to know what to make of that, and Harry found that he was quite content just to sit there and watch her as she glared down at the book in her hands. She was utterly adorable, standing up there at her window, even in that atrocious blue dressing gown of hers. Her hair hung down her back in a single thick braid, and he wondered why it was only just occurring to him now that the entire exchange was extremely irregular. He'd not met her parents, but he could not imagine they would approve of her chatting with an unmarried man in the dark, through her window.

In her dressing gown.

But he was having far too much fun to care, and so he decided that if she wasn't going to concern herself with proprieties, neither would he.

Her eyes narrowed and then she looked back down at the book, her fingers moving stealthily toward the final pages.

"Don't do it," he warned her.

"I just want to see if you're correct."

"Then start at the beginning," he said, mostly because he knew it would vex her.

She let out a groan. "I don't want to read the entire book."

"Why not?

"Because I won't like it, and it will be a waste of my time."

"You don't know you won't like it," he pointed out.

"I know." Said with utter conviction.

"Why don't you like to read?" he asked.

"This is why," she exclaimed, giving *Miss Butterworth* a little shake. "It's complete nonsense. If you gave me the newspaper—now that, I would read. In fact I do. Every word. Every day."

Harry was impressed. It wasn't that he thought women *didn't* read the newspaper. He just hadn't really given the matter much thought. Certainly his mother had never done so, and if his sister did, she never gave any indication in her monthly correspondence.

"Read the novel," he said. "You might surprise yourself and enjoy it."

"Why are you prodding me to read something that you yourself have no interest in?" she asked, with no small degree of suspicion.

"Because—" But he stopped, because he didn't know why he was doing so. Except that he'd given it to her. And he was enjoying teasing her about it. "I'll make a deal with you, Lady Olivia."

She cocked her head to the side expectantly.

"If you read it—all of it, beginning to end—then I will do the same."

"You'll read *Miss Butterworth and the Mad Baron*," she said dubiously.

"I will. As soon as you're through with it."

She looked as if she were about to agree, and indeed she opened her mouth to speak. But then she froze, and her eyes narrowed dangerously.

This, he reminded himself, was a woman with two brothers. She would know how to fight. Deviously.

"I think you should read it *with* me," she said to him.

Harry had all sorts of thoughts about *that*, most of them fed by his usual practice of reading novels before bed.

In bed.

"Buy another copy," she said.

His lovely little daydream popped and disintegrated.

"We shall compare notes. It will be like a reading club. One of those literary salons I am always rejecting invitations to."

"I am flattered beyond imagination."

"As well you should be," she said. "I have never invited anyone else to do the same."

"I don't know that the store will have another copy," he said.

"*I'll* find one for you." She gave him a bit of a smirk. "Trust me, I know how to shop."

"Why am I suddenly frightened?" he murmured.

"What?"

He looked at her and said more loudly, "You scare me."

She appeared to be delighted by that.

"Read me a passage," he said.

"Now? Really?"

He settled himself on the ledge, leaning his back against the window frame. "The beginning, if you will."

She stared down at him for a few moments, then shrugged and said, "Very well. Here we are." She cleared her throat. "*It was a dark and windy night.*"

"I feel as if I've heard that before," Harry commented.

"You're interrupting."

"So sorry. Go on."

She gave him a stare, then continued. "*It was a dark and windy night, and Miss Priscilla Butterworth was certain that at any moment the rain would begin, pouring down from the heavens in sheets and streams, dousing all that lay within her purview.*" She looked up. "This is dreadful. And I'm not sure the author used 'purview' correctly."

"It's close enough," Harry said, although he agreed with her completely. "Continue."

She shook her head but obeyed nonetheless. "*She was, of course, shielded from the weather in her tiny chamber, but the window casings rattled with such noise that there would be no way she would find slumber in this evening. Huddled on her thin, cold bed, she* blah blah blah, hold on, I'll skip to where it gets interesting."

"You can't do that," he scolded.

She held *Miss Butterworth* aloft. "I'm holding the book."

"Toss it down," he said suddenly.

"What?"

He nudged himself off the ledge and stood on the floor, poking his upper body out the window. "Toss it down."

She looked most dubious. "Will you catch it?"

He laid down the gauntlet. "If you can throw it, I can catch it."

"Oh, I can throw," she returned, clearly insulted.

He smirked. "I've never met a girl who could."

At that she hurled it at him, and it was only thanks to his quick reflexes, honed by years on the battlefield, that he managed to get himself in place to catch it.

Which he did. Thank *God*. He was not sure he could have lived with himself had he not.

"Next time try a gentle toss," he grumbled.

"What would be the fun in that?"

Forget *Romeo and Juliet*. This was much closer to *The Taming of the Shrew*. He looked up. She had pulled up a chair and was now sitting right by her open window, waiting with an expression of exaggerated patience.

"Here we are," he said, finding the spot where she'd left off. "*Huddled on her thin, cold bed, she could not help but recall all of the events that had led her to this bleak spot, on this bleak night. But this, dear reader, is not where our story begins.*"

"I hate when authors do that," Olivia announced.

"Shush. *We must begin at the beginning, which is not when Miss Butterworth arrived at Thimmerwell Hall, nor even when she arrived at Fitzgerald Place, her home before Thimmerwell Hall. No, we must begin on the day she was born, in a manger—*"

"A manger!" Olivia nearly shrieked.

He grinned up at her. "I was just making sure you were listening."

"Wretch."

He chuckled and read on. "*. . . the day she was born, in a small cottage in Hampshire, surrounded by roses and butterflies, on the last day before the town was ravaged by pox.*"

He looked up.

"No, don't stop," she said. "It's just starting to get interesting. What sort of pox, do you think?"

"You're a bloodthirsty wench, did you know?"

She cocked her head to the side in a gesture of agreement. "I'm fascinated by pestilence. I always have been."

He skimmed quickly down the page. "I'm afraid you are destined for disappointment. The author gives no medical description whatsoever."

"Maybe on the next page?" she asked hopefully.

"I shall continue," he announced. "*The epidemic took her beloved father, but miraculously spared the baby and her mother. Also among the fallen were her paternal grandmother, both grandfathers, three great-aunts, two uncles, a sister, and a second cousin.*"

"You're having fun with me again," she accused.

"I'm not!" he insisted. "I swear to you, it's all here. It was quite an epidemic there in Hampshire. If you hadn't chucked the book at me, you could see for yourself."

"No one writes that badly."

"Apparently someone does."

"I'm not sure who is worse, the author for writing this drivel, or us, for reading it."

"I'm having great fun," he declared. And he was. It was the most unlikely thing, sitting here at his window, reading an excruciatingly bad novel to Lady Olivia Bevelstoke, the most sought-after young lady of the *ton*. But the breeze was lovely, and he'd been cooped up all day, and sometimes, when he looked up at her, she was smiling. Not at him, although she did that, too. No, the smiles that seemed to tingle through him were the ones on her face when she didn't realize he was looking, when she was simply enjoying the moment, smiling into the night.

She was not just pretty, she was beautiful, with the sort of face that made men weep: heart-shaped, with perfect porcelain skin. And her eyes—women would kill for eyes of that color, that amazing cornflower blue.

She was beautiful, and she knew it, but she did not wield her beauty like a weapon. It was simply a part of who she was, as natural as two hands and feet, ten fingers and toes.

She was beautiful, and he wanted her.

Chapter Twelve

"Sir Harry?" Olivia called out, coming to her feet. She leaned against the sill, peering out past the darkness to his window, where he sat silhouetted against a flickering rectangle of light. He had gone so still, and so suddenly, at that.

He started at the sound of her voice, looking up at her window, but not quite at her. "Sorry," he muttered, and he turned quickly back to the book, searching through the words to find his place.

"No, no, don't be," she assured him. He really did look a little odd, as if he'd just eaten something that had gone off. "Are you all right?"

He looked up at her, and then—it was really quite impossible to describe, or even understand—what happened. His eyes met hers, and even though it was dark, and she couldn't see the color, that rich, warm chocolate—she still knew it. And she felt it. And then, quite simply, she lost her breath. Just lost it. Her balance, too. She stumbled back into her chair, and sat there for a moment, wondering why her heart was racing.

All he'd done was look at her.

And she'd . . . she'd . . .

She'd swooned.

Oh, dear heavens, he must think her an absolute fool. She had never swooned a day in her life, and—and, oh very well, she hadn't really swooned, but that was what it felt like, this strange, floaty thing, all fizzy and queer, and now he was going to think she was one of those ladies who had to carry a vinaigrette with her everywhere she went.

Which was bad enough, except that she'd spent half her life poking fun at those ladies. Oh dear oh dear. She scrambled back to her feet and poked her head out the window. "I'm fine," she called out. "Just lost my footing."

He nodded slowly, and she realized he wasn't entirely with her. His thoughts were far, far away. Then, as if quietly coming back into place, he looked up and begged her pardon. "Woolgathering," he offered as explanation. "It's late."

"It is," she murmured in agreement, although she did not think it could be very much past ten. And all of a sudden she realized that she could not bear to have him say good night, that she was going to have to do it first. Because . . . because . . . Well, she didn't know why, she only knew that it was true.

"I was just about to say that I should really be going," she said, the words tumbling from her lips. "Well, not *going*, I suppose, as I don't really have anywhere to go, since I'm already right here in my room, and I'm not going anywhere but bed, and that's just a few feet away."

She smiled at him, as if that could make up for the nonsense coming from her mouth. "As you said," she continued, "it is growing late."

He nodded again.

And she had to say something more, because he wasn't doing so. "Good night then."

He returned the farewell, but his voice was so soft she didn't really hear it, rather saw the words on his lips.

And again, like his eyes, when he looked at her, she felt it. It started in her fingertips, floating up her arms until she shivered and exhaled, as if she could set the strange feeling free with her breath.

But it stayed with her, tickling her lungs, dancing across her skin.

She was going mad. That had to be it. Or she was overtired. Too tense from a day with a royal prince.

She stepped inside her room, reaching up to pull her window closed, but then—

"Oh!" She poked her head back out. "Sir Harry!"

He looked up. He hadn't moved from his spot.

"The book," she said. "You still have it."

In unison they both looked out at the strip of space between their buildings.

"It's not going to work so well tossing it up," she said, "is it?"

He shook his head, and he smiled, just a little bit, as if he knew he should not. "I shall have to call upon you tomorrow to return it."

And there it came again, that breathless feeling, all

bubbly and strange. "I shall look forward to it," she said, and closed the window.

And shut the curtains.

And then let out a little squeal, hugging her arms to her body.

What a perfect evening this had turned out to be.

The following afternoon, Harry tucked *Miss Butterworth and the Mad Baron* under his arm and prepared to make the extremely short journey to Lady Olivia's sitting room. It was, he thought as he made his way over, nearly as far in vertical distance as horizontal. Twelve steps down to his ground floor, another six to the street, eight up to her front door . . .

Next time he would count the horizontal paces, too. It would be interesting to see how they compared.

He'd quite got over his momentary madness of the night before. Lady Olivia Bevelstoke was astoundingly beautiful; this was not just his opinion, it was a well-accepted fact. Any man would want her, especially one who had been living as monkish an existence as he had these past few months.

The key to his sanity, he was becoming increasingly convinced, was in remembering *why* he was climbing the front steps to her home. The War Office. The prince. National security . . . She was his assignment. Winthrop had all but ordered him to insinuate himself into her life.

No, Winthrop *had* ordered him to insinuate himself into her life. There had been no ambiguity about it.

He was following orders, he told himself as he lifted the knocker at her door. An afternoon with Olivia. For king and country.

And really, she was a damn sight better than that Russian countess with all the vodka.

With such focus on duty, however, one would have thought he'd have been more pleased when he arrived in the sitting room and saw that Lady Olivia was not alone. His other assignment, the incredibly well-postured Prince Alexei of Russia, was right there, sitting across from her, looking smug.

It should have been convenient. Instead, it was annoying.

"Sir Harry," Olivia said, giving him a bright smile as he entered the sitting room. "You remember Prince Alexei, do you not?"

But of course. Almost as well as he remembered his hulking giant of a bodyguard, standing with a deceptive slouch in the corner.

Harry wondered if the fellow followed the prince into his bedroom. That had to be awkward for the ladies.

"What is that in your hand?" the prince asked him.

"A book," Harry replied, setting *Miss Butterworth* down on a side table. "One I promised to lend to Lady Olivia."

"What is it?" the prince demanded.

"Just a silly novel," Olivia put in. "I don't think I will like it, but it was recommended by a friend."

The prince looked unimpressed.

"What do you like to read, Your Highness?" she asked.

"You would not be familiar with it," he said dismissively.

Harry watched Olivia closely. She was good at this, he realized, this playacting that masqueraded as polite society. There was barely a flash of irritation in her eyes before she suppressed it, with an expression so perfectly pleasant and sunny that it *had* to be sincere.

Except that he knew it wasn't.

"I would still like to hear about your reading choices," she said cordially. "I enjoy learning about other cultures."

The prince turned to her, and in doing so, turned his back on Harry. "One of my ancestors was a great poet and philosopher. Prince Antiokh Dmitrievich Kantemir."

Harry found this very interesting; it was well known (among those who knew of Russian culture) that Kantemir had died a bachelor.

"I also read recently all of the fables of Ivan Krylov," Alexei continued. "Every Russian of education must do so."

"We have writers like that, too," Olivia commented. "Shakespeare. Everyone reads Shakespeare. I think it would be almost unpatriotic not to."

The prince shrugged. His opinion of Shakespeare, apparently.

"Do you read Shakespeare?" Olivia asked.

"I have read some of it in French," he said. "But I prefer to read in Russian. Our literature is far deeper than yours."

"I've read *Poor Liza*," Harry said, even though he knew he should have kept his mouth shut. But the prince was such a pompous ass. It was difficult not to try to prick the air from him.

Prince Alexei turned to him with unconcealed surprise. "I did not know that *Bednaya Liza* had been translated into English."

Harry didn't know, either; he'd read it in Russian, years ago. But he'd already made one rash mistake this afternoon. He wasn't going to make another, and so he said, "I think I'm thinking of the right book. The author is . . . oh, I can't think of it . . . begins with a K, I think. Karmazanon?"

"Karamzin," the prince said brusquely, "Nikolai Karamzin."

"Yes, that's the one," Harry said, his tone purposefully breezy. "Poor peasant girl gets ruined by a nobleman, yes?"

The prince gave a curt nod.

Harry shrugged. "Someone must have translated it, then."

"Perhaps I shall try to find a copy," the prince said. "It might benefit to my English."

"Is it very well known?" Olivia put in. "I should love to read it, if we can find a copy in English."

Harry gave her a dubious look. This was the same woman who had claimed not to like either *Henry V* or *Miss Butterworth and the Mad Baron*.

There was the barest hint of a lull in the conversation before Olivia said, "I just called for tea before you arrived, Sir Harry. Will you join us?"

"I would be delighted." Harry took a seat across from the prince, flashing him a bland smile.

"I must confess," Olivia said, "that I am terrible with languages. My governesses despaired of my ever mastering French. I have such admiration for those who can speak more than one. Your English is truly superb, Your Highness."

The prince acknowledged her compliment with a nod.

"Prince Alexei speaks French as well," Olivia said to Harry.

"As do I," he responded, since there didn't seem any reason to hide it. The prince might let something slip in Russian, but he would never do so in French; there were far too many French speakers in London. Besides, after so many years on the Continent, it would have been strange if he hadn't picked up some of the language.

"I didn't realize that," Olivia said. "Perhaps the two of you can converse. Or maybe not." She let out a little laugh. "I quake with terror over what you might say about me."

"Only the deepest of compliments," the prince said smoothly.

"I doubt my skills are up to par with His Highness's," Harry lied. "It would be a frustrating conversation for us both, I am sure."

Again, a lull, and again, Olivia leaped into the breach. "Perhaps you can say something for us in Russian," she said to the prince. "I am not sure that I have ever heard the language spoken aloud. Have you, Sir Harry?"

"I believe so," he murmured.

"Oh, of course you would have done, during your time on the Continent. I imagine you must have heard any number of languages."

Harry nodded politely, but she had already turned back to Alexei. "*Would* you say something? French I do recognize, even if I can hardly understand a word. But Russian—well, I have no idea what it sounds like. Is it a bit like German?"

"*Nyet*," the prince replied.

"Ny-oh!" Olivia beamed. "That must mean no."

"*Da*," the prince said.

"And that must be yes!"

Harry wasn't sure whether he was amused or nauseated.

"Say something more," she urged. "I can't really hear the rhythm of the language from single-syllable words."

"Very well," the prince said. "Let me see . . ."

They waited patiently while he thought of something to say. After a few moments he spoke.

And Harry decided that he had never hated another human being as much as he hated Prince Alexei Gomarovsky of Russia.

"What did you say?" Olivia asked with an expectant smile.

"Only that you are more beautiful than the oceans, sky, and fog."

Or, depending on the translation, *I'm going to pump you until you scream.*

"That's so poetic," Olivia murmured.

Harry did not trust himself to speak.

"Can you say something more?" Olivia entreated.

The prince demurred. "I could not think of anything more—how do you say it?"

Offensive.

"Delicate," the prince finished, looking extremely pleased with his choice of word. "Delicate enough for you."

Harry coughed. It was either that or gag. Or really, it must have sounded like a bit of both, because Olivia looked at him with an expression of panic. He could do nothing but roll his eyes in return. No reasonable man could listen to this drivel without some sort of reaction.

"Oh, here comes the tea," Olivia said, sounding more than a little relieved. "Mary, we will need another setting. Sir Harry has decided to join us."

After Mary had set the tray down and gone off to fetch another cup, Olivia looked over at Harry and said, "You don't mind if I begin to pour, do you?"

"Of course not," he said, and happened to glance at the prince, who was regarding him with nothing less than a smirk.

Harry gave him an equally juvenile look in return. He couldn't help it. And, he reasoned, it would help to maintain the fiction that he was just another jealous suitor. But really, did Alexei think that Olivia signaled her favor by serving him tea before Harry had a cup?

"Do you enjoy our English tea, Your Highness?" Olivia asked. "Although I suppose it isn't really English. But we have made it our own, I think."

"I find it a most pleasant custom," the prince said.

"Do you take milk?"

"Please."

"Sugar?"

"Yes."

She prepared his cup, speaking as she spooned the sugar. "Sir Harry recently told me that tea was what he missed the most while serving in the army."

"Is that so?" Prince Alexei responded.

Harry was not sure who the prince was speaking to but decided to answer nonetheless. "There were many nights when I would have killed for a hot beverage."

"I expect there were many nights when you killed, anyway," the prince returned.

Harry gave him a cool look. "I was armed at various times with a saber, a rifle, and bayonet. I killed frequently."

The prince met his stare with equal measure. "You sound as if you enjoyed it."

"Never," Harry said curtly.

One corner of the prince's mouth curved very slightly. "Evil is sometimes necessary for good to flower, *da*?"

Harry acknowledged this with a single nod.

The prince took a sip of his tea, even though Harry had not yet been served. "Do you fence, Sir Harry?"

"Only passably." This was true. They hadn't had a proper fencing master at Hesslewhite. As a result, Harry's sword skills were far more military than competitive. He was mediocre at the parry, but he knew how to go in for the kill.

"Here is that extra cup," Olivia announced, taking it from the maid, who had just returned. "Sir Harry, you take yours without sugar, do you not?"

"You remember," he murmured.

She smiled at him, a happy, earnest thing that floated across him like a warm breeze. He felt himself smiling back, unbidden, unfeigned. She looked at him, and he at her, and for one breathtaking moment they were alone in the room.

But then she turned away, murmuring something about tea. She busied herself fixing his cup, and he found that he was transfixed by her hands, lovely and elegant, and yet somehow not quite graceful. He liked that. Every goddess needed imperfections.

She looked up again and saw that he had been watching her. She smiled again, and then he had to do the same, and—

And then the damned prince had to go and open his mouth.

Chapter Thirteen

*Five Things I Quite Like About
Sir Harry Valentine
By Olivia Bevelstoke*

*Smile
Wit
Eyes
Will speak to me through a window*

"Vladimir!" the prince suddenly barked out, rendering Olivia's accounting one item short.

Vladimir immediately crossed the room to Prince Alexei, who issued what certainly sounded like an order in Russian. Vladimir grunted his assent and then added his own incomprehensible stream of words.

Olivia looked over at Harry. He was frowning. She supposed she probably was, too.

Vladimir made another gruff sound and returned to his corner, and Harry, who had been watching the entire exchange, looked at the prince and said, "He's very convenient."

Prince Alexei gave him a bored stare. "I do not understand your meaning."

"He comes, he goes, he does whatever you say . . ."

"That is his purpose."

"Well, of course." Harry let his head tilt very slightly to the side. A shoulderless shrug is what it was, and just is careless in appearance. "I did not say otherwise."

"It is necessary for those of royal status to travel with attendants."

"I fully agree," Harry replied, but his agreeable tone only seemed to needle the prince further.

"Here is your tea," Olivia cut in, holding a cup out for Harry. He took it, thanking her quietly before taking a sip.

"I take mine the same way as Sir Harry," she said, to no one in particular. "I used to take sugar, but I've found I've lost the taste for it."

Harry looked at her with a curious expression. Olivia was not surprised; she could not recall the last time she'd made such dull conversation. But surely he realized that she had no choice.

She took a deep breath, trying to navigate the undercurrents of the conversation. The two men detested each other, that much was clear, but she'd been in rooms with people who hated each other before. It wasn't usually quite this palpable.

And while she'd like to think that it was all for jealousy over her, she could not help but feel there was something else afoot.

"I have not been outside yet today," she said, since the weather was always a dependable conversational distraction. "Is it warm?"

"I think it will rain," the prince said.

"Oh well, that is England for you, isn't it? If it isn't raining, it's pouring. And if it isn't pouring . . ."

But the prince had already removed his attention to his rival. "Where is your home, Sir Harry?"

"Lately, next door," Harry said cheerfully.

"I thought that English aristocrats have grand homes in the country."

"They do," Harry replied affably. "Of course, I am not an aristocrat."

"How is the tea?" Olivia asked, a touch desperately.

Both men grunted an answer. Neither was more than one syllable. And neither syllable was particularly intelligible.

"But you are called Sir," Prince Alexei said.

"True," Harry replied, not looking at all concerned by his lack of status. "But it does not make me an aristocrat."

Prince Alexei's lips curved ever so slightly.

"Baronets are not considered part of the aristocracy," Olivia explained, giving Harry an apologetic look. It really was rude of the prince to hammer on about Harry's lower rank, but one did have to make allowances for cultural differences.

"What is this 'baronet'?" the prince asked.

"Endlessly in between," Harry replied with a sigh. "A bit like purgatory, really."

Alexei turned to Olivia. "I do not understand him."

"He means, or at least I think he means"—she shot a peeved look at Harry because she had no idea what he thought he was doing, purposefully antagonizing the prince—"that baronets are not a part of the aristocracy, and yet they are not untitled. That is why he is called Sir."

Prince Alexei still looked confused, so Olivia explained, "In order of rank, beneath royalty, of course, there are dukes and duchesses, marquesses and marchionesses, earls and countesses, viscounts and viscountesses, and finally, barons and baronesses." She paused. "Then baronets and their wives, but they are considered part of the gentry."

"So very low," Harry murmured, having fun with this now. "Miles and miles below someone like you."

The prince glanced at him for barely a second, but it was long enough for Olivia to see the distaste in his eyes. "In Russia, the aristocracy provides a structure for society. Without our great families, we would fall apart."

"Many feel the same way here," Olivia said courteously.

"There would be—how do you say it . . ."

"Revolution?" Harry supplied.

"Chaos?" Olivia guessed.

"Chaos," Alexei selected. "Yes, that is it. Revolution I do not fear."

"We would all be wise to learn from the experiences of the French," Harry said.

Prince Alexei turned on him with fire in his eyes. "The French were stupid. They allowed the bourgeoisie too many freedoms. We do not make this mistake in Russia."

"We do not fear revolution in England, either," Harry said softly, "although I expect it is for different reasons."

Olivia's breath caught. He'd spoken with such quiet conviction, in such contrast to his earlier flippancies. His serious tone could not help but capture the moment. Even Prince Alexei paused and turned to him with an expression that was . . . well, not respect, exactly, for he clearly did not appreciate the comment. But perhaps there was some sort of recognition, an acknowledgment of Harry as a worthy opponent.

"Our conversation grows so serious," she declared. "It is far too early in the day for such talk." And when that failed to garner an immediate response, she added, "I can't bear political discussions when the sun is shining."

Actually, what she couldn't bear was making herself out to be a complete ninny. She adored political discussions, at any time of day.

And the sun wasn't shining, either.

"We are most rude," Prince Alexei said, rising from his seat. He came before her and sank to one knee, leaving her speechless. What was he *doing*?

"Can you forgive us?" he murmured, taking her hand.

"I—I—"

He brought her knuckles to his lips. "Please."

"Of course," she finally got out. "It is—"

"Nothing," Harry put in. "I believe that is the word you're looking for?"

She would have glared at him if she could have seen him around Alexei, who was presently filling her entire breadth of vision. "You are of course forgiven, Your Highness," she said. "I was being silly."

"It is the right of all beautiful women to be silly when they wish."

The prince moved at that point, and Olivia did catch a glimpse of Harry's face. He looked as if he might gag.

"You must have a great many appointments here in London," Harry said, once Alexei had resumed his seat.

"I am given several awards," he said, looking confused and annoyed by the change of subject.

Olivia jumped in to translate. "I think what Sir Harry means is that you must have many commitments, many people to meet."

"Yes," Alexei said.

"Your days must be very busy," Harry added, his voice just a touch impressed and fawning.

Olivia frowned. She had a feeling she knew what he was up to, and it would not end well. "You must lead a very exciting life," she said quickly, trying to shift the conversation.

But Harry was not to be diverted. "Today, for example," he mused. "You must have a terrific schedule. How honored Lady Olivia is that you should take time out to see her."

"I would always make time for Lady Olivia."

"You are ever generous with your company," Harry said. "From what do we take you this afternoon?"

"*You* take me from nothing."

Harry gave a knowing little smile, just to show that the insult, while noticed, had not stung. "Where else could you be this afternoon, Your Highness? With the ambassador? With the king?"

"I could be anywhere I wish."

"Such is the privilege of royalty," Harry mused.

Olivia bit her lip nervously. Vladimir had begun to inch his way over, and if there was to be violence, Harry was not going to emerge the victor.

"I am so honored by your presence," she said—the absolute only sentence she could think of quickly.

"Why, thank you," Harry quipped.

Stop, she mouthed at him.

Why? he mouthed back.

"I think you speak without me," Alexei said angrily.

Vladimir moved ever closer.

"Of course not," Olivia assured him. "I was only trying to remind Sir Harry that his cousin is . . . ehrm . . . expecting him for, er, a meeting."

Alexei looked most dubious. "You said all this?"

Olivia could feel her skin burning. "Quite a bit of it," she mumbled.

"I really must go," Harry said abruptly, standing up.

Olivia stood as well. "Please allow me to escort you to the door," she said, trying not to sound as if it were coming through clenched teeth.

"Please do not trouble yourself," he replied. "I would not dream of asking so beautiful a lady to get up."

Olivia blanched. Did Alexei realize that Harry was mocking him? She looked over at the prince, trying not to be obvious about it. He did not seem to have taken offense; in fact, he looked quite pleased. That is, he looked quite pleased in a rather stiff and reserved sort of way. Perhaps satisfied was a better description.

Harry saw himself out, depriving Olivia of the chance to tell him exactly what she thought of his childish behavior. She gripped the edge of the sofa cushion beneath her, seething. He would not escape so easily. He had no idea what it meant to allow a woman's ire to fester. Whatever she had to say to him, it would be far less pretty tonight than it would have been this afternoon.

In the meantime, however, there was still the prince to attend to. He sat across from her, his expression somewhere between satisfied and smug. He was pleased that Harry had gone, and probably even more pleased that she was now alone with him.

And Vladimir. One really could not forget about Vladimir.

"I wonder where my mother is," Olivia said, because, really, it was odd that she had not made an appearance. The door to the sitting room had been left quite properly open the entire time, so her presence was not needed as a chaperone, but Olivia would have thought that she'd have wanted to greet the prince.

"Is it necessary for her to be here?"

"Well, not really." Olivia glanced over at the open door. "Huntley is right there in hall . . ."

"I am glad we are alone."

Olivia swallowed, not sure what to say to this.

He smiled a little, but his eyes grew heavy. "Are you nervous to be alone with me?"

I wasn't until now.

"Of course not," she said. "I know that you are a gentleman. And besides that, we are not alone."

He blinked several times and then laughed abruptly. "You do not mean Vladimir?"

Olivia felt her eyes dart back and forth across the room, from the prince to his attendant, and then back again, several times. "Well, yes," she said haltingly. "He's right . . . there. And—"

Alexei waved away her concern. "Vladimir is invisible."

Her uneasiness grew. "I don't understand."

"It is like he is not here." He smiled at her, and not in a way that made her comfortable. "If that is how I wish it."

Olivia's lips parted, but she had absolutely nothing to say.

"For example," Alexei continued, "if I were to kiss you—"

Olivia gasped.

"—it would be the same as if we were alone. He would not tell anyone, and you would not feel any more . . . how do you say it . . . uncomfortable."

"I think you should go, Your Highness."

"I should like to kiss you first."

Olivia stood, knocking the table with her shins. "That won't be necessary."

"No," he said, rising to his feet as well. "I think it is necessary. To show you."

"To show me what?" she said, unable to believe she was asking the question.

He gestured to Vladimir. "That it is as if he is not here. I must have protection at all times. He is with me always. Even when—I should not say it in front of a lady."

There was quite a bit already he should not have said in front of a lady. Olivia scooted along the edge of the sofa, trying to make her way out of the seating area and over to the door, but he was blocking her way.

"I will kiss your hand," he said.

"Wh—what?"

"To prove to you that I am a gentleman. You think I will do something else, but I will kiss your hand."

It felt as if her throat were closing up. Her mouth was open, but she didn't seem to be breathing. He had unnerved her completely.

He took her hand. Olivia was still too shocked to pull it back. He kissed it, his fingers stroking hers as he released her.

"Next time," he said, "I will kiss your mouth."

Oh, dear God.

"Vladimir!" Alexei let out a short stream of Russian, and his servant came immediately to his side. Olivia was horrified to realize that she had forgotten that he was there, although she was quite certain this was only because she had been so surprised by the prince's outrageous conversation.

"I will see you tonight," Alexei said to her.

"Tonight?" she echoed.

"You attend the opera, yes? *The Magic Flute*. It is the first performance of the season."

"I—I—" Was she attending the opera? She couldn't think straight. A royal prince had attempted to seduce her in her own sitting room. Or at least had *sort of* attempted to do so. In the presence of his hulking manservant.

Surely she had earned a bit of befuddlement.

"Until then, Lady Olivia." Prince Alexei swept from the room, Vladimir in his wake. And all Olivia could think was, *I need to tell Sir Harry about this.*

Except that she was furious with him.

Wasn't she?

Chapter Fourteen

Harry was in a bad mood. The day had started out perfectly fine, and indeed had promised all sorts of good cheer, until he'd ambled over to Rudland House's sitting room and come across Prince Alexei Gomarovsky, apparent descendant of Russia's most famous bachelor poet.

Or if not most famous, then famous enough.

Then he'd had to watch Olivia fawning over the churl.

Then he'd had to sit there and pretend he didn't understand when the bastard said he wanted to rape her. And then tried to pass the bloody thing off as some nonsense about sky and fog.

Then—as he was sitting at home, trying to figure out what to do about the prince's second statement in Russian, which had been an order to the ever-charming Vladimir to investigate him—he'd received written orders from the War Office to attend that evening's opening of *The Magic Flute*, which would have been marvelous, had he been able to watch the stage instead of his new least favorite person, the aforementioned Alexei of Russia.

Then the bloody prince had left the opera early. *Left*, just as the Queen of the Night was beginning her aria. It was "Hell's Vengeance Boileth in Mine Heart," for heaven's sake. Who left at the beginning of "Hell's Vengeance Boileth in Mine Heart"?

Hell's vengeance, Harry decided, was boilething in his heart as well.

He'd followed the prince (and the ever-present and increasingly menacing Vladimir) all the way to Madame LaRoux's, where Prince Alexei presumably partook of the favors of a lady or three.

At that point, Harry had decided he was well within his rights to go home.

Which he did, but not before getting soaked in a freakishly short but violent rainstorm.

Which was why, when he arrived home and shrugged off his sodden coat and gloves, his only thoughts were of a hot bath. He could see it in his mind, steam rising from the surface. His skin would prickle at the heat, almost painfully, until his body adjusted to the temperature.

It would be heaven. Heaven boilething in a tub.

But sure enough, heaven was not to be his, at least not this night. His coat was still hanging limply off one arm when his butler entered the front hall and informed him that a letter had come for him by special messenger and was waiting on his desk.

And so off to his office he went, his feet splishing

and sploshing in his boots, only to find that the message contained absolutely nothing of immediate importance, only a few bits and pieces of trivia to fill gaps in the prince's history. Harry groaned and shuddered, wishing there was a fire in which to toss the offending missive. Then he could stand in front of it, too. He was so cold and so wet and so bloody annoyed with everything.

And then he looked up.

Olivia. In her window, staring down at him.

Really, this was all her fault. Or at least half of it.

He marched over to his window and wrenched it up. She did the same.

"I've been waiting for you," she said, before he could get word in. "Where have you—what happened to you?"

In the compendium of stupid questions, he decided, that would rank high. But his lips were probably still blue with cold, and there was no way he could say all that. "It rained," he bit off.

"And you decided to go for a walk in it?"

He wondered if, with superhuman effort, he might be able to strangle her from here.

"I need to speak with you," she said.

He realized he could not feel his toes. "Does it have to be right now?"

She drew back, looking terribly offended.

Which did little to improve his disposition. But still, gentlemanly behavior must have been beaten into him as a child, because even though he should have slammed the window shut, he instead explained himself, biting off, "I'm cold. I'm wet. And I'm in a very bad mood."

"Well, so am I!"

"Very well," he ground out. "What has you in a tizzy?"

"A tizzy?" she repeated derisively.

He held up a hand. If she was going to argue over his word choices, he was through with her.

She must have decided to choose a different battle, because she planted her hands on her hips, and said, "All right then, since you asked, *you* are the cause of my tizzy."

This had better be good. He waited for a moment, and then said, dripping with equal parts sarcasm and rainwater, "And. . . ?"

"And your behavior this afternoon. What were you thinking?"

"What was I—"

She actually leaned out of her window and shook a finger at him. "You were deliberately provoking Prince Alexei. Do you have any idea what a difficult situation that put me in?"

He stared at her for a moment, then said simply, "He's an idiot."

"He's not an idiot," she said testily.

"He's an idiot," Harry said again. "One who doesn't deserve to lick your feet. You'll thank me someday."

"I have no intention of allowing him to lick me anywhere," she retorted, then turned utterly red when she realized what she'd said.

Harry began not to feel quite so cold.

"I have no intention of allowing him to court me," she said, her voice hushed yet strangely loud enough to reach him with every syllable crystal clear. "But that does not mean he can be ill-treated in my home."

"Very well. I'm sorry. Are you satisfied?"

She was shocked into silence by his apology, but his triumph was short-lived. After no more than five seconds of her mouth opening and closing, she said, "I don't think you meant it."

"Oh, for God's sake," he burst out. He could not believe she was acting like *he'd* done something wrong. He was only following his bloody orders from the bloody War Office. And even allowing for the fact that she had no idea he had any orders to follow, *she* was the one who had spent the afternoon cooing at a man who had insulted her most viscerally.

Not that she knew that, either.

Still, anyone with a grain of sense could tell that the Prince Alexei was an oily little toad. Very well, an extremely handsome, not-little-at-all toad, but a toad nonetheless.

"Why are you so upset?" she demanded.

It was a damned good thing they were not face to face, because he would have done . . . *some*thing. "Why am I so upset?" he practically spat. "Why am I so *upset*? Because I—" But he realized he could not tell her that he'd been forced to leave the opera early. Or that he had followed the prince to a brothel. Or that he—

No, he could tell her that part.

"I am soaked to the skin, every inch of me ashiver, and I'm arguing with you through a window when I could be in a hot bath."

The last part came out a bit like a bellow, which probably wasn't the wisest thing, given that they were, technically, in public.

She was silent—finally—and then, quietly, she said, "Very well."

Very well? That was it? She was done with a "very well"?

And then, like an idiot, he stood there. She'd given him the perfect opportunity to bid her farewell, shut his window, and march himself upstairs to the bath, but he just stood there.

Looking at her.

Watching the way she hugged her arms to her body, as if she were chilled. Watching her mouth, which he couldn't quite see clearly in the dim light, and yet somehow he knew the precise moment she pressed her lips together, the corners tightening with hidden emotion.

"Where were you?" she asked.

He couldn't stop looking at her.

"Tonight," she clarified. "Where did you go that you got so wet?"

He glanced down at himself, as if only just then re-membering that he was soaked.

How was that possible?

"I went to the opera," he told her.

"Did you?" She hugged her arms more tightly against her body, and although he could not be sure, it looked as if she moved slightly closer to the window. "I was supposed to attend," she said. "I wanted to go."

He moved, too, closer to his window. "Why didn't you?"

She hesitated, her attention moving from his face for a moment before returning as she said, "If you must know, I knew the prince would be there, and I did not wish to see him."

Now this was interesting. He moved closer to the window, then—

There was a knock on his door.

"Don't move," he ordered, pointing up at her. He shut his window, then strode to the door and opened it.

"Your bath is ready, sir," his butler announced.

"Thank you. Could you, ah, have them keep it steaming for me? I'll be a few more minutes."

"I shall instruct the footmen to keep water on the stove. Will you be requiring a blanket, sir?"

Harry looked down at his hands. Funny, he couldn't quite feel them properly. "Er, yes. That would be marvelous. Thank you."

"I will get it at once."

While the butler went off in search of a blanket, Harry hurried back over to the window and wrenched it open. Olivia now had her back to him. She was sitting on the edge of her windowsill, leaning slightly against the side of the aperture. She had also sought a blanket, he noticed, something soft and powdery blue and—

He shook his head. What did her blanket matter? "One more minute," he called up. "Don't go."

Olivia glanced down at the sound of his voice, just in time to see his window close again. She waited another half minute or so, and then he was back, the wood of the window scraping as he pushed it back up.

"Oh, you got a blanket, too," she said, as if that were something significant.

"Well, I was cold," he said, also as if that were important.

They were quiet for a long moment, and then he asked, "Why didn't you want to see the prince?"

Olivia just shook her head. Not because it wasn't true, but because she didn't really think she could talk to him about it. Which was strange, because that afternoon, the first thing she'd thought was that she had to tell him about Prince Alexei's strange behavior. But now, window to window, with him looking up at her with dark, unfathomable eyes, she didn't know what to say.

Or how to say it.

"It's not important," she finally decided.

He did not speak immediately. When he did, his voice was low, with an edge to it that took her breath away. "If he made you uncomfortable, it is very important to me."

"He . . . he . . ." She kept shaking her head as she spoke, until finally she managed to hold herself still and say, "He just said something about kissing me. It's nothing really."

She'd been avoiding looking at Harry, but now she did. He wasn't moving.

"It's not the first time a gentleman has done so," she added. She decided not to mention the part about Vladimir. Frankly, it made her squeamish just to think about it.

"Harry?" she called down.

"I don't want you seeing him again," he said in a low voice.

Her first thought was to tell him that he had no authority over her. And indeed, her mouth opened, the words right there on her lips. But then she remembered something he'd said to her. He'd been teasing, or maybe he hadn't been. Maybe she'd only thought he was teasing when he'd said that she didn't always think before she spoke.

This time she was going to think.

She didn't want to see the prince again, either. What was the point in protesting his statement when they both wanted the same thing?

"I don't know that I will have any choice," she said. It was true. Short of barricading herself in her room, she had no way of avoiding him.

He looked up, his eyes deadly serious. "Olivia, he is not a nice man."

"How do you know?"

"I just—" He raked his hand through his hair, letting out what sounded like a frustrated exhale. "I can't tell you how I know. I mean, I don't know how I know. It's a male sort of thing. I can just tell."

She looked down at him, trying to decipher his words.

He closed his eyes for a moment, rubbing both his hands along his forehead. Finally, he looked up and said, "Don't you know things about other women that men are too dunce-headed to figure out?"

She nodded. He had a point. Quite a good one, actually.

"Just stay away from him. Promise me."

"I can't promise that," she said, although she wished she could.

"Olivia . . ."

"I can promise I will try. You know that's the best I can do."

He nodded. "Very well."

There was a hesitant, nervous silence, and then she said, "You should go have that bath. You're shivering."

"So are you," he said softly.

She was. She hadn't realized it, hadn't noticed that she was shaking, but now . . . now that she knew . . . it seemed to grow worse. And then . . . even worse . . . and she thought she might cry, but she had no idea why. It was just there, inside of her. Too much feeling. Too much . . .

Just too much. It was just too much.

She nodded jerkily. "Good night," she said, rushing out the word. The tears were there, too close, and she didn't want him to see them.

"Good night," he said, but she'd managed to pull down her window before he finished. And then she ran to the bed, and buried her face in her pillow.

But she didn't cry. Even though now she wanted to.

And she still didn't know why.

Harry held the blanket close as he trudged back out of his office. He was no longer quite so cold, but he felt awful. His chest had an unsettling, hollow feeling to it, and it seemed to intensify with each breath, sliding up his throat, drawing his shoulders up into a tense, unyielding shrug.

It wasn't cold, he realized. It was fear.

Prince Alexei had frightened Olivia today. Harry wasn't sure what exactly he'd done or said, and he knew that she would minimize her feelings if he pressed further about them, but something untoward had occurred. And it would happen again, if the prince was allowed free rein.

Harry moved through the front hall, holding the blanket with his left hand while he used his right to rub the back of his neck. He needed to calm down. He needed to catch his breath and think straight. It would be up to the bath, and then into bed, where he could calmly assess the problem and—

His front door began to rattle.

His heart slammed in his chest, and his muscles leaped to readiness, every nerve suddenly poised for a fight. It was late. And he'd been out following mysterious Russians. And . . .

And he was an idiot. If someone was going to break into his house, he'd not use the bloody front door. Harry stalked over, turned the lock, and pulled it open.

Edward fell in.

Harry stared down at his younger brother with disgust. "Oh, for God's sake."

"Harry?" Edward looked up and squinted, and Harry wanted to know who the hell else he was expecting.

"How much have you had to drink?" Harry demanded.

Edward tried to pull himself to his feet, but after a moment gave up and sat right in the center of the hall, blinking as if he weren't quite sure how he'd got into the position. "What?"

If anything, Harry's voice grew quieter. And more deadly. "How much have you had to drink?"

"Uhhhh . . . well . . ." Edward's mouth moved, almost as if he were chewing his cud. He probably was, Harry thought with disgust.

"Don't bother," Harry said curtly. What did it

matter how many drinks Edward had tossed back? It had been enough to render him senseless. The Lord only knew how he'd got himself home. He was no better than their father. The only difference was that Sir Lionel had confined most of his drunkenness to the home. Edward was making an ass of himself all over London.

"Get up," Harry ordered.

Edward stared up at him, his face blank.

"Get. Up."

"Why're you so angry?" Edward muttered, reaching out for a hand. But Harry didn't offer one, and so he struggled to his feet of his own accord, grabbing hold of a nearby table for balance.

Harry fought to keep hold of his temper. He wanted to grab Edward and shake and shake and bloody well scream that he was killing himself, that any day now he'd die the way Sir Lionel had, stupidly and alone.

His father had fallen out a window. He'd leaned too far out and broken his neck. On the table nearby, there had been a glass of wine and an empty bottle.

Or so he'd been told. Harry had been in Belgium. A letter had arrived from his father's solicitor with the details.

From his mother he had heard nothing.

"Go to bed," Harry said in a low voice.

Edward wobbled and smirked. "I don't have to do what you say."

"Fine then," Harry spat. He'd had enough of this. It was like his father all over again, except now he could do something. He could say something. He didn't have to stand there, helpless, and clean up someone else's mess.

"Do what you want," he said, his voice low and shaking. "Just don't puke in my house."

"Oh, you'd like that, wouldn't you?" Edward cried out, lurching forward and then grabbing the wall when he stumbled. "You'd like it if I left, so everything could be neat and tidy. You never wanted me."

"What the hell are you talking about? You're my brother."

"You left. You left!" Edward nearly screamed.

Harry stared at him.

"You left me alone. With him. And her. And no one else. You knew Anne was leaving to get married. You knew I'd have no one."

Harry shook his head. "You were leaving for school. You only had a few months before you would be gone. I made sure of it."

"Oh, that was just—" Edward's face contorted and his head moved about unsteadily, and for a moment Harry was sure he was going to vomit. But no, he was just trying to find the right word, the furious, sarcastic word.

And drunk as he was, he couldn't do so.

"You didn't . . . you didn't even think." Edward shook a finger at him, then shook it again. "What did you think would happen when he dropped me off?"

"You weren't supposed to let him drop you off!"

"How was I supposed to know! I was twelve. Twelve!" Edward shouted.

Harry raced through his memory, trying to recall his good-byes. But he could remember almost nothing. He'd been so eager to get out, to leave it all behind. But he'd given advice to Edward, hadn't he? He'd told him it would all be all right, that he would go to Hesslewhite, and not have to deal with their parents. And he'd told him not to let their father near the school, hadn't he?

"He pissed in his pants," Edward said. "On the first day. He fell asleep on my bed and pissed in his pants. I got him up and changed his clothes. But I didn't have spare bedsheets. And everyone—" His voice choked, and Harry could see the terrified boy in his face, confused and alone.

"Everyone thought it was me," Edward said. "Splendid way to start off, don't you think?" He weaved a bit then, buoyed by bravado. "I was the *most* popular boy after that. Everyone wanted to be friends with *me*."

"I'm sorry," Harry said.

Edward shrugged, then he stumbled. Harry reached out and caught him this time. And then—he wasn't sure how it happened, or why he did it—he pulled his brother close. Gave him a hug. Just a bit of one. Just for long enough to blink back the tears in his eyes.

"You need to get to bed," Harry said, his voice hoarse.

Edward nodded, and he leaned on Harry as he helped him to the stairs. He did all right with the first two, but on the third he tripped.

"Thorry," Edward mumbled, struggling to right himself.

He dropped his *s*'s. Just like their father.

Harry thought he might be sick.

It wasn't quick, and it wasn't pretty, but eventually Harry managed to topple Edward into his bed, boots and all. He laid him carefully on his side with his mouth near the edge of the mattress, in case he threw up. And then he did something he'd never done, in all the years he'd maneuvered his father into a similar position.

He waited.

He stood by the door until Edward's breathing was quiet and even, and then he stayed there for several minutes more.

Because people weren't meant to be alone. And they weren't meant to be scared. Or feel small. And they shouldn't have to count how many times something bad happened, and they shouldn't worry that it might happen again.

And as he stood there in the darkness, he realized what he had to do. Not just for Edward, but for Olivia. And maybe for himself, too.

Chapter Fifteen

By the following morning Olivia was feeling not quite so out of sorts. The light of day and a good night's rest, it seemed, could do a great deal to restore the spirits, even if she hadn't come to any grand conclusions.

Why I Was Crying Last Night
By Olivia Bevelstoke

Actually, I wasn't crying.
But it seemed like it.

She decided to try it from a different angle.

Why I Wasn't Crying Last Night
By Olivia Bevelstoke

She sighed. She had no idea.

But there was always denial. And so she resolved not to think about it, at least until she'd managed to get some breakfast. She was always more levelheaded on a full stomach.

She was halfway through her morning routine, trying to sit still while her maid pinned her hair, when a knock sounded at the door.

"Enter!" she called out, then murmured to Sally, "Did you order chocolate?"

Sally shook her head, and they both looked up as a maid entered, announcing that Sir Harry was waiting for her in the drawing room.

"At *this* time of the morning?" It was nearly ten, so hardly the crack of dawn, but still, unconscionably early for a gentleman to call.

"Shall I have Huntley tell him that you are unavailable?"

"No," Olivia replied. Harry wouldn't call so early without a good reason. "Please inform him that I shall be down straightaway."

"But you haven't had breakfast, my lady," Sally said.

"I'm sure I won't waste away for want of one breakfast." Olivia lifted her chin, regarding her reflection in the mirror. Sally was working on something rather elaborate, involving braids, clips, and at least a dozen pins. "Perhaps something simpler this morning?"

Sally's shoulders slumped with disappointment. "We're more than halfway done, I promise."

But Olivia was already pulling out pins. "Just a little bun, I think. Nothing fancy."

Sally sighed and started to adjust the coiffure. In about ten minutes Olivia was done and heading downstairs, trying to ignore the fact that the rush had meant that a lock of her hair had already fallen free and had to be tucked behind her ear. When she arrived at the drawing room, Sir Harry was seated all the way on the far side, at the small writing table by the window.

He appeared to be . . . working?

"Sir Harry," she said, looking at him with some confusion. "It's so early."

"I have come to a conclusion," he told her, rising to his feet.

She looked at him expectantly. He sounded so . . . *definitive*.

He clasped his hands in front of him, his stance wide. "I cannot allow you to be alone with the prince."

He had said as much the night before, but really, what could he do?

"There is only one solution," he continued. "I shall be *your* bodyguard."

She stared at him, stunned.

"He has Vladimir. You have me."

She continued to stare at him, still stunned.

"I will stay here with you today," he explained.

She blinked several times, finally finding her voice. "In my drawing room?"

"You should not feel that you have to entertain me," he said, motioning to some papers he had set down on the small writing desk. "I brought work with me."

Good heavens, did he intend to move in? "You brought work?"

"I'm sorry, but I really can't lose an entire day."

Her mouth opened, but it was a few seconds before she said, "Oh."

Because really, what else could there possibly be to say to that?

He gave her what she suspected he thought was an encouraging smile. "Why don't you get yourself a book and join me?" he asked, motioning to the seating area in the center of the room. "Oh right, you don't like books. Well, the newspaper will do just as well. Sit down."

Again it took her several moments before she managed to speak. "You're inviting me to join you in *my* drawing room?"

He gave her a steady look, then said, "I'd rather be in my own drawing room, but I hardly think that would be acceptable."

She nodded slowly, not because she was agreeing with him, although she supposed she was, on the last statement at least.

"We are in accord, then," he stated.

"What?"

"You're nodding."

She stopped nodding.

"Do you mind if I sit?" he asked.

"Sit?"

"I really must get back to work," he explained.

"To work," she echoed, because she was clearly at her conversational best this morning.

He looked at her, his brows arching, and it was only then that she realized that what he *meant* was that he could not sit until she did. She started to say, "Please," as in, *Please, do make yourself at home,* because she had had over twenty years of courtesy drummed into her. But good sense (and perhaps a fair bit of self-preservation) took hold, and she switched to, "You really shouldn't feel you need to stay here all day."

His lips pressed together, and tiny lines fanned out from the corners. There was something resolute in his dark eyes, something steely and immovable.

He wasn't asking her permission, she realized. He was telling her what to do.

It should have raised her hackles. It was everything she detested in a man. But all she could do was stand there, feeling . . . fluttery. Her feet were squirming in her slippers, she realized, getting ready to rise to her tiptoes, her body suddenly too light to remain fixed to the ground.

She took hold of the back of a chair. She felt as if she might float away. Maybe she should have eaten breakfast.

Although that really didn't explain the odd sensation that had taken hold somewhat . . . below her stomach.

She looked at him. He was saying something. But she definitely wasn't listening. She didn't even hear him, didn't hear anything but a wicked little voice inside, telling her to look at his mouth, at those lips, at . . .

"Olivia? Olivia?"

"I'm sorry," she said. She squeezed her legs together, thinking that some sort of muscular motion might jolt her from her trance. And she couldn't think of any other body part he couldn't see.

But that just seemed to make her feel . . . squirmier.

His head tilted slightly, and he looked . . . concerned? Amused? It was hard to tell.

She had to get a hold of herself. Now. She cleared her throat. "You were saying. . . ?"

"Are you all right?"

"Perfectly well," she said crisply. She liked the sound of that, brisk and businesslike, with every consonant perfectly enunciated.

He watched her for a few moments, but she could not quite read his expression. Or perhaps she just didn't *want* to read his expression, because if she did, she suspected she'd realize he was looking at her as if she might suddenly start barking like a dog.

She gave him a tight smile, and said again, "You were saying. . . ?"

"I was saying," he said slowly, "that I'm sorry, but I cannot allow you to be alone with that man. And don't say that Vladimir would be here, because he hardly counts."

"No," she said, thinking of her unsettling last conversation with the prince, "I wouldn't say that."

"Good. Then we are in agreement?"

"Well, yes," she said, "about not wanting to be alone with Prince Alexei, but—" She cleared her throat, hoping it might help her regain her equilibrium. She needed to keep a sharper head around this man. He was staggeringly intelligent, and he would run circles around her if she didn't stay on her toes. And that would be *on* her toes, not floating right off them. She cleared her throat again. And then again, because all that clearing was giving her a scratchy throat.

"Do you need something to drink?" he asked solicitously.

"No. Thank you. What I was trying to say was—you do understand that I am not alone here. I have parents."

"Yes," he said, not sounding terribly impressed with her argument, "it is my understanding that you do. I have never seen them, however. Not here, at any rate."

She frowned, glancing over her shoulder into the hall. "I think my mother is still asleep."

"My point exactly," Harry said.

"I am grateful for the gesture," she said, "but I feel I must point out that it is quite unlikely that the prince—or anyone, for that matter—will make a call this early in the morning."

"I agree," he told her, "but it is a chance I am not willing to take. Although . . ." He thought for a moment. "If your brother is willing to come down here and vow to me that he will not allow you out of his sight for the rest of the day, I will happily depart."

"That presupposes that *I* want him in *my* sight for the rest of the day," Olivia said tartly.

"Then you're stuck with me, I'm afraid."

She looked at him.

He looked at her.

She opened her mouth to speak.

He smiled.

She started wondering why she was fighting so hard.

"Very well," she said, finally moving out of the doorway and into the room. "I suppose it can't hurt."

"You won't even know I'm here," he assured her.

That, she highly doubted.

"It's only because I have no other plans for the morning," she informed him.

"I understand."

She gave him a sharp look. It was disconcerting, not being able to tell if he was being sarcastic.

"It's highly irregular," she murmured, but true to his word, he was already back at the desk, carefully reading the papers he'd brought with him. Were those the same documents he had worked on so diligently when she'd been spying on him?

She edged a little closer, grabbing a book off a table. She needed an object in her hands, something to use as a prop if he noticed how closely she was watching him.

"You've decided to read *Miss Butterworth*, then?" he asked, not looking up at her.

Her lips parted. How had he known she'd picked up a book? How had he even known she was watching him? His eyes hadn't left the papers on the desk.

And *Miss Butterworth*? Really? She looked down at the book in her hands in disgust. If she was going to pick up a random object, surely she could have done better than that.

"I'm trying to be more open-minded," she said, settling into the first chair she came across.

"A noble pursuit," he said, not looking up.

She opened the book and looked down, loudly flipping the pages until she found where they'd left off two days earlier. "Pigeons . . . pigeons . . ." she murmured.

"What?"

"Just looking for the pigeons," she said sweetly.

He shook his head, and she thought she saw him smile, but he still didn't look up.

She sighed loudly, then peeked over.

No reaction.

She then reassured herself that the sigh had not been initiated with the intention of trying to attract his attention. She had sighed because she'd needed to exhale, and if it had been loud, well, that was her habit. And since it had been loud, it had made *sense* to peek over . . .

She sighed again. Absolutely not on purpose.

He kept working.

Possible Contents of Sir Harry's Papers
By Olivia Bevelstoke

Sequel to Miss Butterworth *(wouldn't it be delicious if he turned out to be the author?)*
Unauthorized sequel to Miss Butterworth, *because it is highly unlikely that he penned the original, splendid as that would be*
A Secret Diary—with all of his secrets (!!!!!)
Something else entirely
Order for a new hat

She giggled.

"What is so funny?" he asked, finally looking up.

"I couldn't possibly explain," she said, trying not to grin.

"Is the joke at my expense?"

"Only a little."

He quirked a brow.

"Oh very well, it's entirely at your expense, but it's no less than you deserve." She smiled at him, waiting for him to comment, but he did not.

Which was disappointing.

She turned back to *Miss Butterworth*, but even though the poor girl had just broken both legs in a hideous carriage wreck, the novel was less than gripping.

She started drumming her fingers on one of the open pages. The noise grew louder . . . and louder . . . until it seemed to echo through the room.

To her ears, at least. Harry didn't notice.

She let out a loud exhale and went back to Miss Butterworth and her broken legs.

She turned a page.

And read. And turned another. And read. And turned another. And—

"You're on Chapter Four already."

She jumped in her seat, startled by the sound of Harry's voice so close to her ear. How was it possible that he'd got up without her noticing?

"Must be a good book," he said.

She gave a shrug. "It's passable."

"Is Miss Butterworth recovered from the plague?"

"Oh, that was ages ago. She's more recently broken both of her legs, been stung by a bee, and nearly sold into slavery."

"All in four chapters?"

"Closer to three," she told him, motioning to the chapter head visible on her open page. "I've only just started the fourth."

"I finished my work," he said, coming around to the front of the sofa.

Ah. Now, *finally*, she could ask, "What were you doing?"

"Nothing very interesting. Grain reports from my property in Hampshire."

Compared to her imaginings, this was somewhat disappointing.

He sat down on the other end of the sofa, crossing

one ankle over the opposite knee. It was a very informal position; it spoke of comfort, and familiarity, and something else—something that made her giddy and warm. She tried to think of another man who would sit near her in so relaxed a pose. There was no one. Just her brothers.

And Sir Harry Valentine was definitely not her brother.

"What are you thinking about?" he asked, his voice sly.

She must have looked startled, because he added, "You were blushing."

Her shoulders drew back. "I'm not blushing."

"Of course not," he said without hesitation. "It's very warm in here."

Which it wasn't. "I was thinking about my brothers," she said. It was a little bit true, and it ought to put a halt to his imaginings about her alleged blush.

"I quite like your twin," Harry said.

"Winston?" Good heavens, he might have said he liked swinging from trees with monkeys. Or eating their droppings.

"Anyone who can get under your skin can only deserve my respect."

She scowled at him. "And I suppose you were nothing but sweetness and light with *your* sister?"

"Absolutely not," he said with no shame whatsoever. "I was a beast. But"—he leaned forward, his eyes full of mischief—"I always employed stealth."

"Oh please." Olivia had enough experience with siblings of the male persuasion to know that he had *no* idea what he was talking about. "If you are trying to tell me that your sister was not aware of your antics—"

"Oh no, she was most definitely aware." Harry leaned forward. "But my grandmother was not."

"Your grandmother?"

"She came to live with us when I was an infant. I was certainly closer to her than to either of my parents."

Olivia found herself nodding, although she was not sure why. "She must have been lovely."

Harry let out a bark of laughter. "She was many things, but *not* lovely."

Olivia couldn't help but grin as she asked, "What do you mean?"

"She was very . . ." He waved a hand in the air as he considered his words. "Severe. And I would have to say that she was quite firm in her opinions."

Olivia considered that for a moment, then said, "I like women who are firm in their opinions."

"I expect you do."

She felt herself smiling, and she leaned forward, feeling a wonderful, almost effervescent kinship. "Would she have liked me?"

The question seemed to have caught him off guard, and his mouth hung open for a few moments before he finally said, looking almost amused by the question, "No. No, I don't think she would have done."

Olivia felt her own mouth go slack with shock.

"Did you wish for me to lie to you?"

"No, but—"

He waved her protest away. "She had little patience for anyone. She sacked six of my tutors."

"Six?"

He nodded.

"My goodness." Olivia was impressed. "I *would* have liked her," she murmured. "*I* only managed to run off five governesses."

He gave a slow smile. "Isn't it strange how unsurprising I find that?"

She scowled at him. Or rather she meant to scowl. It probably came out something closer to a grin. "How is it," she returned, "that I did not know of your grandmother?"

"You didn't ask."

What did he think, that she ran about asking people about their grandparents? But then it occurred to her—what *did* she know about him, really?

Very little. Very little indeed.

It was odd, because she knew *him*. She was quite certain she did. And then she realized it—she knew the man, but not the facts that had made him.

"What were your parents like?" she said suddenly.

He looked at her with some surprise.

"I didn't ask if you had a grandmother," she said, by way of an explanation. "Shame on me for not thinking of it."

"Very well." But he did not answer right away. The muscles of his face moved—not enough to reveal what he was thinking, but more than enough to let her know that he *was* thinking, that he couldn't quite decide how to answer. And then he said:

"My father was a drunk."

Miss Butterworth, which Olivia had not even realized she was still holding, slipped from her fingers and thunked onto her lap.

"He was a rather amiable drunk, but strangely, that doesn't seem to make it much better." Harry's face betrayed no emotion. He was smiling even, as if it were all a joke.

It was easier that way.

"I'm sorry," she said.

Harry shrugged. "He couldn't help himself."

"It's very difficult," she said softly.

He turned, sharply, because there was something in her voice, something humble, something maybe even . . . understanding.

But she couldn't. She couldn't possibly. She was the one with the tidy, happy family, with the brother who married her best friend, and the parents who actually cared.

"My brother," she said. "The one who married my friend Miranda. I don't think I told you, but he'd been married before. His first wife was horrid. And then she died. And then—I don't know, one would think he'd have been glad to be rid of her, but he just seemed to get more and more miserable." There was a pause, and then she said, "He drank a great a deal."

It's not the same, Harry wanted to say, because it wasn't her parent, it wasn't the person who was supposed to love you and protect you and keep your world a right and steady place. It wasn't the same, because there was no way she'd cleaned up her brother's vomit 127 times. It wasn't a mother who never seemed to have anything to say, and it wasn't . . . *It wasn't the same, damn it. It wasn't—*

"It's not the same," she said quietly. "I don't think it could possibly be."

And with those words, those two short sentences,

everything inside of him, all those feelings that had been thrashing about—they calmed. Settled into a more comfortable place.

She gave him a tentative smile. Tiny, but true. "But I think I can understand. Maybe a little."

He looked down for some reason, down at her hands, which were resting atop the book in her lap, and then at the sofa, covered in a pale green stripe. He and Olivia were not exactly next to each other; there was still room for an entire person between them. But they were on the same piece of furniture, and if he reached out his hand, and if she reached out her hand . . .

His breath caught.

Because she'd reached out her hand.

Chapter Sixteen

He didn't think about what he did. He couldn't have thought about it, because if he had, he never would have done it. But when she reached out her hand . . .

He took it.

It was only then that Harry realized what he had done, and perhaps only then that she realized what she had started, but by then it was far too late.

He brought her fingers to his lips and kissed each of them, right at the base, where she would wear a ring. Where she currently wasn't wearing a ring. Where, in a flash of terrifying imagination, he saw her wearing *his* ring.

It should have been a warning. It should have induced sufficient panic to make him drop her hand, flee the room, the house, her company, forever.

But he didn't. He kept her hand at his lips, unable to part with the touch of her skin.

She was warm, soft.

Trembling.

He looked up, finally, into her eyes. They were wide, gazing at him with trepidation . . . and trust . . . and maybe . . . desire? He couldn't be sure, because he knew *she* couldn't be sure. She wouldn't know desire, wouldn't understand the sweet torture of it, the bodily longing for another human being.

He knew it, and he realized that he'd known it almost constantly since he'd known *her*. There had been that first, electrical moment of attraction, true, but that wasn't meaningful. He didn't know her then, hadn't even liked her.

But now . . . it was different. It wasn't just her beauty he wanted, or the curve of her breast, or the taste of her skin. He wanted *her*. All of her. He wanted whatever it was that made her read newspapers instead of novels, and he wanted that little piece of unconventionality that made her open a window and read silly novels to him across the space between their houses.

He wanted her razor-sharp wit, the triumph on her face when she speared him with a particularly apt retort. And he wanted the look of horrified befuddlement when *he* bested *her*.

He wanted the fire behind her eyes, and he wanted the taste of her lips, and yes, he wanted her beneath him, around him, on top of him . . . in every possible position, in every single way.

He was going to have to marry her. It was that simple.

"Harry?" she whispered, and his gaze fell to her lips.

"I'm going to kiss you," he said softly, without thinking, without even considering that it might be something he should ask her.

He leaned forward, and in that last second before his lips touched hers, he felt washed clean. This was his new beginning.

He kissed her then, the first touch achingly gentle, nothing more than a brush of his lips against hers. But the contact was electric. Breathtaking, in every literal sense of the word. He drew back, just far enough to see her expression. She was gazing at him with a sense of wonder, her cornflower eyes drinking him in.

She whispered his name.

It was his undoing. He pulled her to him again, this time with all the urgency rushing through his veins. He kissed her hungrily, all caution sliding away, and before he knew it, his hands were in her hair, and the pins were falling out, and all he could think was that he wanted to see her again with her hair down.

Her hair down, floating across her skin. And nothing else.

His body, already tight with desire, grew impossibly hard, and in one wretched burst of sanity, he realized that if he did not set her away from him immediately, he was going to rip the clothes from her body and take her right there in her parents' drawing room.

With the door open.

Good God.

He put his hands on her shoulders, not pushing her back so much as he dragged himself away from her.

For a moment they could do nothing but stare at each other. Her hair was tumbling from her coiffure, and she looked adorably, splendidly mussed. She raised one of her hands to her mouth, her three middle fingers touching her lips in wonderment.

"You kissed me," she whispered.

He nodded.

Her lips moved into a hint of a smile. "I think I kissed you back."

He nodded again. "You did."

She looked as if she might say something more, but then she turned toward the open door. And her hand, which had still been up near her face, moved to her hair.

"You'll want to fix that," he said, his own lips quivering toward amusement.

She nodded. And again, she looked as if she might speak, but she didn't. She gathered all of her hair at the back of her neck, using one hand to keep it all bunched together like a pony's tail, and then stood.

"Will you be here when I return?" she asked.

"Do you wish me to be?"

She nodded.

"I shall be here," he said, even though he would have said the same if she had said no.

She nodded yet again, hurrying over to the door. But before she left, she turned one last time and looked at him. "I—" she started to say, but then she just gave her head a shake.

"You what?" he asked, unable to keep the warm amusement from his voice.

She shrugged helplessly. "I don't know."

He laughed. And she laughed. And it was, he decided as he listened to the fading sound of her footsteps, a perfect moment.

In every possible way.

Harry was still sitting on the sofa a few minutes later when the butler stepped into the room. "Prince Alexei Gomarovsky for Lady Olivia," he intoned. He paused, leaning forward as he glanced about the room. "Lady Olivia?"

Harry started to say that she would be back in a moment, but the prince had already stalked into the room. "She will see me," he was saying to the butler.

But she'll be kissing me, Harry wanted to cackle. It was quite a marvelous feeling, this. He had won. And the prince had lost. And although a gentleman did not kiss and tell, Harry was quite certain that by the time Alexei left Rudland house, he'd know who had won Olivia's favor.

Harry stood, feeling just a little evil for how much he was looking forward to this.

He'd never claimed he was an uncompetitive man.

"You," Prince Alexei said. Actually, it sounded a bit like an accusation.

Harry smiled blandly as he stood in greeting. "Me."

"What are you doing here?"

"Visiting Lady Olivia, of course. What are *you* doing here?"

The prince chose to answer this with curled lip. "Vladimir!" he barked.

Vlad the Impaler (as Harry had taken to calling him), thumped heavily into the room, sparing Harry a surly glance before turning back to his master, who was asking him (in Russian, of course) what he had discovered so far about Harry.

"*Poka nitchevo.*"

Nothing yet.

For which Harry was immensely grateful. It was not well known that he spoke Russian, but it was not well hidden, either. It would not require much investigation to discover that Harry's grandmother had come from an extremely old and noble Russian family.

Which didn't *necessarily* mean that he had learned the language, but Prince Alexei would have to be an idiot not to wonder. And while Alexei was rude, and lecherous, and most probably without any redeeming social qualities, he was not an idiot, regardless of what Harry might have called him in the past.

"Have you had a pleasant morning, Your Highness?" Harry asked in his friendliest voice.

Prince Alexei speared him with a stare, clearly intending that to be his reply in its entirety.

"I am having a lovely morning," Harry continued, sitting back down.

"Where is Lady Olivia?"

"I believe she went upstairs. She had something to . . . ah . . . attend to." Harry made a little motion near his hair, which he decided to let the prince interpret how he wished.

"I will wait for her," Alexei said in his usual clipped tones.

"Please do," Harry said affably, motioning toward the seat across from him. For this he received another furious stare, probably earned, since it wasn't his place to act as host.

Still, it was immensely entertaining.

Alexei flipped his coattails and took a seat, his mouth pressed shut in a firm, unyielding line. He stared straight ahead, *clearly* intending to ignore Harry completely.

Which would have been just fine with Harry, since he had no great desire for interaction with the prince himself, except that he was feeling just a trifle superior, since *he* was the one Olivia had chosen to kiss and *not* the prince, despite Harry's position outside royalty, outside the aristocracy, outside all that Prince Alexei held dear.

And when one combined this with Harry's current directive from the War Office, which one *could* interpret to mean that he ought to do his best to be a thorn in the Russian prince's side, well . . .

Far be it from Harry Valentine to shirk his patriotic duty.

Harry stood up just enough to reach *Miss Butterworth* on the table, then sat back down, humming to himself as he found the page where they'd left off two days earlier, with poor Priscilla losing her family to pox.

Hmm hmm hmmm hmmmmmm hm hm . . .

Alexei shot him a sharp, annoyed glance.

" 'God Save the King,' " Harry informed him. "In case you were wondering."

"I was not."

"God save our gracious King, Long live our noble King, God save the King."

The prince's lips moved, but his teeth remained clenched as he ground out, "I am familiar with the tune."

Harry let his voice rise slightly in volume. "*Send him victorious, Happy and glorious, Long to reign over us: God save the King.*"

"Cease your infernal singing."

"I'm just being patriotic," Harry said, launching right back in with, "*O Lord, our God, arise, Scatter his enemies, And make them fall.*"

"If we were in Russia, I would have you arrested."

"For singing my own country's anthem?" Harry murmured.

"I would need no reason beyond my own indulgence."

Harry considered this, shrugged, and continued: "*Confound their politics, Frustrate their knavish tricks, On Thee our hopes we fix, God save us all.*"

He stopped, deciding that the final verse was not needed. He rather liked ending on "knavish tricks."

"We are an extremely fair-minded people," he said to the prince. "If you'd like to be included in the 'all.'"

Alexei did not answer, but Harry noticed that both of his hands were balled into tight fists.

Harry turned back to *Miss Butterworth*, deciding that he did not mind this part of the espionage trade. He hadn't had this much fun annoying someone since . . .

Ever.

He smiled to himself at that. Even his sister had not been so delightful to torture. And Sebastian never took anything seriously; it was almost impossible to annoy him.

Harry hummed the first few bars of "La Marseillaise," just to gauge the prince's reaction (brilliantly red-faced with fury), then settled in to read. He flipped ahead, quickly deciding that he had no interest in Priscilla Butterworth's formative years, and finally settled on page 144, which appeared to contain madness, disfigurement, insult, and tears—all the requirements for a cracking good novel.

"What are you reading?" Prince Alexei demanded.

Harry looked up absently. "I beg your pardon?"

"What are you reading?" he snapped.

Harry glanced down at the book, and then back up at the prince. "I was under the assumption you did not wish to speak with me."

"I don't. But I am curious. What is that book?"

Harry held the book up so that Prince Alexei could see the front cover. "*Miss Butterworth and the Mad Baron.*"

"Is that what is popular in England?" Alexei sneered.

Harry thought about that. "I don't know. Lady Olivia is reading it. I thought I might do so as well."

"Is that not the book she said she would not like?"

"I believe so, yes," Harry murmured. "Can't say I blame her."

"Read it to me."

Score one to the prince. Harry would have been only slightly more surprised if the prince had come over and kissed him square on the lips.

"I don't think you'll enjoy it," Harry said.

"Do you like it?"

"Not really," Harry replied with a shake of his head. It wasn't precisely true; he very much enjoyed listening to Olivia read it aloud. Or reading it aloud to Olivia. But somehow he doubted the words would share the same magic when shared with Prince Alexei Gomarovsky of Russia.

The prince lifted his chin, tilting his face ever so slightly to the side. It was as if he were posing for a portrait, Harry realized. The man spent his whole life holding himself as if he were posing for a portrait.

Harry might have felt sorry for him if he weren't such an ass.

"If Lady Olivia is reading it," the prince said, "then I want to do so, as well."

Harry paused, digesting that. He supposed he could sacrifice *Miss Butterworth* for the sake of Anglo-Russian relations. He shut the book and held it out.

"No. You read it to me."

Harry decided to obey. It was such a bizarre request he couldn't bring himself to say no. Also, Vladimir had taken two steps in his direction and begun to growl.

"As you wish, Your Highness," Harry said, once again settling down with the book. "I assume you would like to begin at the beginning?"

Alexei answered with a single, regal nod.

Harry turned back to the opening. "*It was a dark and windy night,*" he read, "*and Miss Priscilla Butterworth was certain that at any moment the rain would begin, pouring down from the heavens in sheets and streams, dousing all that lay within her purview.*" He looked up. " 'Purview' is not used correctly, by the way."

"What are these 'sheets'?"

Harry looked back down at the words. "Er, just an expression. Rather like raining cats and dogs."

"This I find stupid."

Harry shrugged. He'd never been fond of the idiom himself. "Shall I continue?"

Again the nod.

"*She was, of course, shielded from the weather in her tiny chamber, but the window*—"

"Mr. Sebastian Grey," came the butler's voice.

Harry looked up from the book with some surprise. "Here to see Lady Olivia?" he asked.

"Here to see you," the butler informed him, sounding vaguely put out by the whole thing.

"Ah. Well. Show him in, then."

Sebastian entered a moment later, already halfway through his sentence: "—told me to find you here. I must say, it's very convenient." He stopped short and blinked a few times, staring at the prince with surprise. "Your Highness," he said, bowing.

"My cousin," Harry said.

"I recall," Alexei said icily. "Clumsy with champagne."

"So dreadful of me," Sebastian said, settling into a chair. "I'm an absolute dunce, you know. Spilled wine on the Chancellor of the Exchequer just last week."

Harry was fairly certain that Sebastian had never had cause to be in the same room as the Chancellor of the Exchequer, much less close enough to hurl wine on his boots.

But this he kept to himself.

"What are you fine gentlemen doing this afternoon?" Sebastian asked.

"Is it afternoon?" Harry inquired.

"Only just."

"Sir Harry is reading to me," the prince said.

Sebastian looked at Harry with unconcealed interest.

"He speaks the truth," Harry said, holding up *Miss Butterworth*.

"*Miss Butterworth and the Mad Baron*," Sebastian said approvingly. "Excellent choice."

"You have read this?" Alexei asked.

"It's not as good as *Miss Davenport and the Dark Marquis*, of course, but worlds better than *Miss Sainsbury and the Mysterious Colonel*."

Harry found himself rendered speechless.

"I'm reading *Miss Truesdale and the Silent Gentleman* right now."

"Silent?" Harry echoed.

"There is a noticeable lack of dialogue," Sebastian confirmed.

"Why are you here?" the prince asked bluntly.

Sebastian turned to him with a sunny expression, as if he did not notice that the prince quite palpably detested him. "Needed to speak with my cousin, of course." He settled into his seat, looking for all the world as if he expected to be there all day. "But it can wait."

Harry had no ready response to that. Neither, apparently, did the prince.

"Go on," Sebastian urged.

Harry had no idea what he was talking about.

"With the book. I thought I might give it a listen. I haven't read it in ages."

"You're going to sit here while I read aloud to you?" Harry asked dubiously.

"And to Prince Alexei," Sebastian reminded him. He closed his eyes. "Don't mind me. It helps to picture the scene."

Harry had not thought that anything could bring about a sense of kinship with the prince, but as they exchanged glances it was clear that both of them thought Sebastian was insane.

Harry cleared his throat, backed up to the beginning of the sentence, and read: "*She was, of course, shielded from the weather in her tiny chamber, but the window casings rattled with such noise that there would be no way she would find slumber this evening.*"

Harry looked up. The prince was listening intently, despite the bored expression on his face. Sebastian was completely enrapt.

Either that or asleep.

"*Huddled on her thin, cold bed, she could not help but recall all of the events that had led her to this bleak spot, on this bleak night. But this, dear reader is not where our story begins.*"

Sebastian's eyes popped open. "You're only on the first page?"

Harry quirked a brow. "Did you expect that His Highness and I had been meeting each evening, conducting secret reading sessions?"

"Give me the book," Sebastian said, reaching out and snatching it from Harry's hands. "You recite dreadfully."

Harry turned to the prince. "I have little training."

"*It was a dark and windy night,*" Sebastian began, and Harry had to admit he did bring a great deal of drama to it. Even Vladimir was leaning forward to listen, and he didn't speak English.

"*—Miss Priscilla Butterworth was certain that at any moment the rain would begin, pouring down*

*from the heavens in sheets and streams, dousing all
that lay within her purview.*"

Dear God, it almost sounded like a sermon. Sebastian had clearly missed his calling.

"'Purview' is not used correctly," Prince Alexei said.

Sebastian looked up, his eyes flashing with irritation. "Of course it is."

Alexei jabbed a finger in Harry's direction. "He said it is not."

"It's not," Harry said with a shrug.

"What's wrong with it?" Sebastian demanded.

"It implies that what she sees is under her power or control."

"How do you know it's not?"

"I don't," Harry admitted, "but she doesn't seem in control of anything else." He looked over at the prince. "Her mother was pecked to death by pigeons."

"That happens," Alexei said with a nod.

Both Harry and Sebastian looked over at him in shock.

"It is not accidental," Alexei demurred.

"I may need to revisit my desire to see Russia," Sebastian said.

"Swift justice," Alexei stated. "It is the only way."

Harry couldn't believe he was asking, but it had to be said. "Pigeons are swift?"

Alexei shrugged, quite possibly the least clipped and precise gesture Harry had seen him make. "Justice is swift. The punishment, not so much."

This was met with silence and a stare, then Sebastian turned back to Harry and said, "How did you know about the pigeons?"

"Olivia told me. She read ahead."

Sebastian's lips pressed together disapprovingly. Harry felt his own part in surprise. It was a singularly odd expression to see on his cousin's face. Harry couldn't recall the last time Sebastian had disapproved of anything.

"May I continue?" Sebastian asked, voice dripping with solicitousness.

The prince gave his nod, and Harry murmured, "Please do," and they all settled in for a listen.

Even Vladimir.

Chapter Seventeen

Olivia's second coiffure of the day took considerably more time to arrange than the first. Sally, still irritated at having been cut off mid-braid, took one look at Olivia's hair and had not gone lightly with the "I told you so's."

And although it went against Olivia's nature to sit meekly and take such abuse, sit meekly she did, since she couldn't very well tell Sally that the only reason her hair was falling from its bun in huge messy chunks was because Sir Harry Valentine had had his hands in it.

"There," Sally declared, inserting the final pin with what Olivia deemed unnecessary force. "This will stay in all week if you're so inclined."

Olivia would not have been surprised had Sally painted her with glue, just to keep every hair in place.

"Don't go out in the rain," Sally warned.

Olivia stood and headed toward the door. "It's not raining."

"It could."

"But it's—" Olivia cut herself off. Good heavens, what was she doing, standing there arguing with her maid? Sir Harry was still downstairs, waiting for her.

Just the thought of him made her giddy.

"Why are you skipping?" Sally asked suspiciously.

Olivia paused, her hand on her doorknob. "I wasn't skipping."

"You were doing"—Sally did a funny little hopping movement—"this."

"I am walking sedately out of the room," Olivia announced. She stepped into the hall. "Very sedately! Like a pallbearer I am . . ." She turned, ascertained that Sally was out of earshot, and dashed down the stairs.

Upon reaching the ground floor, she did opt for a sedate, pallbearish pace, and it was perhaps because of this that her footfalls were so quiet, and she reached the drawing room without making anyone aware of her approach.

What she saw . . .

There were really no words to describe it.

She stood in the doorway, thinking this would be a fine time to create a list titled *Things I Do Not Expect To See in My Drawing Room*, but she was not sure she could come up with anything that topped what she *did* see in her drawing room, which was Sebastian Grey, standing atop a table, reading (with great emotion) from *Miss Butterworth and the Mad Baron*.

If that weren't enough—and it really ought to have

been enough, since what was Sebastian Grey doing at Rudland House, anyway?—Harry and the prince were sitting side by side on the sofa, and neither appeared to have suffered bodily harm at the hands of the other.

That was when Olivia noticed the three housemaids, perched on a settee in the corner, gazing at Sebastian with utter rapture.

One of them might even have had tears in her eyes.

And there was Huntley, standing off to the side, openmouthed, clearly overcome with emotion.

"'*Grandmother! Grandmother!*'" Sebastian was saying, his voice higher pitched than usual. "'*Don't go. I beg of you. Please, please don't leave me here all by myself.*'"

One of the housemaids began to quietly weep.

"*Priscilla stood in front of the great house for several minutes, a small, lonely figure watching her grandmother's hired carriage speed down the lane and disappear from view. She had been left on the doorstep at Fitzgerald Place, deposited like an unwanted bundle.*"

Another housemaid began to sniffle. All three were holding hands.

"*And no one*"—Sebastian's voice dropped to a breathy, dramatic register— "*knew she was there. Her grandmother had not even knocked upon the door to alert her cousins of her arrival.*"

Huntley was shaking his head, his eyes wide with shock and sorrow. It was the most emotion Olivia had ever seen the butler display.

Sebastian closed his eyes and placed one hand on his heart. "*She was but eight years old.*"

He closed the book.

Silence. Utter silence. Olivia looked about the room, realizing no one knew she was there.

And then—

"Bravo!" Huntley was the first to cheer, clapping his hands with great fervor. The maids joined in next, sniffling through their applause. Even Harry and the prince clapped, although Harry's face held more amusement than anything else.

Sebastian opened his eyes, and he was the first to see her. "Lady Olivia," he said with a smile. "How long have you been standing there?"

"Since Priscilla begged her grandmother not to leave."

"She was a heartless woman," Huntley said.

"She did what needed to be done," the prince argued.

"With all due respect, Your Highness—"

Olivia's mouth dropped open. Her butler was arguing with *royalty*?

"—if she had tried a little harder—"

"—she would not have been able to feed the child," the prince interrupted. "Any fool could see that."

"It was heartbreaking," one of the maids said.

"I cried," said another.

The third nodded, apparently unable to speak.

"You are a wonderful speaker," the first one continued.

Sebastian gave the three of them a melting smile. "Thank you for listening," he murmured.

They sighed.

Olivia rubbed her eyes, still trying to make sense of

the scene. She turned to Harry with a searching look. Surely he had an explanation.

"It's really quite a bit better with Sebastian reading it," he told her.

"It really couldn't have been worse," she murmured.

"This should be made into Russian," the prince said. "It would be very much a success."

"I thought you said your literature had a deeper tradition," Olivia said.

"This is very deep," he replied. "As a trench."

"Shall I begin the next chapter?" Sebastian asked.

"Yes!" came the resounding response.

"Oh, please," begged one of the maids.

Olivia still stood unmoving, only her eyes darting back and forth. As splendid as Sebastian's performance was, she was not sure she could sit through an entire chapter of it without laughing. Which would not endear her to . . . well . . . anyone. She certainly didn't want to fall into Huntley's disfavor. Everyone knew he ran the house.

Maybe this meant she could slip away. She still hadn't had breakfast. And she hadn't finished with the newspaper, either. If Sebastian was entertaining all of the guests (and the household staff, too, but Olivia was willing to overlook this), then she could escape to the breakfast room and read.

Or maybe go shopping. She did need a new hat.

She was pondering her options when Vladimir suddenly spoke. In Russian, of course.

"He says you should have been on the stage," Alexei said to Sebastian.

Sebastian gave a pleased smile and bowed in Vladimir's direction. "*Spasibo*," he said, thanking him.

"You speak Russian?" the prince said, turning sharply in Sebastian's direction.

"Only the very basics," Sebastian quickly replied. "I can say thank you in fourteen languages. Alas, please in but twelve."

"Really?" Olivia asked, far more interested in this than the *Miss Butterworth* recitation. "Which languages?"

"I also find it useful to know 'I need a drink,'" Sebastian said to the prince.

"*Da*," he said approvingly. "In Russian, it is *Ya nuzhdayus v napitkyeh*."

"*Spasibo*," Sebastian replied.

"No, really," Olivia said, even though no one was paying her any attention. "I want to know which languages."

"Does anyone know what time it is?" Harry asked.

"There's a clock on the mantel," Olivia said without looking at him. "Mr. Grey," she persisted.

"One moment," he said to her, before turning back to the prince. "I am very curious about your servant," he said. "He does not speak English, does he? How did he follow the recitation?"

The prince and Vladimir shared a quick conversation in Russian, and then the prince turned back to Sebastian and said, "He says that he can follow the emotion in your voice."

Sebastian looked delighted.

"And also he knows a few words," the prince added.

"Still," Sebastian murmured.

"Portuguese," Olivia said, wondering if anyone planned to pay her any attention that afternoon. "You must have learned some Portuguese in the army. How do you say 'thank you' in Portuguese?"

"*Obrigado*," Harry said.

She turned to him with some surprise.

He gave a little shrug. "I learned a bit, too."

"*Obrigado*," she repeated.

"*Obrigada* for you," he said. "Not that you are likely to be mistaken for a man."

It was not the most resounding of compliments, but she decided to take it, nonetheless.

"What is the strangest language you can thank people in?" she asked Sebastian.

He thought about that for a moment, then said, "*Köszönöm*."

She looked at him expectantly.

"Magyar," he said, and at her blank expression added, "It's spoken in parts of Hungary."

"Why do you know that?"

"I have no idea," he said.

"It was a woman," the prince said knowingly. "If you don't remember, it was a woman."

Olivia decided it was not worth the effort to feel insulted for that.

"*Kiitos*," Prince Alexei said, giving Sebastian a *top that* sort of look, before adding, "Finnish."

"My heartfelt thanks to you," Sebastian said. "My repertoire now numbers fifteen."

Olivia thought about saying *merci*, but decided she'd only look desperate.

"What can you do?" the prince asked Harry.

"Yes, Harry," Sebastian said. "What can you do?"

Harry gave his cousin a cool look, then answered, "I'm afraid I've got nothing out of the ordinary."

Olivia had the feeling that there had been some sort of unspoken conversation between the two cousins, but she was not given the opportunity to consider it further, because Sebastian turned back to the prince and asked, "How does one say 'please' in Finnish?"

"*Ole hyvä*."

"Excellent." He nodded once, apparently tucking the small piece of knowledge into the back of his mind. "One never knows when one might come across a lovely lady from Finland."

Olivia was wondering how she might possibly regain control of her drawing room, when she heard a knock at the front door. Huntley immediately excused himself to go answer it.

He returned moments later with a young man she had never met. Although . . . a little taller than average, dark brown hair . . . He was almost certainly—

"Mr. Edward Valentine," Huntley announced. He raised his brows. "Here to see Sir Harry Valentine."

"Edward," Harry said immediately, standing up. "Is everything all right?"

"Yes, of course," Edward replied, looking awkwardly about the room. He clearly had not expected so many people. He handed Harry an envelope. "This came for you. I was told it was urgent."

Harry took the envelope and placed it in his coat pocket, then introduced his brother to everyone in the room, even the three housemaids, who were still sitting in a neat little row on the settee.

"Why is Seb standing on a table?" Edward asked.

"Entertaining the troops," Sebastian replied, saluting him.

"Sebastian was reading from *Miss Butterworth and the Mad Baron*," Harry explained.

"Oh," Edward exclaimed, his face lighting with enthusiasm for the first time since he'd entered the room. "I've read that."

"Did you like it?" Sebastian asked.

"Brilliant. Great fun. The writing is a bit spotty in places, but the story is fantastic."

Sebastian seemed to find that very interesting. "Fantastic good, or fantastic like fantasy?"

"A bit of both, I suppose," Edward replied. He looked about the room. "Do you mind if I join you?"

Olivia opened her mouth to say, "Of course not," but she was beaten to the punch by Sebastian, Harry, *and* the prince.

Really, whose home *was* this?

Edward looked over at her—it was interesting, he looked nothing like Harry save for the coloring, which was identical—and said, "Er, do you plan to come in, Lady Olivia?"

She realized that she was still standing near the doorway. All the rest of the gentlemen were sitting down, but it was unlikely that Edward, who had only just met her, would do so while she still stood.

"Actually, I thought I might go out to the garden," she said, her voice trailing off when she realized that no one was protesting her departure. "Or I'll sit down."

She found a seat off to the side, not so far from the three maids, who gave her nervous looks.

"Please," she said to them, "stay. I couldn't possibly ask you to miss the rest of the performance."

They thanked her with such devotion that Olivia could only wonder how she would explain this to her mother. If Sebastian came by each afternoon to read (for surely he would not attempt the entire novel in one swoop), and the maids came to listen, that would be quite a few fireplaces that did not get cleaned out.

"Chapter Two," Sebastian announced. A reverent hush fell over the room, prompting a most irreverent giggle from Olivia.

The prince shot her a dirty look, as did Vladimir and Huntley.

"Sorry," she mumbled, and placed her hands primly in her lap. It was time, apparently, to be on her best behavior.

Satisfying Endings for Miss Butterworth
By Olivia Bevelstoke

The baron is quite sane, but Priscilla is mad!
Reemergence of pox. New, deadlier strain.
Priscilla leaves the baron and devotes her life
to the care and feeding of carrier pigeons.
The baron eats the pigeons.
The baron eats her.

The last one would be a bit of a stretch, but there was no reason why the baron could not have gone mad while exploring in the darkest jungle, where he fell in with a society of cannibals.

It could happen.

She looked over at Harry, trying to see what he

thought of the performance. But he looked distracted; his eyes were narrowed in thought but not focused on Sebastian. And his fingers were drumming along the arm of the sofa—a sure sign of a wandering mind.

Was he thinking of their kiss? She hoped not. He did not look remotely transported into rapturous bliss.

Good heavens, she was beginning to sound like Priscilla Butterworth.

Gad.

Several pages into Chapter Two, Harry decided it would not be impolite to quietly excuse himself so that he could read the letter Edward had brought over, presumably from the War Office. He glanced over at Olivia before he left the room, but she was seemingly lost in her own thoughts, staring straight ahead at a blank spot on the wall.

Her lips were moving, too. Not much, but he tended to notice the finer details of her lips.

Edward, too, seemed well situated. He was kitty-corner to the prince, watching Sebastian with a great, big loopy smile on his face. Harry had never seen his brother smile like this before. He laughed, even, when Sebastian mimicked a particularly annoying character. Harry *knew* he'd never heard his brother laugh.

Once in the hall, he tore open the envelope and pulled out a single sheet of paper. Apparently, Prince Alexei was no longer suspected of wrongdoing. Harry was to stop his assignment at once. There was no explanation as to *why* the prince was no longer of interest to the War Office, nothing saying how they had come to this determination. Just an order to stop. No please, no thank you.

In any language.

Harry shook his head. Couldn't someone have figured this out before sending him on such a ridiculous assignment? This was why he stuck to translations. This sort of thing drove him batty.

"Harry?"

He looked up. Olivia had slipped out of the drawing room and was walking toward him, her eyes soft with concern.

"Not bad news, I hope," she said.

He shook his head. "Just unexpected." He folded up the paper and placed it back into his pocket. He could dispose of it later, when he was back home.

"I had to leave," she said, her lips pressed together in what he imagined was her attempt not to smile. She motioned with her head to the open door of the drawing room, through which they could hear snatches of *Miss Butterworth*.

"Sebastian is that bad, eh?"

"No," she said, sounding quite amazed. "He's really quite good. That's the problem. The *book* is so bad, but no one seems to realize it. They're all staring at him like he's Edmund Kean, performing Hamlet. I just couldn't keep a straight face any longer."

"I'm impressed you managed for as long as you did."

"And the prince," she added, shaking her head with disbelief. "He's positively entranced. I can't believe it. I would never have thought he'd like this sort of thing."

The prince, Harry thought. Now there was a relief. He wouldn't have to deal with the bastard ever again.

He wouldn't have to follow him, he wouldn't have to speak with him . . . Life would return to normal. It would be lovely.

Except . . .

Olivia.

He watched her as she tiptoed back to the doorway and peeked in. Her movements were a little blocky, and for a moment he thought she might trip. She wasn't clumsy, not exactly. But she moved in her own inimitable way, and he realized he could watch her for hours, do nothing but sit and stare at the way her hands carried out mundane tasks. He could watch her face, enjoying every play of emotion, every movement of her brow, of her lips.

She was so beautiful it made his teeth ache.

He made a mental note not to attempt poetry.

She let out a little, "Oh!" and leaned in farther.

He took a step forward and murmured in her ear, "For someone who is not interested, you're quite interested."

She hushed him, then gave him a little shove so that he wasn't crowding her.

"What's going on?" he asked.

Her eyes widened, and her face took on an expression of delight. "Your cousin is performing a death scene. Your brother has got up on the table, too."

"Edward?" he asked doubtfully.

She nodded, taking another peek. "I can't tell who is killing whom—Oh, never mind. Edward's dead."

That was quick.

"Oh, wait—" She craned her neck. "No, he's dead. Sorry." She turned. Smiled at him.

He felt it everywhere.

"He was rather good at it," she murmured. "I think he takes after your cousin."

He wanted to kiss her again.

"Clutched his heart"—she clutched hers—"groaned, and then, when it was all done, he let out one last shudder, and it wasn't really all done." She grinned again. "And then it was done."

He had to kiss her. Now.

"What's that room over there?" he asked, pointing to a door.

"My father's office, why?"

"What about that one?"

"Music room. We never use it."

He grabbed her hand. They were using it now.

Chapter Eighteen

Olivia barely had time to catch her breath before she found herself in Rudland House's small music room with the door closed behind her. And after that, she managed only the "*Wh*" in *What are you doing?* before it was perfectly clear what he was doing.

His hands were back in her hair, and her back was to the wall, and he was kissing her. Madly, passionately, bone-meltingly kissing her.

"Harry!" she gasped, when his lips left hers to nibble on her ear.

"I can't help it," he said, his words ticklish against her skin. She could hear the smile in his voice. He sounded happy.

She *felt* happy. And more.

"You were there," he said, one of his hands moving down her side, around her back. "You were there, and I had to kiss you, and that's all there was to it."

Forget the flowery words of Miss Butterworth's mad baron. That was the most romantic thing Olivia had ever heard.

"You exist," he said, his voice deepening with desire. "Ergo, I need you."

No, *that* was the most romantic thing.

And then he whispered something in her ear. Something about lips and hands, and the heat of her body, and she had to wonder if maybe *that* was the most romantic of all.

She had been desired by men before. Some had even claimed they loved her. But this—this was different. There was an urgency in his body, in his breath, in the pulse of his blood under his skin. He wanted her. He *needed* her. It went beyond words, beyond anything he might try to explain. But it was something she understood, something she felt deep within.

It made her feel deliciously powerful. And at the same time powerless, because whatever it was that was racing through him, it was spreading to her as well, causing a quickness inside in her veins, an inability to draw breath. It felt as if her entire body were rushing through her, moving from the inside out until she could do nothing but touch him. She had to grab him, squeeze him. She needed him close, and so she reached around with her hands, entwining herself around his neck.

"Harry," she whispered, and she heard the delight in her voice. This moment, this *kiss*—it was everything she'd been waiting for.

It was everything she wanted.

And a million things more.

His hands slid down her back, pulling her from the

wall, and they turned and swirled across the carpet until they both fell over the arm of the sofa. He landed atop her, the warm, solid weight of his body pinning her to the cushions. It should have been the strangest sensation. It should have been terrifying—her body compressed, her movement diminished. But instead it just felt like the most normal, natural thing in the world, that she would be on her back, and this man on top of her, hot, powerful, and *hers*.

"Olivia," he whispered, his mouth trailing fire down the side of her neck. She arched beneath him, her pulse jumping when his lips found the thin, sensitive skin over her collarbone. He was moving lower, lower, to the wispy, lacy edge of her bodice. And at the same time his hands were moving higher, sliding along her side, catching her in the cradle of his thumb and forefinger until he reached her breast.

She gasped with shock. His hand had slid around to her front, and now he was cupping her through the thin muslin of her dress. She moaned his name, and then she moaned something else, something unintelligible and completely without thought or meaning.

"You're so . . . good," he groaned. He squeezed her gently, closing his eyes as his entire body shook with desire. "So good."

She grinned. Right there in the middle of her seduction, she grinned. She loved that he didn't call her beautiful or pretty or radiant. She loved that he was so out of his mind for her that "good" was the most complicated word he could manage.

"I want to touch you," he whispered, his lips moving against her cheek as he spoke. "I want to feel you . . . on my skin . . . in my hand." His fingers stole upward until they reached the edge of her dress, and he pulled, tugged gently, and then not so gently, until the fabric slid over her shoulder, and then down—down more—until she was bared to him.

She didn't feel wanton. She didn't feel wicked. She just felt right. Like herself.

His breath—hard and fast—was the only sound. The air around them seemed to crackle with urgency, and then she didn't just hear his breath, she felt it on her skin, cool at first, and then hot, as his mouth grew closer.

And then he was kissing her. She nearly screamed—from the shock of it, then from the fire of it, and the curls of pleasure it brought forth from within. "Harry," she gasped, and now she did feel wanton. She felt wicked, utterly and thoroughly. His head was at her breast, and all she could seem to do was sink her fingers into his hair, not sure whether she was trying to pull him away or bind him to her forever.

His hand moved to her leg, squeezing, stroking, moving higher, and then—

"What was that?" Olivia shot up into a sitting position, knocking Harry right off her. There had been a tremendous crash. It had sounded like wood splintering and glass breaking, and there had definitely been a scream.

Harry sat on the floor, trying to catch his breath. He looked at her, his eyes still hot, and she realized her dress was awry. She yanked it up, quickly, and crossed her arms protectively over her, each hand clutching the opposite shoulder. It wasn't that she feared him, but after that noise she was terrified that anyone might come running in.

"What happened?" she asked.

He was shaking his head as he rose to his feet. "It came from the drawing room."

"Are you sure?"

He nodded, and her first thought was relief, although she had no idea why. Her second thought went in quite the opposite direction. If she'd heard the crash, then other people in the house would have heard it, too. And if this other person happened to be upstairs, as her mother was, she might come running down to investigate. And if she did that, she might enter the wrong room.

Finding her daughter in a state of considerable *dishabille*.

But in truth her mother would probably head first to the drawing room. The door would be open, and it was the first room one came across at the bottom of the stairs. But if she did that, she would find three gentlemen, a hulking bodyguard, the butler, three housemaids . . .

And no Olivia.

She jumped to her feet, immediately awash in panic. "My hair!"

"—is remarkably intact," he finished for her.

She looked at him with patent disbelief.

"No, really," he said, looking somewhat astonished himself. "It's really almost" —he moved his hands near his head as if to indicate . . . *some*thing— "the same."

She hurried over to the mirror over the fireplace and stood on her tiptoes. "Oh my goodness," she said. Sally had outdone herself. Barely a lock was out of place, and she could have sworn that Harry had pulled the whole mass of it down.

Olivia pulled two hairpins out, repositioned and fastened them, then stood back to inspect her reflection. Aside from her flushed cheeks, she looked entirely respectable. And really, any number of things could have caused that. Plague, even, although she probably needed to start coming up with a new excuse.

She looked over at Harry. "Do I look presentable?"

He nodded. But then he said, "Sebastian will know."

Her mouth opened in shock. "What? How?"

Harry gave a one shouldered shrug. There was something elementally male about the gesture, as if to say—*a woman might answer your question in exhaustive detail, but this will do for me.*

"How will he know?" Olivia repeated.

He gave her another one of those looks. "He just will. But don't worry, he won't say anything."

Olivia looked down at herself. "Do you think the prince will know?"

"What does it matter if the prince knows?" Harry returned, a little snappishly.

"I have my—" She had been about to say that she had her reputation to consider. "Are you jealous?"

He looked at her as if she was slightly deranged. "Of course I'm jealous."

Her legs started to feel rather liquid, and she sighed. "Really?"

He shook his head, clearly impatient with her sudden dreaminess. "Tell everyone I've gone home."

She blinked, unsure of what he was talking about.

"You don't want everyone to know what we've been doing in here, do you?"

"Er, no." Said perhaps a little haltingly, since it wasn't as if she was ashamed. Because she wasn't. But she did wish for her activities to remain private.

He walked over to the window. "Tell them you saw me off ten minutes ago. You can say that I had matters to attend to at home."

"You're going out the window?"

He already had one leg over the sill. "Do you have any better ideas?"

She might, if he gave her a few moments to think about it. "There's a drop," she pointed out. "It's—"

"Don't forget to shut the window after me." And he was gone, hopping right out of sight. Olivia rushed over and peered out. Actually, there hadn't been much of a drop at all. Certainly no more than Priscilla Butterworth had had to deal with when she'd hung out the ground-floor window, and heaven knew Olivia had mocked her for her silliness.

She started to ask Harry if he was all right, but he was already making his way up and over the wall that separated their properties, clearly uninjured by the drop.

And besides, Olivia didn't have time for any more conversation. She could hear someone coming down the stairs, so she hurried out, just in time to reach the front of the hall at the same time as her mother.

"Did someone scream?" Lady Rudland asked. "What is going on?"

"I have no idea," Olivia replied. "I was in the washroom. There is a bit of a performance—"

"A performance?"

"In the drawing room."

"What on earth are you talking about? And why" —her mother reached out and plucked something from her hair—"is there a feather in your hair?"

"I cannot explain," Olivia said, taking the feather in her hands for later disposal. It must have popped out through the upholstery on one of the pillows. They were all stuffed with feathers, although Olivia had always thought that the quills were removed first.

She was saved from further comment by Huntley, who had come into the hall, looking terribly embarrassed. "My lady," he said, bowing toward Olivia's mother. "There has been an accident."

Olivia scooted around Huntley, hurrying into the drawing room. Sebastian was on the floor, his arm twisted at an unnatural angle. Behind him a vase appeared to have tipped over, leaving shattered glass, cut flowers, and water all over the floor.

"Oh my heavens!" she exclaimed. "What happened?"

"I think he broke his arm," Edward Valentine told her.

"Where's Harry?" Sebastian gasped. His teeth were grit together, and he was sweating from the pain.

"He went home," Olivia told him. "What happened?"

"It was part of the performance," Edward explained. "Miss Butterworth was on a cliff, and—"

"Who is Miss Butterworth?" Olivia's mother asked from the doorway.

"I'll explain later," Olivia promised. That idiotic novel was going to be the death of someone. She turned back to Sebastian. "Mr. Grey, I think we should call for a surgeon."

"Vladimir will fix it," Prince Alexei announced.

Sebastian looked up at Olivia, eyes wide with alarm.

"Mother," Olivia called out, motioning her to come over. "I think we need the surgeon."

"Vladimir!" the prince barked, letting loose a stream of Russian.

"Don't let him touch me," Sebastian hissed.

"Do not think that you shall go to bed tonight without explaining every last detail," Lady Rudland murmured in Olivia's ear.

Olivia gave a nod, grateful that she'd have a bit of time to come up with a plausible explanation. She had a feeling that nothing could top the truth, however. Or at least the truth with a few carefully selected deletions. She was very grateful that Huntley had got caught up in the drama of the afternoon; that, at least, would explain why Lady Rudland had not been informed of her daughter's many visitors.

"Get Harry," Sebastian said to Edward. "Now."

The young man excused himself and ran off with alacrity.

"This is what Vladimir does," Prince Alexei said, shoving his way close. Vladimir was right next to him, looking down at Sebastian with narrowed, assessing eyes.

"He mends broken arms?" Olivia asked, looking over at him with considerable doubt.

"He does many things," Alexei replied.

"Your Highness," Lady Rudland murmured, bobbing a quick curtsy. He was, after all, royalty, and protocol must be observed, regardless of twisted limbs.

"*Pereloma ruki u nevo nyet,*" Vladimir said.

"He says the arm is not broken," Alexei said, grabbing hold of Sebastian's shoulder. Sebastian yelled out with such force that Olivia flinched.

Vladimir said something more, to which Alexei murmured a response that was clearly a question. Vladimir gave a nod, and then, before anyone had a chance to react, both men caught hold of Sebastian, Alexei around his middle and Vladimir at his arm, a bit above the elbow. Vladimir gave a pull and a twist—or maybe it was a twist and a pull. There was a horrific sound of bone on—good Lord, Olivia didn't know what the bone was on, but it must have been something hideous, because Sebastian let out a blood-curdling cry.

Olivia thought she might be sick.

"Better?" Prince Alexei asked, looking down on his shuddering patient.

Sebastian looked too stunned to speak.

"He is better," Alexei said confidently. He then said to Sebastian, "It will hurt for several days. Maybe longer. You . . . ah . . . how do you say it?"

"Dislocated," Sebastian whimpered, tentatively moving his fingers.

"*Da*. The shoulder."

Olivia shifted her weight to get a better look past Vladimir, who was blocking her view. Sebastian looked *awful*. His entire body was shaking, he seemed to be breathing too rapidly, and his skin . . .

"Do you think he looks a bit green?" she asked, of no one in particular.

Beside her, Alexei nodded. Her mother stepped forward, too, saying, "Perhaps we should—oh!"

Sebastian's eyes had rolled back, and the next *thunk* they heard was his head hitting the carpet.

Harry was at the bottom of Rudland House's front steps when he heard the scream. It was cry of pain, that he knew instantly, and it sounded like a woman.

Olivia.

His heart leaped with terror, and without a word to Edward, he charged up the steps and into the front hall. He didn't knock, he didn't even stop running until he skidded into the drawing room, barely able to breathe.

"What the hell happened here?" he gasped. Olivia looked fine. In perfect health, actually. She was standing next to the prince, who was speaking in Russian to Vladimir, who was on his knees, tending to . . . Sebastian?

Harry looked at his cousin with some concern. He was sitting up, propped against the leg of a chair. His skin was pasty and he was clutching his arm.

The butler was fanning him with the splayed-open copy of *Miss Butterworth and the Mad Baron.*

"Seb?" Harry asked.

Sebastian held up a hand, shaking his head, which Harry took to mean, *Don't mind me.*

So he didn't. "Are you all right?" he asked Olivia. His heart was still racing with terror that she'd been hurt. "I heard a woman scream."

"Ah, that would have been me," Sebastian said.

Harry looked down on his cousin, face frozen in disbelief. "*You* made that noise?"

"It *hurt*," Sebastian bit off.

Harry fought not to laugh. "You scream like a leettle girl."

Sebastian glared at him. "Is there any reason you're saying that with a German accent?"

"None whatsoever," Harry replied, little snorts of barely suppressed laughter popping from his mouth.

"Er, Sir Harry," came Olivia's voice behind him.

He turned, took one look at her and burst out laughing. For no reason except that he'd been holding it in, and when he saw her he simply couldn't do it any longer. She seemed to have that effect on many of his emotions lately. And Harry was coming to realize this wasn't a bad thing at all.

Olivia, however, was not laughing. "May I introduce my mother," she said weakly, motioning to the older woman next to her.

He sobered instantly. "I'm so sorry, Lady Rudland. I did not see you there."

"It was quite a scream," she said dryly. Harry had only seen her up to now from across a room, but up close he could see that she did indeed look quite like her daughter. Her hair had some silver in it, and there were faint lines on her face, but the features were remarkably similar. If Lady Rudland was any indication, Olivia's beauty would not dim.

"Mother," Olivia said, "this is Sir Harry Valentine. He has let the house to the south."

"Yes, I'd heard," Lady Rudland said. "I am pleased to finally meet you."

Harry could not tell if he heard a warning in her voice. *I know you have been cavorting with my daughter?*

Or perhaps: *Don't think we will ever let you near her again.*

Or maybe he was imagining the whole thing.

"What happened to Sebastian?" Harry asked.

"He dislocated his shoulder," Olivia explained. "Vladimir fixed it."

Harry didn't know whether to be worried or impressed. "Vladimir?"

"Da," Vladimir said proudly.

"It was . . . really . . . quite . . ." Olivia searched for words. "Remarkable," she finally decided.

"I might have described it differently," Sebastian put in.

"You were very brave," she said, giving him a motherly nod.

"He has done this many times," Alexei said, motioning to Vladimir. He looked down at Sebastian, who was still sitting on the floor, and said, "You will need—" He made a motion with his hand, then looked at Olivia. "It is for the pain."

"Laudanum?"

"Yes. That is it."

"I have some at home," Harry confirmed. He put his hand on Sebastian's shoulder.

"Aaaaaah!"

"Oh, sorry. Meant to grab your other shoulder." Harry looked up at the rest of the room's inhabitants, most of whom were looking at him as if he were a criminal. "I was trying to be reassuring. You know, pat on the shoulder and all that."

"Perhaps we should take Seb back," Edward suggested.

Harry nodded, helping his cousin to his feet. "You'll stay with us for a few days?"

Sebastian nodded gratefully. As he headed for the door, he turned to Vladimir and said, "*Spasibo*."

Vladimir smiled proudly and said that it was an honor to help such a great man.

The prince translated, then added, "I must agree. Your performance was magnificent."

Harry exchanged an amused glance with Olivia. He couldn't help it.

But Alexei was not done. "It would be my honor if you would be a guest at the party next week. It is to be at my cousin's home. The ambassador. A celebration of Russian culture." He looked back to the rest of the crowd. "You are all invited, of course." He turned to Harry, and their eyes met. He shrugged, as if to say— *even you*.

Harry nodded his reply. It seemed he wasn't to be done with the Russian prince just yet. If Olivia was going, he was going. That was all there was to it.

Lady Rudland thanked the prince for his kind invitation, then turned to Harry and said, "I think Mr. Grey needs to lie down."

"Of course," Harry murmured. He said his goodbyes and helped Sebastian to the drawing-room door. Olivia walked alongside, and when they reached the front door, she said, "Will you let me know how he is doing?"

He flashed her a very small, very secret smile. "Be at your window at six in the evening."

He should have left right then. There were too many people milling about, and Sebastian was clearly in pain, but he could not resist one last look at her face.

And in that moment he finally understood what people meant when they said someone's eyes lit up.

Because when he told her to be at her window at six, she smiled. And when he looked into her eyes, it was as if the whole world was bathed in a soft, happy glow, and all of it, every little bit of good and fun and happiness—it all came from her. From this one woman, standing next to him at her front door in Mayfair.

And that was when he knew. It had happened. It had happened right there, in London.

Harry Valentine had fallen in love.

Chapter Nineteen

That evening, promptly at six, Olivia opened her window, leaned on the sill, and looked out.

And there was Harry, leaning on his windowsill, gazing up. He looked utterly delicious, his lips curved into the perfect smile, a little bit boyish, a little bit sly. She liked him like this, happy and relaxed. His dark hair was no longer neatly styled, and she was struck by a sudden urge to touch it, to run her fingers through, to muss it up even more.

Good heavens, she must be in love.

It should have been a revelation. She should have been struck down with the shock of it. But instead she just felt lovely. Perfectly, fabulously wonderful.

Love. *Love*. LOVE. She tested the word out in her mind, in different pitches and tones. They all sounded splendid.

Really, the emotion had a great deal to recommend it.

"Good evening," she said, a silly grin on her face.

"Good evening to you."

"Have you been waiting long?"

"Just a moment or two. You're quite fantastically prompt."

"I don't believe in keeping people waiting," she said. She leaned forward, and *almost* had enough courage to lick her lips. "Unless they deserve punishment."

That seemed to intrigue him. He edged farther out his window, too, until they were both hanging just a little bit too far out. He looked as if he were going to speak, but then some devil must have overtaken him, because he burst out laughing.

And then she did, too.

And they were both just . . . giggling, really, until they had tears in their eyes.

"Oh my," Olivia gasped. "Do you think that perhaps . . . sometime . . . we ought to have some sort of proper meeting?"

He wiped his eyes. "Proper?"

"Like at a dance."

"We've already danced," he told her.

"Only once, and you didn't like me then."

"You didn't like me, either," he reminded her.

"You didn't like me *more*."

He thought about that, then nodded. "That's true."

Olivia winced. "I was rather horrid, wasn't I?"

"Well, yes," he admitted, rather quickly, too.

"You're not supposed to *agree* with me."

He grinned. "It's good that you can be horrid when necessary. It's a useful skill."

She leaned on her elbow, settling her chin onto her hand. "Funny, my brothers never seemed to think so."

"Brothers are like that."

"Were you?"

"Me? Never. I encouraged it, actually. The more horridly my sister behaved, the more opportunity there was to watch her get in a great deal of trouble."

"You're very crafty," she murmured.

He answered with a shrug.

"I'm still curious," she said, refusing to allow a change of topic. "How is it useful to know how to be horrid?"

"That is a very good question," he said solemnly.

"You haven't an answer, have you?"

"I have not," he admitted.

"I could be an actress," she suggested.

"And lose your respectability?"

"A spy, then."

"Even worse," he said, with great firmness

"You don't think I could be a spy?" She was being an utter flirt, but she was having far too much fun to hold back. "Surely England could have used someone like me. I should have had the war tidied up in no time."

"Of that I have no doubt," he said, and strangely enough, he sounded as if he might have meant it.

But something made her pull back. She was being too playful, about a topic that wanted no humor. "I should not joke about such things," she said.

"It's all right," he said. "Sometimes one has to."

She wondered what he had seen, what he had done. He'd been in the army for many years. It could not all have been regiment parades and girls swooning over uniforms. He would have fought. Marched. Killed.

It was almost impossible to imagine. He rode superbly, and after this afternoon, she had firsthand knowledge of his strength and power, but still, she somehow saw him as more cerebral than athletic. Perhaps it was all those afternoons she'd seen him bent over papers at his desk, his quill moving swiftly across the page.

"What do you do in there?" she asked.

"What?"

She motioned toward him. "In your office. You spend a great deal of time at your desk."

He hesitated, then said, "This and that. Translations, mostly."

"Translations?" Her mouth opened with surprise. "Really?"

He shifted position, looking, for the first time that evening, a little bit uncomfortable. "I told you I spoke French."

"I had no idea you did so so well."

He shrugged modestly. "I was on the Continent for many years."

Translations. Good heavens, he was even more clever than she'd thought. She hoped she could keep up. She thought she could; she liked to think she was a great deal more intelligent than most people considered her. It was because she didn't feign interest in every topic that crossed her path. And she didn't bother to pursue topics or activities at which she had no aptitude.

It was how any sensible person would behave.

In her opinion.

"Is it very different," she asked, "translating?"

He cocked his head to the side.

"As opposed to just speaking," she clarified. "I can't manage anything but English, so I really wouldn't know."

"It's quite different," he confirmed. "I don't really know how to explain it. One is . . . unconscious. The other almost mathematical."

"Mathematical?"

He almost looked sheepish. "I told you I didn't know how to explain it."

"No," she said thoughtfully, "I think it might make sense. You have to fit together pieces of a puzzle."

"It's a bit like that."

"I like puzzles." She paused for a moment, then added, "Oh, but I hate maths."

"It's the same thing," he told her.

"No. It's not."

"If you can say that you must have had very poor teachers."

"*That* goes without saying. I ran off five governesses, if you recall."

He smiled at her, slow and warm, and she tingled inside. If someone had told her just this morning that talk of maths and puzzles would make her shiver with delight, she'd have laughed her head right off. But now, looking at him, all she wanted was to reach out, to float across the space between them, and settle into his arms.

This was madness.

And bliss.

"I should let you go," he said.

"Where?" She sighed.

He chuckled. "Wherever you need to go."

To you, she wanted to say. Instead she placed her hand on her window, getting ready to pull it shut. "Shall we meet at the same time tomorrow evening?"

He bowed, and her breath caught. There was something so graceful about his movements, almost as if he were a medieval courtier, and she, his princess in a tower.

"It would be my honor," he said.

That night, when Olivia crawled into bed, she was still smiling.

Yes, love had a great deal to recommend it.

A week later, Harry was sitting at his desk, staring at a blank piece of paper.

Not that he had any intention of writing anything down. But he tended to do his best thinking at his desk, with a piece of paper laid squarely in the middle of his blotter. And so, after he'd lain in his bed, making a remarkably thorough study of his ceiling as he tried in vain to figure out the best way to propose marriage to Olivia, he'd moved here, hoping for inspiration.

It was not striking.

"Harry?"

He looked up, grateful for the interruption. It was Edward, standing in the doorway.

"You'd asked me to remind you when it was time to begin getting ready," Edward said.

Harry nodded and thanked him. It had been a week since that strange and wonderful afternoon at Rudland House. Sebastian had all but moved in, having declared Harry's home far more comfortable (and with considerably better food) than his own. Edward was spending more time at home, too, and hadn't come home drunk even once. And Harry hadn't had to give one bit of serious thought to Prince Alexei Ivanovich Gomarovsky.

Well, until now. There was that celebration of Russian culture he was committed to attend that evening. But Harry was actually looking forward to it. He liked Russian culture. And the food. He hadn't had decent Russian food since his grandmother had been alive to scream at the cooks in the Valentine kitchen. He supposed it was unlikely that there would be caviar, but he was hoping, nonetheless.

And of course Olivia would be there.

He was going to ask her to marry him. Tomorrow. He hadn't yet worked out the details, but he refused to wait any longer. The past week had been bliss and torture, all rolled up into one sunny blond, blue-eyed woman.

She had to have guessed his intentions. He'd been quite obviously courting her all week—all the proper things, like walks in the park and interviews with her family. And many of the improper ones as well— stolen kisses and midnight conversations through open windows.

He was in love. He'd long since recognized it. All that remained was for him to propose.

And for her to accept, but he thought she would. She hadn't said she loved him, but she wouldn't have done, would she? It was up to the gentleman to declare himself first, and he had not yet done so.

He was just waiting for the right moment. They needed to be alone. It ought to be in the daytime; he wanted to be able to see her face clearly, to imprint every play of emotion into his memory. He would declare his love for her and ask her to marry him. And then he'd kiss her senseless. Maybe kiss himself senseless as well.

Who knew he was such a romantic?

Harry chuckled to himself as he got up and wandered over to his window. Olivia's curtains were open, and so was her window. Curious, he pushed his own up and popped his head out into the warm spring air. He waited for a moment, in case she'd heard his window going up, then whistled.

Within seconds she appeared, bright-eyed and cheerful. "Good afternoon!" she called out.

"Were you waiting for me?" he asked.

"Of course not. But if I was to be in my room, I saw no reason not to leave the window open." She leaned on the ledge, and smiled down at him. "It's almost time to get ready."

"What are you wearing?" Good God, he sounded like one of her gossipy friends. But he didn't care. It was simply too pleasant to gaze up at her to worry over such things.

"My mother was pressing for red velvet, but I wanted something you could see."

It was ridiculous how much he loved that she eschewed red and green for his benefit.

"Blue, perhaps?" she mused.

"You do look lovely in blue."

"You're very complimentary this afternoon."

He shrugged, still sporting what he was sure must be an exceedingly silly grin. "I'm in an exceedingly good mood."

"Even though you must spend the evening with Prince Alexei?"

"He will have three hundred guests. Ergo, no time for me."

She chuckled. "I thought you were beginning to like him better."

Harry supposed that he was. He still thought the prince was a bit of an ass, but he *had* fixed Sebastian's shoulder. Or to be more precise, he'd had his manservant do so. Still, it amounted to the same thing.

And, more important, he had finally accepted defeat and ceased calling upon Olivia.

Unfortunately for Harry, the prince's infatuation with Olivia had been replaced with a friendly devotion toward Sebastian. Prince Alexei had decided that Seb must be his new best friend and had been calling daily to check on his recuperation. Harry made a point of being in his office during such visits and had been regaling Olivia with the details, as told to him by Sebastian. All in all, it had been quite amusing, and all the more proof that Prince Alexei was mostly harmless.

"Oh, there's my mother," Olivia said, twisting to look behind her. "She's calling me from down the hall. I must go."

"I shall see you tonight," Harry said.

She smiled. "I can't wait."

Chapter Twenty

$\mathcal{B}$y the time Harry arrived at the ambassador's residence, the ball was in full swing. He couldn't quite determine what aspects of Russian culture were being celebrated; the music was German and the food was French. But no one seemed to care. The vodka was flowing freely, and the room echoed with peals of laughter.

Harry immediately looked for Olivia, but she was nowhere to be seen. He was fairly certain she would have already arrived; her carriage had left her house over an hour before his had departed. But it was a crowded room. He'd find her soon.

Sebastian's shoulder was nearly improved, but he had insisted upon wearing a sling under his coat— the better to attract the women, he'd told Harry. And indeed, it worked. They were mobbed instantly, and Harry was happy to stand back, watching with amusement as Sebastian basked in the worry and concern of London's fair ladies.

Harry noted that Sebastian did not give an accurate depiction of the accident. In fact, all details were rather vague. There was certainly nothing about standing atop a table, acting out a cliff scene from a gothic novel. It was hard to tell exactly what Sebastian *had* said, but Harry heard one lady whisper to another that he'd been attacked by footpads, the poor, *poor* dear.

Harry fully expected to hear that Sebastian had fought off an entire French regiment by the end of the evening.

Harry leaned over to Edward as Sebastian graciously accepted the heartrending concern of one particularly buxom widow. "Whatever you do, don't tell anyone how this really happened. He'll never forgive you."

Edward nodded, but just barely. He was far too busy watching and learning from Seb to pay attention to Harry.

"Enjoy the leavings," Harry said to his brother, smiling to himself as he realized that he was through with Sebastian's left-over females.

Life was good. Very good. As perfect and fabulous as it had ever been, in fact.

Tomorrow he would propose, and tomorrow she would say yes.

She would, wouldn't she? He couldn't possibly be so misguided about her feelings.

"Have you seen Olivia?" he asked Edward.

Edward shook his head.

"I'm going to try to find her."

Edward nodded.

Harry decided that it was useless to attempt to conduct a conversation with his brother with so many young ladies flitting about, and he moved away, trying to see above the crowd as he walked over to the opposite side of the ballroom. There was a small knot of people near the punch bowl, Prince Alexei at the center, but he did not see Olivia. She'd said she would be wearing blue, which would make her easier to spot, but it was always harder for him to distinguish colors in the evening.

Her hair . . . Now, that was a different story. Her hair would shine like a beacon.

He kept moving through the crowd, looking this way and that, and then finally, just when he was starting to get frustrated, he heard from behind him:

"Looking for someone?"

He turned, and it was as if his life was illuminated by her smile. "Yes," he said, feigning perplexity, "but I can't quite find her . . ."

"Oh, stop," Olivia said, batting him lightly on the arm. "What has taken you so long? I have been here for hours."

He raised a brow at that.

"Oh, very well, one hour at least. Probably ninety minutes."

He glanced over at his cousin and brother, still holding court across the room. "We had difficulties adjusting Sebastian's sling with his coat."

"And people say women are fussy."

"While I would have to argue on behalf of my gender, I am always happy to impugn my cousin."

She laughed at that, a bright, musical sound, then grabbed his hand. "Come with me."

He followed her through the crowds, impressed by

her single-minded determination to get to wherever it was she was going. She weaved this way and that, laughing all the way, until she reached an arched door at the far side of the room.

"What's this?" he murmured.

"Shhhh," she directed. He followed her out into the hall. It wasn't empty; there were several small groups of people congregating here and there, but it was much less crowded than the main room.

"I've been exploring," she said.

"Apparently so."

She turned another corner, and another, and the crowds grew progressively thinner, until finally she stopped in a quiet gallery. One side had doors interspersed with tall portraits—perfectly ordered, two paintings between each door. The other side held a neat row of windows.

She stopped directly in front of one of the windows. "Look out," she urged.

He did, but saw nothing out of the ordinary. "Shall I open it?" he asked, thinking this might offer more clues.

"Please do."

He found the lock and undid it, then lifted the window. It glided up without sound, and he poked his head out.

He saw trees.

And her. She had poked her head out right beside him.

"I must confess to confusion," he said. "What am I looking at?"

"Me," she said simply. "Us. Together. On the same side of a window."

He turned. He looked at her. And then . . . He had to do it. He couldn't not. He reached for her, and he pulled her to him, and she came willingly, with a smile that spoke of the lifetime they had waiting ahead of them.

He leaned down and kissed her, his lips eager and hungry, and he realized he was shaking, because this was more than a kiss. There was something sacred about this moment, something honorable and true.

"I love you," he whispered. He hadn't meant to say it yet. All his plans had been to tell her when he proposed. But he had to. It had grown and spread inside of him, bubbling with warmth and strength, and he just could not keep it back. "I love you," he said again. "I love you."

She touched his cheek. "I love you, too."

For several seconds he could do nothing but stare at her, holding the moment in reverence, letting every speck of it wash over him. And then something else took over, something primal and fierce, and he crushed her to him, kissing her with the urgency of a man who must claim his own.

He couldn't get enough of her, her touch, her feel, her scent. Tension and need were spiraling within him, and he could feel his grip slipping—on his control, on sense of propriety, on everything except *her*.

His fingers were grasping at her clothing, desperate to feel her skin, warm and smooth. "I need you," he groaned, his mouth moving to her cheek, her jaw, her neck.

They twisted and turned away from the window, and Harry found himself leaning up against a door. He took the knob in his hand, turned, and they fell in, stumbling and tumbling, but managing to remain upright.

"Where are we?" Olivia asked, her breath shaking her body.

He shut the door. Locked it. "I don't care."

He grabbed her then, pulled her to him. He should have been gentle, he should have been tender. But he was beyond that now. For the first time in his life, he was moved by something beyond his control. He was moved *to* something he could not resist. His world became nothing but this woman, and their bodies, and showing her, in the most fundamental way possible, how much he loved her.

"Harry," she gasped, her body arching against his. He could feel every curve through their clothing, and he had to—he couldn't stop—

He had to feel her. He had to *know* her.

He said her name, barely recognizing his own voice, grown hoarse with need. "I want you," he said. And when she moaned incoherently in response, her lips finding his earlobe as his had done hers, he said it again.

"I want you *now*."

"Yes," she said. "Yes."

With a shuddering breath, he pulled away from her and took her face in his hands. "Do you understand what I'm saying?"

She nodded.

But that wasn't good enough. "Do you understand?" he asked, urgency making him sound almost strident. "I need you to say it."

"I understand," she whispered. "I want you, too."

Still, he held off, unable to let himself cut that last thread of sanity, of propriety. He knew he was ready to commit his very life to her, but he had not sworn it in a church, before her family. But by God, if she was going to stop him now, she was going to have to stop him *now*.

She went very still; for a moment even her breathing seemed to stop, and then she took his face in her hands, the very same position he held with her. Their eyes met, and in her face he saw a love and a trust so big and so deep that it nearly paralyzed him with fear.

How could he possibly be worthy of this? How could he keep her safe and happy and make sure that every second of every day she knew how much he loved her?

She smiled. At first it was sweet, and then it grew clever, and maybe a little bit mischievous. "You're going to ask me to marry you," she murmured, "aren't you?"

His lips parted with shock. "I—"

But she placed one of her hands against his mouth. "Don't say anything. Just nod if it's yes."

He nodded.

"Don't ask me now," she said, and she looked almost serene, as if she were a goddess and the mortals around her were doing exactly what she asked of them. "This isn't the time or the place. I want a proper proposal."

He nodded again.

"But if I *know* that you plan to ask me, I might be convinced to act in a manner . . ."

It was all the permission he needed. He pulled her back for another searing kiss, his fingers finding the cloth-covered buttons at the back of her gown. They slipped easily through the buttonholes, and in seconds the fabric pooled and rustled at her feet.

She was standing before him in her chemise and corset, the pale fabric glowing softly in the moonlight filtering through the uncurtained upper half-moon of the room's only window. She looked so beautiful, so ethereal and pure—he found himself wanting to stop and drink in the sight of her, even as his body burned for closer contact.

He shrugged off his own coat, then loosened the folds of his cravat. Through it all she just stood there, silently watching him, her eyes wide with wonder and excitement. He undid the first few buttons on his shirt, just enough to pull it over his head and, with whatever last grasp on rational thought he had left, he laid it neatly on a chair so it wouldn't wrinkle. She let out a little giggle, clasping her hand to her mouth.

"What?"

"You're so neat," she said, looking almost embarrassed to be pointing it out.

He glanced pointedly over his shoulder. "There are four hundred people on the other side of this door."

"But you're ruining me."

"I can't do it neatly?"

Another snort of laughter burst from her mouth. She reached down, picked up her dress, and handed it to him. "Would you mind folding this as well?"

He pressed his lips together to keep from laughing. Wordlessly, he reached out and took it.

"If you are ever short of funds," she said, watching him lay the dress over the back of a chair, "there are always opportunities for a conscientious lady's maid."

He turned, one corner of his mouth tipping up in a wry salute. He tapped his left temple, close to his eye, murmuring, "Blind to color, if you recall."

"Oh, dear." She clasped her hands together, looking terribly proper. "That would be a problem."

He took a step toward her, his eyes devouring her. "I might be able to make up for my lack with excessive devotion to my mistress."

"Loyalty and fidelity is always prized amongst servants."

He came close, very close, until his lips were almost touching the corner of her mouth. "And amongst husbands?"

"It's very prized amongst husbands," she whispered. Her breathing was growing erratic, and just the touch of it on her skin made his blood race.

His hand went to the ties of her corset. "I am very loyal."

She nodded jerkily. "That's good."

He tugged on the ribbon, first undoing the bow, and then slipping his finger under the knot below. "I can say 'fidelity' in three languages."

"Really?"

Really, and he didn't care if she knew. He planned to make love to her in all three, but for the first time, he thought he would stick to English. Well, mostly.

"Fidelity," he whispered. "*Fidelité. Vyernost.*"

He kissed her then, before she could ask more. He

would tell her everything, but not now. Not when he was shirtless, and her corset was undone and sliding from her body. Not when his fingers were working the two buttons of her chemise, unhooking the straps that held it in place over her shoulders.

"I love you," he said, leaning forward to place one kiss on the hollow over her collarbone.

"I love you," he said again, moving up to the elegant line of her neck.

"I love you." And this time he whispered it, hot at her ear as he let go of the straps and allowed her last garment to fall from her body.

Her arms came to cover herself, and he kissed her once, lightly, on the lips as his fingers moved to the fastening of his breeches. He was aching for her, hot and heavy with need, and he had no idea how he got his boots off so fast, but before he could even take another breath, he'd lifted her into his arms and was carrying her over to the divan.

"You should have a proper bed," he murmured, "with proper sheets and proper pillows . . ."

But she just shook her head, clasping her fingers behind his neck to pull him down for a kiss. "I don't want to be proper right now," she said, whispering the words into his ear. "I only want you."

It had been inevitable. He'd known that for some time now, since the moment she'd slyly asked him if he planned to propose. But even so, something seemed to tip at that moment, sending him over the edge of restraint, transforming this from a seduction to sheer madness.

He set her down on her back and immediately covered her body with his. The touch was electric. They were skin to skin, pressed up against each other with breathtaking intimacy. And he wanted so much just to bury himself inside her, to have her, to *know* her, but he could not allow himself to rush. He did not know if he could bring her to completion; he'd never made love to a virgin before, and he had no idea if it was even possible. But by God, he would make this good for her. When they were through, she would know that she had been worshipped.

She would know that she was loved.

"Tell me what you like," he murmured, kissing her on the lips before moving to her throat.

He heard her breath, raspy, excited, and perhaps a little confused. "What do you mean?"

He cupped her breast with his hand. "Do you like this?"

He heard the swift intake of her breath.

"Do you?" he asked softly, trailing his lips down to the base of her neck.

She nodded, quick frantic movements. "Yes."

"Tell me what you like," he said again, and his mouth found the tip of her breast. He blew a little air on it, then circled the edge with his tongue before finally capturing her with his lips.

"I like that," she gasped.

So do I, he thought, and he moved to the other side, telling himself it was for balance. But really it was for him, and for her, and because he couldn't bear to leave one inch of her untouched.

She arched beneath him, pressing up against his mouth, and he slid one of his hands down, wrapping around her bottom. He squeezed, then moved, his fingers finding the soft skin of her inner thigh. And when he squeezed again, his fingers were close, so close to the very center of her, so close that he could feel her heat.

His mouth moved back to hers just as his fingers found her, stroked her, entered her.

"Harry!" she cried out, surprised, but not, he thought, upset.

"Tell me what you like," he said again.

"That," she managed to get out. "But I don't . . ."

He moved deeper, in and out, her wetness making him burn with need for her. "You don't what?" he asked.

"I don't know."

He smiled. "You don't know what?"

"I don't know what I don't know," she practically snapped.

He bit back a laugh, and his fingers stilled for a moment.

"Don't stop!" she cried.

And so he didn't. He didn't stop when she moaned his name, and he didn't stop when she grabbed his shoulders so hard he was sure he'd be bruised. And he absolutely did not stop when she convulsed around him, so fast and so hard that she nearly pushed him out of her.

A gentleman might have stopped then. She had climaxed, and she was still a virgin, and he was probably a beast for wanting to make love to her fully, but he simply couldn't . . . not.

She was his.

But not, he was coming to realize, quite as much as he was hers.

Before she came down from her climax, before she could collapse from the power of it, he pulled his fingers out and positioned himself at her opening. "I love you," he said, his voice husky and hoarse with emotion. "I have to tell you. I need you to know. *Right now* I need you to know."

He pushed forward then, expecting resistance. But she was so excited, so well loved, that he slid inside with ease. He shuddered at the pleasure of it, of the exquisite joining of their bodies. It was as if he'd never done this before—his desire took over and he lost all control. And then, in what would have been shameful speed had he not just pleasured her, he cried out and stiffened, and then, finally, collapsed.

Chapter Twenty-one

Olivia left first.

She wasn't sure how long they had lain there on the divan, trying to regain their sanity, and then, once they were able to breathe normally, it had taken some time to right their appearances. Harry couldn't get his tie folded with the same crisp precision as his valet had done, and Olivia had found that one handkerchief was not up to the task of . . .

Good heavens, she couldn't even *think* the words. She did not regret what she had done. She could never; it was the most wonderful, amazing, spectacular experience of her life. But now she was . . . sticky.

Their departure was also delayed by several stolen kisses, at least two lustful glances that had threatened to send them right back to the divan, and one extremely mischievous pinch on the behind.

Olivia was still congratulating herself on that one.

But eventually they managed to look respectable enough to rejoin polite society, and it was decided that Olivia would depart first. Harry would follow five minutes later.

"Are you certain my hair looks presentable?" she asked as she placed her hand on the doorknob.

"No," he admitted.

She felt her eyes widen with alarm.

"It does not look bad," he said, with a man's typical inability to accurately describe coiffure, "but I don't think it looks precisely the same as it did when you arrived." He smiled weakly, clearly aware of his shortcomings in this regard.

She rushed back over to the room's lone mirror, but it was over the mantel, and even on her tiptoes she couldn't quite catch a glimpse of her entire face. "I can't see a thing," she grumbled. "I am going to have to find a washroom."

And so their plans changed. Olivia would leave, find a washroom, and then remain there for at least ten minutes, so that Harry could leave five minutes after she departed and arrive back at the ballroom five minutes before she arrived.

Olivia found the subterfuge exhausting. How did people manage such things, sneaking about like thieves? She would make a terrible spy.

Her frustration must have shown on her face, because Harry came over and kissed her once, softly, on the cheek. "We shall be married soon," he promised, "and we will never have to do this again."

She opened her mouth to point out that her mother would insist upon a three-month engagement at the very least, but he held up a hand and said, "Don't worry, that's *not* your proposal. When I propose, you'll know it. I promise."

She smiled to herself and murmured her farewell, peeking out the door first to make sure no one was coming, then slipping out into the quiet, moonlit gallery.

She knew the location of the washroom; she'd been there once already that evening. She tried to walk at precisely the correct speed. Not too fast; she did not want to look as if she was rushing. Not too slowly, either; it was always best to appear as if one had a purpose.

She encountered no one on her way to the washroom, for which she was grateful. When she opened the door, however, and stepped into the outer chamber, where ladies could wash their hands and check their appearances, she was met with:

"Olivia!"

Olivia nearly jumped out of her skin. Mary Cadogan was standing at the mirror, pinching her cheeks.

"Good heavens, Mary," Olivia said, trying to catch her breath. "You gave me a start." She desperately did not want to get caught up into a conversation with Mary Cadogan, but on the other hand, if she had to run into someone, she was grateful it was a friend. Mary might wonder at Olivia's mussed appearance, but she would never suspect the truth.

"Is my hair an absolute fright?" Olivia asked, reaching up to pat it. "I slipped. Someone spilled champagne."

"Oh, I hate that."

"What do you think?" Olivia asked, hoping that she

had successfully diverted Mary from asking any more questions.

"It's not so bad," Mary said consolingly. "I can help you. I've dressed my sister's hair dozens of times." She pushed Olivia into a chair and began to adjust her pins. "Your dress looks as if it suffered no harm."

"I'm sure the hem is stained," Olivia said.

"Who spilled the champagne?" Mary asked.

"I'm not sure."

"I'll bet it was Mr. Grey. He has one arm in a sling, you know."

"I saw," Olivia murmured.

"I heard he was pushed down a flight of stairs by his uncle."

Olivia just barely managed to contain her horror at the rumor. "That can't be true."

"Why not?"

"Well . . ." Olivia blinked, trying to come up with an acceptable answer. She didn't want to say that Sebastian had fallen off a table in her house—Mary would positively *pummel* her with questions if she knew that Olivia had any special knowledge of the incident. Finally she settled on: "If he'd fallen down a flight of stairs, don't you think he'd have suffered more serious injury?"

Mary appeared to consider this. "Maybe it was a short flight of stairs. His front steps, perhaps."

"Perhaps," Olivia said, hoping that would be the end of it.

"Although," Mary continued, putting an end to Olivia's hopes, "one would think there would be witnesses if it had happened outside."

Olivia decided not to comment.

"I suppose it could have happened at night," Mary mused.

Olivia was beginning to think that Mary ought to consider writing a *Miss Butterworth*-style novel of her own. She certainly possessed the imagination for it.

"There," Mary declared. "As good as new. Or almost. I couldn't quite recreate the little curl over your ear."

Olivia was impressed (and perhaps a little alarmed) that Mary had remembered the curl over her ear; Olivia certainly hadn't. "Thank you," she said. "I very much appreciate it."

Mary smiled warmly. "I'm happy to be of help. Shall we head back to the party?"

"You go ahead without me," Olivia said. She motioned toward the other, more private, section of the washroom. "I need a moment."

"Would you like me to wait for you?"

"Oh, no no no," Olivia said, hoping her surfeit of no's sounded more conversational than desperate. She really needed a few moments to herself—just a bit of time to collect her thoughts, to breathe deeply, and to attempt to regain her equilibrium.

"Oh, of course. I shall see you later, then." Mary gave her a nod and exited the small room, leaving Olivia on her own.

Olivia closed her eyes for a moment and took that deep breath she'd been waiting for. She still felt tingly and lightheaded, shocked by her own behavior and, at the same time, giddy with delight.

She wasn't sure what shocked her more—that she had just given up her virginity in the home of the Russian ambassador or that she was preparing to rejoin the party as if nothing had happened.

Would people see it on her face? Did she look fundamentally different? Heaven knew, she *felt* fundamentally changed.

She leaned forward a few inches, trying to examine her reflection more closely. Her cheeks were pink; there was no hiding that. And maybe her eyes looked a little brighter, almost glittery.

She was being fanciful. No one would know.

Except Harry.

Her heart jumped. Literally jumped in her chest.

Harry would know. He would remember every last detail, and when he looked at her, his eyes hot with desire, she would melt anew.

And suddenly she was no longer so sure she would be able to carry this off. No one would know what she'd been doing from looking at her. But if someone happened to look at her while she was looking at Harry . . .

She stood. Squared her shoulders. Tried to be resolute. She could do this. She was Lady Olivia Bevelstoke, comfortable in any social situation, wasn't she? She was Lady Olivia Bevelstoke, soon to be . . .

She let out a little squeal at the thought of it. Soon to be Lady Valentine. She liked that. Lady Valentine. It was so romantic. Really, names didn't get much better than that.

She turned toward the door. Reached for the knob.

But someone opened it first. So she stepped back to avoid being hit by the door.

But she couldn't avoid—

"Oh!"

* * *

Where the hell was Olivia?

Harry had been back at the party for more than half an hour and he still hadn't caught a glimpse of her. He'd played his part to perfection, chatting with any number of bright young ladies, even dancing with one of the Smythe-Smiths. He'd checked on Sebastian, not that he needed it—his shoulder had not been troubling him for several days.

Olivia had said that she was planning to go to the ladies' retiring room to check on her appearance, so he'd not expected her to arrive promptly, but still, shouldn't she have been done by now? He'd thought she'd looked rather nice when he'd last seen her. What more could she have needed to do?

"Oh, Sir Harry!"

He turned at the sound of a female voice. It was that young lady Olivia had been sitting with in the park. Blast, what was her name?

"Have you seen Olivia?" she asked.

"No," he said. "I haven't been in the ballroom long, though."

The young woman frowned. "I don't know where she could be. I was with her earlier."

Harry regarded her with increased interest. "You were?"

She nodded, waving one of her hands off to the side, presumably to indicate another location. "I was helping her with her hair. Someone spilled champagne on her dress, you know."

Harry was not sure how that related to her hair, but he knew better than to ask. Whatever story Olivia had concocted, it had convinced her friend, and he wasn't going to contradict.

The young lady frowned, tilting her head this way and that as she glanced out over the crowd. "I really needed to tell her something."

"When did you last see her?" Harry asked, keeping his tone polite, almost paternal.

"Goodness, I'm not sure. An hour ago? No, it couldn't have been that long." She continued her visual search of the dance floor, but Harry couldn't tell if she was looking for Olivia or merely inspecting the guest list.

"Do you see her?" Harry murmured, mostly because it was damned awkward, standing there next to her while she looked at everyone in the room besides him.

She shook her head, and then, apparently spotting someone she deemed of greater importance, said, "Do let her know I'm looking for her when you find her." With a little wave, she headed back into the crowd.

That was singularly unhelpful, Harry decided, as he moved toward the doors to the garden. He didn't think Olivia would have gone outside, but the ballroom was sunken, and one had to ascend three steps to reach the doors. He'd be much more likely to be able to see her from there.

But when he reached his vantage point, he was once again stymied. Everyone else he knew seemed to be in attendance, but Olivia was nowhere to be found. There was Sebastian, still charming the ladies with his made-up tales of derring-do. Edward was at his elbow, trying to appear older than he really was. Olivia's friend (whose name he still could not recall) was sipping a glass of lemonade, pretending she was listening to the elderly gentleman who was shouting something at her. And there was Olivia's twin brother, leaning against the back wall, his expression bored.

Even Vladimir was there, walking across the ball-room with great purpose, not bothering to excuse himself as he shoved aside various lords and ladies. He did look rather serious, Harry thought, and he was wondering if he ought to investigate when he realized the giant Russian was heading for him.

"You come with me," he said to Harry.

Harry started. "You speak English?"

"Nyeh tak khorosho, kak tiy govorish po-russki."

Not as well as you speak Russian.

"What is going on?" Harry asked. In English, just to be careful.

Vladimir's eyes met his with steely purpose. "I know Winthrop," he said.

It was almost enough to convince Harry to trust him.

And then Vladimir said, "Lady Olivia has disap-peared."

Suddenly it didn't matter if he trusted him or not.

Olivia had no idea where she was.

Or how she'd got there.

Or why her hands were tied behind her back, and her feet were bound together, and a gag had been wrapped around her mouth.

Or, she thought, blinking frantically to adjust to the dim light, why she *hadn't* been blindfolded.

She was lying on her side, on a bed, staring at a wall. Maybe whoever had done this to her had figured that if she couldn't move or make a noise, it wouldn't matter what she saw.

But who? Why? What had happened to her?

She tried to think, tried to calm her racing mind. She'd been in the washroom. Mary Cadogan had been there, and then she'd left, and Olivia had been alone for how long? At least a few minutes. Maybe as many as five.

She'd finally summoned the nerve to go back to the party, but the door had opened and then . . .

What happened? What happened?

Think, Olivia, think.

Why couldn't she remember? It was as if a big gray smudge had been wiped across her memory.

She started to breathe more heavily. Quick and deep. Panicked. She couldn't think straight.

She started to struggle, even though she knew it was fruitless. She managed to flip over, away from the wall. She couldn't seem to calm down, to focus, to—

"You're awake."

She froze. In an instant she went still, her only movement the rapid rise and fall of her chest.

She did not recognize the voice. And when its owner came closer, she did not recognize the man, either.

Who are you?

But of course she couldn't speak. He saw the question, however; saw it in her panicked eyes.

"It does not matter who I am," he said, his voice carrying some sort of accent. But she couldn't tell where he was from. Just as she'd always been terrible with languages, she never could place accents, either.

The man drew closer, then sat in a chair near her. He was older than she was, although not as old as her parents, and his graying hair was clipped close to his head. His eyes—she couldn't tell what color they were in the darkness. Not brown. Something lighter.

"Prince Alexei has taken quite a fancy to you," he said.

Her eyes widened. *Prince Alexei* had done this to her?

Her captor chuckled. "You do not hide your emotions well, Lady Olivia. It was not the prince who brought you here. But it will be the prince"—he leaned closer, menacingly, until she could smell his breath—"who will pay to bring you back."

She shook her head, grunting, trying to tell him that the prince had not taken a fancy to her, or that if he had, he didn't any longer.

"If you're smart, you won't struggle," the man said. "You won't free yourself, so why waste your strength?"

And yet she couldn't seem to *stop* struggling. Absolute terror was building up within her, and she didn't know how to keep it still.

The gray-haired man stood, gazing down at her with a tiny curve of his lips. "I will bring you food and drink later." He left the room, and Olivia thought her throat would close in panic as she heard the click of the door shutting, followed by the turns of two locks.

She wasn't going to be able to get out of here. Not by herself.

But did anyone even know she was gone?

Chapter Twenty-two

*W*here is she?"

That was all Harry managed to get out before he launched himself at the prince. He had followed Vladimir to a room at the back of the house, his panic rising with each step. He knew he was being foolish; this could be a trap. Someone obviously knew he worked for the War Office; how else would Vladimir have known he spoke Russian?

He could be walking toward his own execution.

But it was a chance he had to take.

Still, when he saw the prince standing there, illuminated by a single candle on a bare table, Harry snapped. His fear made him even stronger, and when they both hit the floor, it was with stunning force.

"Where is she?" Harry yelled again. "What have you done with her?"

"Stop!" Vladimir wedged himself between the two men, pulling them apart. It was only when Harry was standing again, held an arm's length from the prince, that he realized Alexei had not fought back.

The terror in the pit of his stomach grew. The prince looked pale, grim. Frightened.

"What is going on?" Harry whispered.

Alexei handed him a piece of paper. Harry took it over to the candle and looked down. It was written in Cyrillic; Harry didn't protest. This was not the time to pretend he could not read it.

The lady will live if you cooperate. She will be expensive. Tell no one.

Harry looked up. "How do we know it's her? They don't mention her by name."

Wordlessly, Alexei held out his hand. Harry looked down. It was a lock of hair. Harry wanted to say that it might not be hers, that there could be another woman with hair that color, that unbelievable shade of sun and butter, with the same amount of curl, not a ringlet but more than a wave.

But he knew.

"Who wrote this?" he asked. In Russian.

Vladimir spoke first. "We think—"

"You *think*?" Harry roared. "You *think*? You had better start knowing, and damned soon. If anything happens to her . . ."

"If anything happens to her," the prince cut in with icy precision, "I will cut out their throats myself. There will be justice."

Harry turned to him slowly, trying to hold back the

roiling acid in his belly. "I don't want justice," he said, his voice low and flat with rage. "I want *her*."

"And we will get her," Vladimir said quickly. He shot the prince a look of warning. "She will not come to harm."

"Who *are* you?" Harry demanded.

"It does not matter."

"I think it does."

"I work also for the War Office," Vladimir said. He shrugged a little. "Sometimes."

"Pardon me if you fail to capture my trust."

Vladimir looked at him again, that hard, direct stare that had unnerved Harry back in the ballroom. It was clear that he was much more than the menacing manservant he pretended to be.

"I know Fitzwilliam," Vladimir said in a low voice.

Harry froze. No one knew Fitzwilliam—not unless he wanted them to. His mind reeled. Why would Winthrop have ordered him to observe Prince Alexei if they already had Vladimir in place?

"Your man Winthrop did not know about me," Vladimir said, anticipating Harry's next question. "He is not high enough to know about me."

As far as Harry knew, the only person higher up than Winthrop was Fitzwilliam himself. "What is going on?" he asked, struggling to keep his voice even.

"I am not a sympathizer of Napoleon," Prince Alexei said. "My father was, but I"—he spat on the floor—"am not."

Harry looked at Vladimir.

"He does not work with me," Vladimir said, motioning with his head toward the prince. "But he is

. . . supportive. He has given money. And the use of his land."

Harry shook his head. "What does this have to do with—"

"There are those who would seek to use him," Vladimir interrupted. "He is valuable, alive or dead. I protect him."

It was amazing. Vladimir really was Alexei's bodyguard. One tiny truth in a web of lies.

"He is here to visit his cousin, just as he says," Vladimir continued. "It is a convenient way for me to meet with my associates in London as well. Unfortunately, the prince's interest in Lady Olivia did not go unnoticed."

"Who took her?"

Vladimir looked away for a moment, and Harry knew it was bad. If he could not look him in the eye, Olivia was in grave danger indeed.

"I am not certain," Vladimir finally said. "I can't tell yet if there are political considerations or it is just for money. The prince is a man of considerable wealth."

"I was told his fortunes had declined," Harry said curtly.

"They have," Vladimir confirmed, raising a hand to stop Alexei from defending himself. "But he still has much. Land. Jewels. More than enough for a criminal to wish to ransom someone close to him."

"But she's not—"

"Someone thinks I was planning to ask her to marry me," Alexei cut in.

Harry turned on him. "Were you?"

"No. I might have considered it once. But she—" He

waved a hand dismissively through the air. "She is in love with you. I do not need a woman who will love me. But I will not tolerate one who loves someone else."

Harry crossed his arms. "Apparently your intentions were not made clear to your enemies."

"For that I would apologize." Alexei swallowed, and for the first time since Harry had known him, he looked uncomfortable. "I cannot control what others think of me."

Harry turned to Vladimir. "What do we do now?"

Vladimir gave him a look that told him he would not like what came next. "We wait," he said. "We will be contacted again."

"I'm not going to stand here and—"

"And what do you suggest we do instead? Interview every last guest? The note said to tell no one. We already disobeyed when we told you. If these are men like I think they are, we do not want to make them upset with us."

"But—"

"Do you want to give them a reason to hurt her?" Vladimir demanded.

Harry felt himself choking. It was as if someone had reached up from his belly and was strangling him from the inside out. He knew Vladimir was right, or at least he knew that *he* didn't have any better ideas.

It was killing him. The fear. The helplessness. "Someone has to have seen something," he said.

"I am going to investigate," Vladimir said.

Harry immediately made for the door. "I am going with you."

"No," Vladimir said, putting up a hand to stop him. "You have too much emotion. You will not make good decisions."

"I can't do nothing," Harry said. He felt small again, young and powerless, staring down a problem only to find there were no good solutions.

"You won't," Vladimir assured him. "You will do much. But later."

Harry watched as Vladimir went to the door, but before he could leave, he shouted, "Wait!"

Vladimir turned around.

"She went to the washroom," Harry said. "She went to the washroom after . . ." He cleared his throat. "I know that she went to the washroom."

Vladimir gave a slow nod. "This is good to know." He slipped out the door and was gone.

Harry looked at Alexei.

"You speak Russian," Alexei said.

"My grandmother," Harry said. "She refused to speak English to us."

Alexei nodded. "My grandmother, she was from Finland. She was the same."

Harry gave him a long look, then sank into a chair, his head in his hands.

"It is good that you speak our language," Alexei said. "Very few of your countrymen do."

Harry tried to ignore him. He had to think. He didn't know where to start, what he might possibly know that could help to determine Olivia's whereabouts, but he knew that he had to scour his brain.

But Alexei would not stop talking. "I am always surprised when—"

"Shut up!" Harry burst out. "Just shut up. Don't speak. Do not say a single bloody word unless it is about finding Olivia. Do you understand me?"

Alexei was very still for a moment. Then, silently, he crossed the room to a bookcase and pulled down a bottle and two glasses. He poured a liquid—vodka, probably—into both glasses. Without speaking, he set one of the glasses down in front of Harry.

"I don't drink," Harry said, not bothering to look up.

"It will help you."

"No."

"You say you are Russian? You don't drink vodka?"

"I don't drink anything," Harry said curtly.

Alexei regarded him with some curiosity, then took a seat on the far side of the room.

The glass sat untouched for nearly an hour, until Alexei, finally accepting that Harry spoke the truth, picked it up and drank it himself.

After about ten minutes, Olivia finally managed to calm her body down enough to allow her mind to work properly. She had absolutely no idea what she could possibly do to aid in her rescue, but it seemed prudent to gather whatever information she could.

It was impossible to figure out where she was being held. Or was it? She scooched herself up into a sitting position and examined the room as best she could. It was almost impossible to see anything in the dim light. There had been a candle but the man had taken it with him.

The room was small, and the furnishings were sparse, but it was not shabby. Olivia nudged herself closer to the wall and squinted at the plaster. Then she rubbed her cheek against it. Neat and tidy, with no chips or peeling paint. Looking up, she saw a crown molding where the walls met the ceiling. And the door—it was difficult to tell from where she sat on the bed, but the knob looked to be of high quality.

Was she still in the ambassador's residence? It seemed possible. She bent over, placing her cheek against the bare skin of her arms. Her skin was warm. Wouldn't she feel chilled if she'd been taken outside? Of course, she did not know how long she had been unconscious. It was possible she'd been here for hours. Still, she didn't *feel* as if she'd been outside.

A panicked bubble of laughter threatened to burst from her throat. What was she *thinking*? She didn't *feel* as if she'd been outside? What did *that* mean? Was she going to start making decisions based on gut feelings on what may or may not have happened when she was unconscious?

She forced herself to pause. She needed to calm down. She wasn't going to be able to accomplish anything if she succumbed to hysterics every five minutes. She was smarter than that. She could keep a calm head.

She *had* to keep a calm head.

What did she know about the ambassador's residence? She had been there twice, first during the day, when she was presented to Prince Alexei, and then at night, for the ball.

It was a huge building, a veritable mansion right in the middle of London. Surely there were myriad rooms where a person could be hidden. Perhaps she was in the servants' quarters. She frowned, trying to remember the servants' rooms at Rudland House. Did they have crown moldings, too? Were the doorknobs of as high a quality as the rest of the house?

She had no idea.

Damn it. Why didn't she know that? Shouldn't she know that?

She turned to the far wall. There was one window, but it was obscured by heavy velvet curtains. Dark red, maybe? Dark blue? It was impossible to tell. The night was sucking all of the color out of her surroundings. The only light coming in was from the moon, filtering through the semicircular window above the curtained rectangle.

She paused, thinking. Something was tapping at her memory.

She wondered if she might be able to see out the window, if she were able to maneuver herself off the bed. It would be difficult. Her ankles had been tied so tightly together there was little hope of making even baby steps. And she hadn't realized how off balance she would feel with her hands bound behind her back.

Not to mention that she had to do everything in total silence. It would be a disaster if her captor came back and found her anywhere but on the bed, right where he'd left her. Very carefully, and *very* slowly, she swung her legs off the bed, inching her way toward the edge until her feet touched the floor. Keeping her movements similarly controlled, she was able to maneuver herself to a standing position, and then, by leaning on various pieces of furniture, she made her way toward the window.

The window. Why did the window seem so familiar?

Probably because it was a *window*, she told herself impatiently. They weren't exactly replete with unique architectural detail.

When she reached her destination, she leaned carefully forward, trying to push the curtains aside with her face. She started with her cheek, then, once she had them pushed a bit to the side, she rolled her face forward, trying to hook the edge of the curtains with her nose. It took her four tries, but eventually she managed it, even jabbing her shoulder forward to block the curtains from falling back into place.

Resting her head against the glass, she saw . . . nothing. Just the fog from her breath. She moved her head to the side again, using her cheek to rub the mist away. When she faced front again, she held her breath.

Still, she couldn't see much. The only thing she could determine for sure was that she was fairly high up, perhaps on a fifth or sixth floor. She could see the roofs of other buildings and not much else.

The moon. She could see the moon.

She had seen the moon in the other room, the one where she'd made love with Harry. She'd seen it through the fanlight window.

The fanlight window!

She edged back, very carefully so as not to lose her balance. This window also had a fanlight at the top. Which didn't mean _much_, except there was a pattern to it, mullions spreading out from the center point on the bottom, making it look rather like a handheld fan.

Exactly like the one downstairs.

She was still in the ambassador's residence. It was possible that she'd been brought to another building with the exact same window pattern, but that was unlikely, wasn't it? And the ambassador's residence was huge. Practically a palace. It was not in central

London but rather out past Kensington, where there was quite a bit more room for such grand buildings.

She moved back toward the window, hooking her head around the edge of the curtains again, this time succeeding on the first try. She placed her ear against the glass, listening for . . . anything. Music? People? Shouldn't there be some indication that there was a massive party going on in the same building?

Maybe she *wasn't* in the ambassador's residence. No, no, it was a huge building. She could easily be far enough away not to hear anything.

But she could hear footsteps. Her heart slammed in her chest, and she half shuffled, half jumped her way to the bed, managing to flop herself down just as she heard the two locks clicking undone.

As the door opened she began to struggle. It was the only thing she could think of that might explain why she was out of breath.

"I told you not to do that," her captor scolded. He was carrying a tray with a teapot and two cups. Olivia could smell the tea steeping from across the room. The scent was heavenly.

"I am very civilized, yes?" he asked, lifting the tray slightly before setting it down on a table. "I have worn such a gag before." He motioned to the one wrapped around her head. "It does make the mouth very dry."

Olivia just stared at him. She wasn't sure how she was meant to respond. Literally, *how*. Surely he knew she could not speak.

"I will remove that so you may have some tea," he said to her, "but you must remain quiet. If you make a noise, anything louder than a whispered thank you, I will have to make you again unconscious."

Her eyes widened.

He shrugged. "It is easy enough to do. I did it once, and quite well I must say. You do not even have a headache, I am guessing."

Olivia blinked. She *didn't* have a headache. What had he done to her?

"You will be quiet?"

She nodded. She needed him to remove the gag. Maybe if she could speak with him, she could convince him that this was all a mistake.

"Do not try anything heroic," he warned her, although his eyes were somewhat amused, as if he could not imagine her startling him in any way.

She shook her head, trying to keep her eyes earnest. They were her only means of communication until he removed the gag.

He leaned forward, reaching out his arms, then he stopped, drawing back. "I think the tea is done," he said. "We wouldn't want it to over . . . how do you say it?"

He was Russian. With that one phrase—*How do you say it?*—Olivia was finally able to recognize his accent and determine his nationality. He sounded exactly like Prince Alexei.

"Silly me," the man said, pouring out two cups of tea. "You cannot say anything." Finally, he moved to her side and removed the gag.

Olivia coughed, and it took her several moments before her mouth was moistened enough to speak, but when she did, she looked directly at her captor and said, "Oversteep."

"I beg your pardon?"

"The tea. You didn't want it to oversteep."

"Oversteep." He repeated the word, appearing to test it out on his tongue and in his mind. He made an expression of approval, then handed her a cup.

She grimaced and gave a little shrug. How did he think she would hold it? Her hands were still tied behind her back.

He smiled, but it wasn't a cruel smile. It wasn't even condescending. It was almost . . . rueful.

Which gave Olivia hope. Not much, but some.

"I'm afraid I don't trust you enough to untie your hands," he said.

"I promise I won't—"

"Don't make promises you can't keep, Lady Olivia."

She opened her mouth to protest, but he cut her off. "Oh, I do not think you realize you make false promises, but you will see something you think is an opportunity, and you will be unable to pass it by, and then you will do something foolish, and I will have to hurt you."

It was an effective way to end the discussion.

"I thought you would come to see my opinion," he said. "Here, do you trust me enough to allow me to hold your cup?"

She shook her head slowly.

He laughed. "A smart woman. The very best kind. I do not have patience for stupidity."

"Someone I very much respect told me never to trust a man who tells me to trust him," Olivia said quietly.

Her captor chuckled some more. "That person—is it a man?"

Olivia nodded.

"He is a good friend."

"I know."

"Here." He brought the cup to her lips. "You have no choice but to trust me in this occasion."

She took a sip. She didn't really have a choice, and her throat *was* dry.

He set the cup down and picked up his own. "They were poured from the same pot," he said, taking a sip. When he was finished he added, "Not that you should trust me."

She raised her eyes to meet his and said, "I have no connection to Prince Alexei."

One corner of his mouth tilted up. "Do you think I am foolish, Lady Olivia?"

She shook her head. "He was courting me, it is true. But he is not any longer."

Her captor leaned forward a few inches. "You disappeared for nearly an hour this evening, Lady Olivia."

Her lips parted. She could feel herself blush and prayed that he could not see it in the darkness.

"So did Prince Alexei."

"He was not with me," she said quickly.

The gray-haired man took a leisurely sip of his tea. "I do not know how to say this without insulting you," he murmured, "but you smell like . . . how do you say it?"

Olivia had a feeling he knew *exactly* how to say it. And as mortifying as it was, she had no choice but to say, "I was with a man. A different man. *Not* Prince Alexei."

This caught his interest. "Really?"

She nodded once, curtly, so as to show him that she did not intend to elaborate.

"Does the prince know?"

"It's not any of his business."

He took another sip of tea. "Would he disagree with you about that?"

"I beg your pardon?"

"Would Prince Alexei think that it was his business? Would he be angry?"

"I don't know," Olivia said, trying to be honest. "He has not called upon me for over a week."

"A week is not such a very long time."

"He is acquainted with the other gentleman, and I believe he is aware of my feelings for him."

Her captor sat back, assessing this new information.

"May I have some more tea?" Olivia asked. Because it was good. And she was thirsty.

"Of course," he murmured, holding forth her cup again.

"Do you believe me?" Olivia asked, once she was done with her drink.

He spoke slowly. "I do not know."

She waited for him to ask her Harry's identity, but he did not, which she found curious.

"What will you do with me?" she said quietly, praying she wasn't a fool for asking.

He had been looking at a spot over her shoulder, but his gaze shifted swiftly back to her face. "That depends."

"On what?"

"We will see if Prince Alexei still values you. I don't think we will tell him of your indiscretions. Just in case he still hopes to make you his wife."

"I don't think he—"

"Don't interrupt, Lady Olivia," he said, his voice

holding just enough warning to remind her that he was not her friend, and this was no ordinary tea party.

"I'm sorry," she murmured.

"If he still desires you, it is in your best interests that he thinks you are a virgin. Do you not agree?"

Olivia held still until it became apparent that this was not a hypothetical question. Finally, she gave a single nod.

"After he pays to get you back"—he gave a fatalistic sort of shrug—"then you can sort it out as you wish. It will be of no interest to me." He watched her with silent intensity for several moments, then said, "Here, take one more sip of tea before I cover your mouth again."

"Must you?"

"I am afraid I must. You are far more clever than I had imagined. I cannot leave any weapons at your disposal, including your voice."

Olivia took her final sip of tea, and then closed her eyes as her captor reaffixed the gag. When he was done, she lay back down, staring stonily at the ceiling.

"I would recommend that you take a rest, Lady Olivia," he said from the doorway. "It is the only good use of your time here."

Olivia did not bother to look at him. Surely he did not expect a reply, even one made with only her eyes.

He made no more comment as he shut the door. Olivia listened to the clicks of the two locks, and then finally, for the first time during her ordeal, she wanted to cry. Not to struggle, not to rage, just to cry.

She felt the tears, silent and hot, slide along each temple, down to the pillow below. She couldn't wipe her face. Somehow that seemed the worst sort of indignity.

What was she supposed to do now? Lie here and wait? *Rest*, as her captor had suggested? It was impossible; the inaction was killing her.

Harry must have noticed that she was gone by now. Even if she had only been unconscious for a few minutes, he would have had to have noticed. She'd been locked in this room for at least an hour.

But would he know what to do? He had been a soldier, it was true, but this was no battlefield, with clear, well-labeled enemies. And if she was still in the ambassador's residence, how would he question anyone? More than half of the servants spoke only Russian. Harry could say please and thank you in Portuguese, but that wasn't going to get him far.

She was going to have to save herself, or at the very least, do her best to make it easy for someone else to save her.

She swung her legs off the bed and sat up, placing her moment of pity firmly behind her. She couldn't sit here and do nothing.

Perhaps there was something she could do about her bindings. They were firmly tied, but not so tight as to dig into her skin. Maybe she could reach her ankles with her hands. It would be awkward, since she'd have to bend backwards, but it was worth a try.

She lay on her side and curled her legs up behind her, reaching back . . . back . . .

There. She had it. It wasn't rope but rather a strip of fabric, tied in an extremely tight knot. She groaned. It was the sort of thing she'd more likely cut through than attempt to work open.

She'd never had patience for this sort of thing. It went with the embroidery she hated, and the lessons she'd skipped . . .

If she could get this knot undone, she'd learn French. No, she'd learn Russian! That would be even more difficult.

If she could get it undone, she'd finish *Miss Butterworth and the Mad Baron*. She'd even find the one about the mysterious colonel and read that one, too.

She'd write more letters, and not just to Miranda. She'd deliver charity boxes, not just pack them. She would bloody well complete *everything* she started.

Everything.

And there was no way she was going to fall in love with Sir Harry Valentine and not marry him.

No way at all.

Chapter Twenty-three

Harry sat in silence while Alexei downed his second shot of vodka. He said nothing when he took his third, or even his fourth, which was actually the one he'd originally poured for Harry. But when the prince reached for the bottle for his fifth shot—

"Don't," Harry snapped.

Alexei looked at him with surprise. "I beg your pardon."

"Do not take another drink."

Now the prince appeared merely confused. "You are telling me not to drink?"

One of Harry's hands clenched into a fist, hard and tense. "I am telling you that if we need your assistance in finding Olivia, I don't want you stumbling and puking down the hallway."

"I can assure you, I never stumble. Or—what is this puke?"

"Put the bottle down."

Alexei did not comply.

"Put. It. Down."

"I think you forget who I am."

"I never forget anything. You would do well to take note of that."

Alexei merely stared at him. "You make no sense."

Harry stood. "You do not want to provoke me right now."

Alexei regarded him for a moment, then turned back to the glass and bottle in his hands. He started to pour.

Harry saw red.

It was the first bloody time in his life he'd seen the color, but he would have sworn that the entire world seemed to turn a different, hotter hue. His ears roared and tensed on the inside, as if he'd climbed to the top of a mountain. And he no longer had control. Of anything. His body leaped forward of its own volition, and his mind certainly wasn't doing anything to stop it. He landed on the prince like a human cannonball, and they crashed against a table and then onto the floor, the vodka spilling on them both.

Harry nearly gagged at the heavy scent of the alcohol. It soaked his clothes, and it was cold, so cold against his skin.

But it didn't stop him. Nothing could have stopped him. He couldn't say anything, couldn't think of anything to say. For once in his life he had no words. He had nothing but rage. It poured through him, pulsed with fury, and when he raised his fist, ready to slam it into the prince's face, all that came forth was a cry of fury. And—

"Stop it!"

It was Vladimir, stepping nimbly into the fray, yanking Harry off Alexei and shoving him toward the opposite wall. "What the hell are you doing?"

"He is insane," Alexei hissed, rubbing his throat.

Harry did nothing but breathe, but it was a rough, furious sound.

"Shut up," Vladimir said. He glared at Harry, as if anticipating an interruption. "Both of you. Now listen to me." He stepped forward, and his foot met with the bottle on the floor. It skittered across the room, spraying what was left of the vodka. Vladimir grunted in disgust but made no comment. After eyeing both men assessingly, he continued speaking. "I have inspected the building, and I believe that Lady Olivia is still inside."

"Why do you think that?" Harry asked.

"There are guards at every door."

"For a party?"

Vladimir shrugged. "There are many reasons to protect the contents of the house."

Harry waited for more, but Vladimir did not elaborate. God above, it was just like talking with Winthrop. Harry hadn't realized until this very moment how much he hated it—all those vague sentences and *We have our ways.*

"None of the guards saw her depart," Vladimir continued. "The only door she might have exited without detection is the main one, where the party is."

"She did not return to the party," Harry said, then clarified: "She went to the washroom, but she did not return to the party."

"Are you certain?"

He gave one sharp nod. "I am."

"Then we must assume she did not leave the building. We don't know if she reached the washroom—"

"She did," Harry interrupted. He felt like an idiot for not mentioning this sooner. "She was there for some time. Her friend told me she saw her there."

"Who is this friend?" Vladimir asked.

Harry shook his head. "I can't recall her name. But she won't have any useful information. She said she left before Olivia did."

"She may have seen something. Find her," Vladimir ordered. "Bring her to me. I will question her."

"That's a bad idea," Harry told him. "Unless you're prepared to hold *her* hostage. She could not keep a secret if her *own* life depended upon it, never mind someone else's."

"You question her, then. We will meet back here." Vladimir turned back to Alexei. "You stay here. In case they send another message."

Alexei said something in response, but Harry did not hear him. He was already well down the hall, in search of that girl—whatever her name was.

"Stop!" Vladimir called.

Harry skidded to a halt and turned impatiently. They didn't have time to waste.

"You don't need to look for her," Vladimir said gruffly. "It was a ruse to get you out of the room and leave him"—he jerked his head toward the small salon where Alexei waited—"in."

Harry's mind raced but his voice was even when he asked, "Do you suspect him of involvement?"

"*Nyet.* But he will be a nuisance. You, I think, now that you have had time to calm down . . ."

"Do not mistake this for calm," Harry bit off.

Vladimir's brows rose; nonetheless, he reached into his coat and pulled out a gun, handle first. He held it out to Harry. "I do not think you will do something stupid."

Harry's hand wrapped around the handle of the gun, but Vladimir did not let go. "Will you?" he asked.

Do something stupid? "No," Harry said. And he prayed it would be true.

Vladimir kept his hand in place for several seconds more, then abruptly let go, waiting while Harry inspected the weapon. "Come with me," he ordered, and the two of them moved swiftly down the hall and around a corner. Vladimir stopped in front of a door, glanced both ways, and then ducked into an empty room, motioning for Harry to follow. Vladimir held a finger over his lips, then inspected the room, making sure it was empty.

"The ambassador has her," he said. "Or rather, his men do. He is still at the party."

"What?" Harry had never met the man, save for that evening's receiving line, but still, it was hard to believe.

"He needs money. He will be recalled to Russia soon, and he has little resources of his own." Vladimir shrugged, then waved one his arms expansively, indicating their opulent surroundings. "He has become used to living in this palace. And he has always been jealous of his cousin."

"What makes you think he took Olivia?"

"I have other men here," Vladimir said cryptically.

"And that is all you're going to tell me," Harry said disgustedly, finally fed up with never being told 100 percent of a story.

"That is all I am going to tell you, my friend," Vladimir said. He shrugged again. "It is safer that way."

Harry did not speak. He did not trust himself to do so.

"Lady Olivia's parents have noticed her disappearance," Vladimir said.

Harry was not surprised. It had been well over an hour.

"As far as I know, it has not been noticed by anyone else," Vladimir continued. "There is much vodka in the room. I do not think they realize there is some in the lemonade."

Harry looked at him sharply. "What?"

"Did you not know?"

He shook his head. How many glasses had he had? Bloody hell. His head felt clear, but then again, would he even know the difference? He had never been drunk, never even the slightest bit impaired.

"It has also been noticed that the prince is gone," Vladimir continued. "Her parents are worried that they are together."

Harry's lips pressed into a flat, firm line. His chest burned at the insinuation, but this was not the time for jealousy.

"They wish to keep this quiet. They are with the ambassador right now."

"They are with him? Has he—"

"He is playing the concerned host to perfection." Vladimir spit on the floor. "I have never trusted him."

Harry stared down at the wet spot on the floor with some surprise. It was the largest show of emotion he had seen him display. When he looked back up, it was clear that Vladimir had noticed his curiosity.

The huge Russian looked at him with steely eyes. "I especially detest men who prey on women."

There was a world of history behind that remark, but Harry knew better than to ask. He nodded once—a show of respect—and then asked, "What now?"

"It is known where the prince is. That is where they will deliver a note. He has strict instructions not to do anything, and I think he is wise enough to do as I say."

Harry hoped this was true. He thought it was, but then again, Prince Alexei had been drinking.

"While he waits, we search."

"How big is this bloody mausoleum?"

Vladimir shook his head. "I do not precisely know. More than forty rooms, to be sure. Perhaps more. But if I were to hold someone, I would take her to the north wing."

"What is in the north wing?"

"It is more remote. And the rooms are smaller."

"But wouldn't he think that that would be the first place we'd look?"

Vladimir moved to the door. "He would not know anyone is looking. He thinks me a stupid servant." He looked over at Harry with a heavy-lidded stare. "And he knows nothing of you." He placed his hand on the knob. "Are you ready?"

Harry's fingers tightened on his gun. "Lead the way."

It took nearly half an hour, and Olivia was quite sure her shoulders were both falling out of their sockets, but finally her fingers slipped under a piece of the knot and she was able to get it partially undone. She paused, listening attentively—were those footsteps she'd heard?

She stretched out straight, assuming the same position she'd held when her captor had left.

But no, nothing. There was no unclicking of locks, no opening of the door. She squirmed herself back around until she could feel the knot at the back of her ankles again. It was definitely smaller, but she still had work. Lots of it. She couldn't be certain, but it felt like a double square. Well, one and a half, now. But if she could get the next section undone, she'd be . . .

She'd still be stuck.

She let out a long sigh, deflating in body *and* spirit. If it had taken her that long just to do one small part of the knot . . .

No, she berated herself. She had to keep going. If she could get the next *two* bits undone, *then* the rest ought to slip open with a little squirming on her part.

She could do this. She could.

She grit her teeth and got back to work. Maybe this one would go faster now that she knew what she was doing. She knew how to move her fingers, wedging one in the crease and then wiggling back and forth, back and forth, trying to loosen the knot.

Or maybe it would go faster because her shoulders had gone numb. Surely the lack of pain would be to her benefit.

She wedged . . . and wiggled . . . and wedged . . . and wiggled . . . and arched her back . . . and stretched . . . and rolled . . . and rolled back . . .

And lost her balance.

She landed on the floor with a loud thump. A really loud thump. She winced, praying that the change in the bindings around her ankles wasn't noticeable as she listened for the clicks of the locks.

But there was nothing.

Could he not have heard her? It seemed impossible. Olivia had never been graceful; tie both her hands and her feet and she was a complete gawk. Needless to say, she had not landed quietly.

Maybe no one was out there. She had assumed that her captor was sitting in a chair outside her door, but truthfully, she had no idea why she thought that. He certainly couldn't have thought she might escape, and Olivia was fairly certain that this section of the building was deserted. The only footsteps she'd heard had been immediately followed by the appearance of the gray-haired man.

She waited at her spot on the floor by the bed for another minute, just in case anyone came in, then shoved herself across the wood to the door, where she could peer underneath. There was a sliver of space there, no more than three-quarters of an inch, and she couldn't see much—the hall was only the slightest bit better lit than her room. But she thought she might see shadows, if there were any.

And she didn't think there were.

So she wasn't guarded. This had to be a useful bit of information, although given her currently bound state, she wasn't certain how. And she really wasn't certain how she might maneuver herself back onto the bed. She could try to prop herself up against one of the legs, but the table with the teapot was still blocking the one by the head of the bed, and—

The teapot!

A surge of excitement and strength burst through

her, and she literally flipped herself over in her haste to get back to the table. From there it was a scoot, scoot, shove, and—

She was there. Now how would she send it crashing down? If she could break the pot, she could use a shard to cut through her bindings.

With great effort she managed to get her feet beneath her. Using the side of the bed for support, she rose slowly, her muscles screaming, until finally she was standing. She took a moment to catch her breath, then backed up to the small table, bending at the knees until her hands were at just the right height to grab the teapot handle.

Please don't let there be anyone out there please don't let there be anyone out there.

She needed to get good force. She couldn't just drop the thing on the floor. She glanced around the room, looking for inspiration. She started to spin.

Please please please.

She spun faster and faster, and then—

She let fly.

The teapot hit the wall with a mighty crack, and Olivia, terrified that someone might burst through the door, hopped back to the bed and lay on her back, although how she might explain the broken teapot on the far wall, she had no idea.

But no one entered.

She held her breath. She started to rise. Her shoes touched the floor and then—

Footsteps. Fast, moving toward her.

Oh God.

Voices, too. In Russian. They sounded urgent. Angry.

They wouldn't hurt her, would they? She was too valuable. She was to be ransomed to Prince Alexei, and—

And what if Prince Alexei had said good riddance? He was no longer courting her. And he knew that she was smitten with Harry. What if he felt spurned? What if he felt vengeful?

She scooted back on the bed, cowering in the corner. It would be so nice to be brave, to face whatever was coming with a curl of the lip and flip of the hair, but she was no Marie Antoinette, dressing in white for a beheading, regally begging the pardon of her executioner when she accidentally stepped on his foot.

No, she was Olivia Bevelstoke, and she did not want to die with dignity. She didn't want to be here, she didn't want to feel this awful terror, clawing at her gut.

Someone started pounding on the door—hard, rhythmic, and brutal.

Olivia started to shake. She curled into the tiniest ball she could manage, burying her head between her knees. *Please please please*, she chanted in her head, over and over. She thought of Harry, of her family, of—

The wooden door began to splinter.

Olivia prayed she would not lose control.

And then it all came crashing in.

She screamed, the sound ripping from the back of her throat. It felt as if the gag was clawing at her tongue, as if a puff of dry, scorching air was whipping through her windpipe.

And then someone said her name.

The air was obscured by dust and darkness, and all

she could see was the massive figure of a man moving toward her.

"Lady Olivia." The man's voice was gruff and deep. And accented. "Are you hurt?"

It was Vladimir, Prince Alexei's hulking and usually silent manservant. Suddenly all she could think of was the way he'd yanked and twisted on Sebastian Grey's arm, and oh dear God, if he could do that, he could break her right in two, and—

"Let me help you," he said.

He spoke English? Since when had he spoken English?

"Lady Olivia?" he repeated, his deep voice barely a grunt. He pulled out a knife, and she cringed, but he just brought it to the back of her gag and sliced through it.

She coughed and choked, barely hearing him as he shouted something in Russian again.

Someone replied, also in Russian, and she heard footsteps . . . running . . . coming closer . . . and then—

Harry?

"Olivia!" he cried, running toward her.

Vladimir said something to him—*in Russian*—and Harry gave a curt reply.

Also in Russian.

She stared at both of them in shock. What was happening? Why was Vladimir speaking in English?

Why was Harry speaking in Russian?

"Olivia, thank God!" Harry said, his hands cupping her face. "Tell me you haven't been hurt. Please, tell me what happened?"

But she couldn't move, could barely even think.

When he'd spoken in Russian—it was as if he had been an entirely different person. His voice had been different, and his *face* had been different, the mouth and the muscles moving in a completely different way.

She shrank from his touch. Did she know him? Did she even know him? He'd told her that his father had been a drunk, that his grandmother had brought him up—had any of that been true?

What had she done? Oh dear Lord, she had given herself to someone she did not know, could not trust.

Vladimir handed something to Harry, who nodded and said something else in Russian.

Olivia tried to back away, but she was already at the wall. She was breathing fast, and she was cornered, and she didn't want to be here, not with this man who wasn't Harry, and—

"Hold still," he said, and then he raised a knife.

Olivia looked up, saw the glint of metal as it came toward her, and screamed.

It was a sound Harry never wanted to hear again.

"I'm not going to hurt you," he said to her, trying to sound as calm and reassuring as possible. His hands were steady as he cut through her bindings, but on the inside, he was still shaking.

He'd known he loved her. He'd known he needed her, couldn't possibly be happy without her. But until that moment, he hadn't understood the breadth of it, the depth of it, the absolute knowledge that without her, he was nothing.

And then her scream, her fear . . . of *him*.

He'd nearly choked on the anguish of it.

He freed her ankles first, then her wrists, but as he

reached out to comfort her, she made an almost in-human sound, and leaped off the bed. She moved so quickly he wasn't able to stop her, and then, when she hit the floor—her feet must have been burning with pins and needles—her knees buckled, and she tumbled to the floor.

Dear God, she was terrified of him. Of *him*. What had they said to her? What had they done to her?

"Olivia," he said cautiously, and he reached out to her, keeping his movements slow and even.

"Don't touch me," she whimpered. She tried to crawl away, dragging her useless feet behind her.

"Olivia, let me help you."

But it was as if she did not hear him.

"We need to go," Vladimir said, saying the words in gruff Russian.

Harry didn't even bother to look at him as he insisted on another minute, the Russian words rolling off his tongue without a thought.

Olivia's eyes widened, and she looked frantically toward the door, clearly intending to make a break for it.

"I should have told you," Harry said, suddenly realizing the cause of her panic. "My grandmother was Russian. It was all she spoke to me when I was a child. It was why—"

"We do not have time for explanations," Vladimir said harshly. "Lady Olivia, we must go *now*."

She must have responded to the authority in his voice, because she nodded and, still looking unsteady and scared, allowed Harry to help her to her feet.

"I will explain everything soon," he told her. "I promise you."

"How did you find me?" she whispered.

He looked down at her as they hurried from the room. Her eyes had changed; she still looked shaken, but he could see *her* again in their depths. Before, there had been nothing but terror.

"We heard your noise," Vladimir said, holding his gun at the ready as he checked around a corner. "That was very fortunate of you. Possibly very foolish, too. But it is good that you did it."

Olivia nodded, and then, to Harry, she said, "Why is he speaking English?"

"He is a bit more than a bodyguard," Harry said, hoping that would be enough for now. It wasn't the time to unravel the entire story.

"Come," Vladimir said, motioning for them to follow.

"Who is he?" Olivia whispered.

"I really couldn't say," Harry replied.

"You will never see me again," Vladimir said, almost offhandedly.

As much as Harry was beginning to like and respect the man, he fervently hoped that was true. This was *it*. When they got out of here, he was giving notice at the War Department. He would marry Olivia, they'd move out to Hampshire and have a passel of little multilingual babies, and he'd sit at his desk every day doing nothing more exotic than adding numbers in a ledger.

He liked boring. He *craved* boring.

But boring, unfortunately, was not to be the watchword of the rest of the evening . . .

Chapter Twenty-four

$\mathcal{B}$y the time they reached the ground floor, the feeling had returned to Olivia's feet, and she didn't have to lean quite so hard on Harry.

But she didn't let go of his hand.

She was still in a panic, heart racing and blood pounding, and she didn't understand why he was speaking Russian or holding a gun, and she wasn't sure if she should trust him, and even worse, she didn't know if she could trust *herself*, because she feared she might have fallen in love with a mirage, a man who didn't even exist.

But still, she didn't let go of his hand. It was, in that terrifying moment, the one true thing in her life.

"This way," Vladimir said curtly, leading the way. They were heading to the ambassador's office, where her parents waited. They still had a way to go, or so Olivia assumed from the silence in the halls. When she could hear the hum of the party, then she would know that she was close.

But they were not moving quickly. At every corner, and at the top and bottom of each staircase Vladimir would stop, placing one finger to his lips as he pressed himself against the wall and peered carefully around the corner. And every time, Harry followed suit, pushing her behind him, guarding her with his body.

Olivia understood the need for caution, but she felt as if something inside of her were about to burst, and she just wanted to break free and run, to feel the air whistling past her face as she flew through the halls.

She wanted to go home.

She wanted her mother.

She wanted to take off this dress and burn it, to wash herself, to drink something sweet or sour or minty—whatever would most quickly wipe the taste of fear from her mouth.

She wanted to curl up in her bed, and pull the pillow over her head—she didn't want to think about any of this. She wanted, for once in her life, to be *in*curious. Maybe tomorrow she'd want all of the whys and wherefores, but for right now, she just wanted to close her eyes.

And hold Harry's hand.

"Olivia."

She looked over at him, and it was only then that she realized that she *had* closed her eyes. And nearly lost her balance.

"Are you all right?" he whispered.

She nodded, even though she wasn't. But she thought

she might be all right *enough*. Enough for this night, for whatever it was she needed to do.

"Can you do this?" he asked.

"I have to." Because, really, what other choice did she have?

He squeezed her hand.

She swallowed, looking down at where they touched, his skin against hers. His grip was warm, almost hot, and she wondered if her fingers felt like sharp little icicles in his palm.

"It's not much farther," he assured her.

Why were you speaking Russian?

The words hovered on her lips, almost tumbled out. But she caught them, held them inside. This wasn't the time to ask questions. She had to focus on what she was doing, what *he* was doing for her. The ambassador's residence was enormous, and she'd been unconscious when she'd been brought to her little upstairs room. She couldn't find her way back to the ballroom herself, could she—at least not without getting lost along the way?

She had to have faith that he would deliver her to safety. She had no choice.

She had to trust him.

She had to.

Then she looked at him, really looked at him for the first time since he and Vladimir had rescued her. The strange gauzy fog that had washed over her began to lift, and she realized that her mind was finally clear. Or rather, she thought with a funny, rueful little twitch of her lips, it was clear enough.

Clear enough to know that she did trust him.

It wasn't because she had to. It was simply because she did. Because she loved him. And maybe she didn't know why he hadn't told her he spoke Russian, but she knew *him*. When she looked at his face, she saw him reading from *Miss Butterworth*, scolding her for interrupting. She saw him sitting in her drawing room, insisting that she needed protection from the prince.

She saw him smiling.

She saw him laughing.

And she saw his eyes, open to his soul, as he told her he loved her.

"I trust you," she whispered. He didn't hear her, but it didn't matter. She hadn't said the words for him.

She'd said them for herself.

Harry had forgotten just how much he hated this. He'd fought in enough battles to know that some men thrived on danger. And he'd fought in more than enough to know that he was not one of them.

He could keep his head, act with calm and rational intent, but afterward, when safety had settled around him like a shroud, he began to shake. His breath came faster and faster, and more than once, he'd lost his belly.

He didn't like fear.

And never in his life had he been more afraid.

The men who had taken Olivia were ruthless, or so Vladimir had told him when they were searching for her. They had served the ambassador for years and had been amply rewarded for their misdeeds. They were loyal and violent—a terrifying combination. The only consolation was that they were unlikely to hurt Olivia if they thought she was of value to Prince Alexei. But now that she had escaped, who knew how they might judge her? They might consider her soiled goods, completely expendable.

"It is not much farther now," Vladimir said in Russian as they reached the bottom of the stairs. They had only to make it down the long gallery and over to the public section of the house. Once there, they would be safe. The party was still in full swing, and no one would dare attempt violence with several hundred of England's most prominent citizens as witnesses.

"It's not much farther," Harry whispered to Olivia. Her hands were like ice, but she seemed to have regained most of her spirit.

Vladimir edged forward. They had taken the service stairs, which, unfortunately, ended at a closed door. He pressed his ear against the wood and listened.

Harry tugged Olivia closer.

"Now," Vladimir said quietly. He opened the door very slowly, stepped out, then motioned for them to follow.

Harry took a step out, and then another, Olivia one pace behind.

"Quickly now," Vladimir whispered.

They moved swiftly, silently, keeping to the walls, and then—

Crack!

Harry pulled hard on Olivia's hand, his first instinct to shove her to safety, but there was nowhere, no shelter, no refuge. There was nothing but the wide-open hallway, and someone, somewhere, with a gun.

"Run!" Vladimir shouted.

Harry let go of Olivia's hand—she'd be able to run faster with both arms free—and he yelled, "Go!"

And they ran. They tore down the hallway, skidding around the corner after Vladimir. From behind them, a voice shouted in Russian, ordering them to stop.

"Keep going!" Harry yelled to Olivia. Another shot rang out, and this one came close, slicing the air near Harry's shoulder.

Or maybe it sliced his shoulder. He couldn't tell.

"This way!" Vladimir ordered, and they followed him around another corner, and then down a hall. The shots had stopped, and there were no more footsteps racing behind them, and then, somehow, they were all tumbling into the ambassador's office.

"Olivia!" her mother shrieked, and Harry watched as they embraced, as Olivia, who had not shed a tear, at least not one that he'd seen, collapsed in her mother's arms, weeping.

Harry leaned against the wall. He felt dizzy.

"Are you all right?"

Harry blinked. It was Prince Alexei, looking at him with concern.

"You're bleeding."

Harry looked down. He was holding his shoulder. He hadn't realized he'd been doing that. He lifted his hand and looked down at the blood. Strange, it didn't hurt. Maybe that was someone else's shoulder.

His knees buckled.

"Harry!"

And then . . . it wasn't blackness, really. Why did everyone say things went to black when one fainted? This was red. Or maybe green.

Or maybe . . .

Two days later

Experiences I Hope Never to Repeat
By Olivia Bevelstoke

Olivia paused in her thoughts as she took a sip of tea, sent up to her bedroom along with a large plate of biscuits by her concerned parents. Really, where did one start with a list such as that? There was the being rendered unconscious (apparently with some sort of drug-soaked cloth to the mouth, she had later learned). And one could not forget the gag, or the tied ankles, or the tied hands.

Oh, and she could not leave off being fed steaming hot tea by the very same man responsible for all of the above. That one had been more of an affront to her dignity than anything else, but it would be rather high up the list.

Olivia was fond of her dignity.

Let's see, what else . . . Being eye- and ear-witness to a door being kicked down. She had not enjoyed that. The expressions on her parents' faces when she was finally brought back to their care—there had been relief, that was true, but that sort of relief required commensurate terror, and Olivia did not want anyone she loved to feel that way ever again.

And then, dear God, this had been the worst: watching Harry as he'd slumped to the floor of the ambassador's office. She hadn't realized that he'd been shot. How could she not have realized that? She'd been so busy sobbing in her mother's arms, she hadn't seen that he'd gone deathly pale, or that he was clutching his shoulder.

She'd thought she'd been afraid before, but nothing—nothing—could have compared to the terror of those thirty seconds between the time he went down and Vladimir assured her it was nothing but a flesh wound.

And indeed, that was all it was. True to Vladimir's word, Harry was up and about the very next day. He'd arrived at her home while she was eating breakfast, and then he explained everything—why he hadn't told her he could speak Russian, what he'd really been doing at his desk when she had spied upon him, even why he had called upon her with *Miss Butterworth and the Mad Baron* that first crazy, wonderful afternoon. It hadn't been to be neighborly, or because he had had any feelings for her other than disdain. He had been *ordered* to do so. By no less an authority than the War Office.

It was a lot to take in over coddled eggs and tea.

But she'd listened, and she'd understood. And now everything was settled, every loose end neatly tied. The ambassador had been detained, as had the men who worked for him, including her gray-haired captor. Prince Alexei had sent over a formal letter of apology, on behalf of the entire Russian nation, and Vladimir, true to his word, had disappeared.

And yet she hadn't seen Harry in over twenty-four hours. He had left after breakfast, and she'd assumed he'd call again, but . . .

Nothing.

She wasn't worried. She wasn't even concerned. But it was odd. Quite odd.

She took another sip of her tea, then set the cup down on its saucer. Then she picked up both dishes and set them atop *Miss Butterworth*. Because she kept reaching for the book.

And she didn't want to pick it up. Not without Harry.

She hadn't finished the newspaper yet, anyway. She'd read the last half of it, and was rather interested in getting on to the more serious news at the front. There had been rumors that Monsieur Bonaparte was in exceedingly ill health. She supposed he couldn't have actually died yet; that would have been reported on the front page, with a headline prominent enough that she couldn't have missed it.

Still, there might be something of note, so she picked up the paper again, and had just found an article to read when she heard a knock on the door.

It was Huntley, carrying a small piece of paper. When he approached, she realized it was actually a card, folded in thirds and sealed at the center with dark blue wax. She murmured her thanks, examining the seal while the butler left the room. It was quite simple: just a V, in a rather elegant script, starting with a swirl and then finishing with a flourish.

She slid her finger underneath and loosened the wax, carefully unfolding the card.

Come to your window.

That was all. Just one sentence. She smiled, looking down at the words for a few seconds more before sliding herself to the edge of her bed. She hopped down, her feet lightly hitting the floor, but she paused for a few seconds before crossing the room.

She needed to wait. She wanted to stand here and savor this moment because . . .

Because *he* had made it. Harry had created the moment. And she loved him.

Come to your window.

She found herself grinning, almost giggling. She didn't ordinarily like being ordered about, but in this case it was delightful.

She walked to the window and pulled her curtains open. She could see him through the glass, standing in his own window, waiting for her.

She pushed her window open.

"Good morning," Harry said. He looked very solemn. Or rather, his mouth looked solemn. His eyes looked like they were up to something.

She felt her own eyes begin to twinkle. Wasn't that odd? That she could feel it. "Good morning," she said.

"How are you feeling?"

"Much better, thank you. I think I needed time to rest."

He nodded. "One needs time after a shock."

"You are speaking from experience?" she asked. But she needn't have done so; from his expression she knew that he was.

"When I was in the army."

It was funny. Their conversation was simple, but it wasn't flat. They weren't awkward; they were merely warming up.

And Olivia was already feeling the first tingles of anticipation.

"I bought another copy of *Miss Butterworth*," he said.

"You did?" She leaned on the ledge. "Did you finish it?"

"Indeed."

"Does it get any better?"

"Well, she does go into surprising detail about the pigeons."

"*No.*" Good heavens, she *was* going to finish that wretched novel. If the author actually showed the death by pigeons . . . well now, that was worth her time.

"No, really," Harry said. "It turns out Miss Butterworth was witness to the sad event. She relives it in a dream."

Olivia shuddered. "Prince Alexei is going to adore it."

"Actually, he's hired me to translate the entire book into Russian."

"You're joking!"

"No." He gave her a look that was both sly and satisfied. "I'm working on the first chapter right now."

"Oh, how exciting. I mean, awful, too, since you actually have to read it, but I suppose it's a different task altogether when you're being paid to do so."

Harry chuckled. "It's a change from the War Office documents, I must say."

"Do you know, I think I would like those better." Dull, dry facts were much more to her taste.

"You likely would," he agreed. "But then again, you're an odd sort of female."

"Charming as always with the compliments, Sir Harry."

"As I am a scholar of words, that is only to be expected."

She realized she was grinning. She was hanging half out of her window, grinning. And she was quite happy to be there.

"Prince Alexei pays quite handsomely," Harry added. "He feels that *Miss Butterworth* will be a huge success in Russia."

"He and Vladimir certainly enjoyed it."

Harry nodded. "It means I may retire from the War Office."

"Is that what you wished to do?" Olivia asked. She'd only just found out about his work; she'd not got a sense as to whether he enjoyed it.

"Yes," he replied. "I don't think I realized just how much until these last few weeks. I'm tired of all the secrets. I enjoy translation, but if I can keep to gothic novels—"

"*Lurid* gothic novels," Olivia corrected.

"Indeed," Harry agreed. "I—oh, excuse me, our other guest has arrived."

"Our other—" She glanced this way and that, blinking with confusion. "Someone else is here?"

"Lord Rudland," Harry said, nodding deferentially at the window below and to the left of Olivia's.

"Father?" Olivia looked down, startled. And perhaps a bit mortified as well.

"Olivia?" Her father poked the upper half of his body out the window, twisting awkwardly to see her. "What are you doing?"

"I was going to ask you the same thing," she admitted, the sheepishness of her tone taking an edge off her impertinence.

"I received a note from Sir Harry requesting my presence at this window." Lord Rudland twisted back around to face Harry. "What is this about, young man? And why is my daughter hanging out of her window like a fishwife?"

"Is Mother here?" Olivia asked.

"Your mother is here, too?" her father blustered.

"No, I was just wondering, since *you're* here, and—"

"Lord Rudland," Harry interrupted, his voice loud enough to cut the both of them off, "I would like to request the honor of your daughter's hand in marriage."

Olivia gasped, then squealed, then jumped up and down, which turned out to be a bad idea. "Ow!" she yelped, smacking her head on the window. She poked her head back out and beamed down at Harry with tears in her eyes. "Oh, Harry," she sighed. He'd promised her a proper proposal. And here it was. Nothing could have been so splendid as this.

"Olivia?" her father asked.

She looked down, wiping at her eyes.

"Why is he asking me this through a window?"

Olivia considered the question, considered her possible answers, and decided that honesty was her best alternative. "I am fairly certain you do not wish to know the answer to that question," she told him.

Her father closed his eyes and shook his head. She had seen that gesture before. It meant he didn't know what to do with her. Luckily for him, she was about to be taken off his hands.

"I love your daughter," Harry said. "And I like her very much as well."

Olivia put her hand over her heart and squeaked.

She didn't know why she squeaked; it just came out, like a little bubble of pure joy. His words—they were quite simply the most perfect declaration of love imaginable.

"She is beautiful," Harry went on, "so beautiful it makes my teeth ache, but that's not why I love her."

No, *that* was more perfect, aching teeth and all.

"I love that she reads the newspaper every day."

Olivia looked down at her father. He was staring at Harry as if he'd gone mad.

"I love that she has no patience for stupidity."

It was true, Olivia thought with a silly smile. He knew her so well.

"I love that I'm a better dancer than she is."

Her smile disappeared, but she had to acknowledge the truth of that as well.

"I love that she's kind to small children and large dogs."

What? She looked at him in askance.

"I'm guessing," he admitted. "You seem like the sort."

She pressed her lips together so she wouldn't laugh.

"But most of all," Harry said, and although he was looking squarely at Olivia's father, it felt as if he were looking at her, "I love *her*. I adore her. And I would like nothing more than to spend the rest of my days standing beside her as her husband."

Olivia looked back down at her father. He was still staring at Harry with an expression of great shock.

"Father?" she asked hesitantly.

"This is highly irregular," her father said. But he didn't sound angry, just dazed.

"I would give my life for her," Harry said.

"You would?" she asked, her voice small, and hopeful, and thrilled. "Oh, Harry, I—"

"Hush," he said, "I'm talking to your father."

"I approve," Lord Rudland suddenly said.

Olivia's mouth fell into an indignant *O*. "Because he told me to hush?"

Her father looked up. "It is indicative of uncommon good sense."

"*What?*"

"And a healthy dose of self-preservation," Harry added.

"I like this man," her father announced.

And then, quite suddenly, Olivia heard another window opening.

"What is going on?" It was her mother, in the drawing room, precisely three windows over from her father. "Who are you talking to?"

"Olivia is getting married, dear," her father said.

"Good morning, Mama," Olivia added.

Her mother looked up, blinking. "What are you doing?"

"Apparently getting married," Olivia said, with a rather silly grin.

"To me," Harry said, just to clarify.

"Oh, Sir Harry, er . . . lovely to see you again." Lady Rudland looked over at him, blinking a few times. "I didn't see you there."

He nodded graciously at his future mother-in-law.

Lady Rudland turned to her husband. "She's marrying him?"

Lord Rudland nodded. "With my heartfelt approval."

Lady Rudland considered this for a moment, then turned back to Harry. "You may have her in four months." She looked up at Olivia. "We have much to plan, you and I."

"I was thinking more along the lines of four weeks," Harry said.

Lady Rudland turned to him sharply, the index finger of her right hand pointed straight up. It was a gesture Olivia also knew quite well. It meant that the recipient was to argue at his own peril.

"You have a great deal to learn, my boy," Lord Rudland said.

"Oh!" Harry exclaimed. He motioned up to Olivia. "Don't move."

She waited, and a moment later he returned with a small jeweler's box. "A ring," he said, even though it was quite obvious. He opened the box, but Olivia was too far away to see anything but a bit of sparkle.

"Can you see it?" he asked.

She shook her head. "I'm sure it's lovely."

He poked his head farther out the window, his eyes narrowing as he measured the distance. "Can you catch it?" he asked.

Olivia heard her mother gasp, but she knew there was only one suitable reply. She gazed upon her future husband with a most supercilious expression and said, "If you can throw it, I can catch it."

He laughed. And he threw.

And she missed. On purpose.

It was better that way, she thought, when they met

in the middle to search for the ring. A proper proposal deserved a proper kiss.

Or, as Harry murmured to her in full sight of both of her parents, perhaps an improper one . . . ?

Improper, Olivia thought, as his lips touched hers. *Definitely* improper.

Think you know Sebastian Grey?

THINK AGAIN.

Don't miss
Julia Quinn's next bestseller.

Coming Summer 2010

From

Avon Books